Be Careful What You Wish For

Gemma Crisp developed her love of books and magazines while growing up on a sheep farm in the middle of Tasmania in the prehistoric days before the internet. It wasn't until she'd hit the bright lights of London some years later that she realised she could get paid to write about mascara, threesomes and celebrities (not necessarily all at once!). After acing her first magazine internship, thanks to being a photocopying and coffee-fetching ninja, Gemma moved to Sydney and has spent more than a decade working for some of Australia's glossiest magazines, including *New Woman*, *Girlfriend*, *OK!*, *Cosmopolitan Bride* and *NW*. She popped her editorship cherry at teen bible *DOLLY*, then moved to the editor's chair at *CLEO*, where she spent her days fending off wannabe Eligible Bachelors, wrangling celebrity publicists and attempting to craft the perfect coverline. Gemma is now based in London again, where she's trying not to buy Topshop out of shoes.

GEMMA CRISP

Be Careful What You Wish For

ALLEN&UNWIN
SYDNEY • MELBOURNE • AUCKLAND • LONDON

The characters and events in this book are fictitious. Any similarity to real persons, alive or dead, is coincidental and not intended by the author.

First published in 2013

Copyright © Gemma Crisp 2013

All rights reserved. No part of this book may be reproduced or transmitted in any form or by any means, electronic or mechanical, including photocopying, recording or by any information storage and retrieval system, without prior permission in writing from the publisher. The Australian *Copyright Act* 1968 (the Act) allows a maximum of one chapter or 10 per cent of this book, whichever is the greater, to be photocopied by any educational institution for its educational purposes provided that the educational institution (or body that administers it) has given a remuneration notice to Copyright Agency Limited (CAL) under the Act.

Allen & Unwin
Sydney, Melbourne, Auckland, London

83 Alexander Street
Crows Nest NSW 2065
Australia
Phone: (61 2) 8425 0100
Email: info@allenandunwin.com
Web: www.allenandunwin.com

Cataloguing-in-Publication details are available from the National Library of Australia
www.trove.nla.gov.au

ISBN 978 1 74237 891 6

Typeset in 12.5/18.5pt Joanna MT Std by Bookhouse, Sydney
Printed and bound in Australia by the SOS Print + Media Group.

10 9 8 7 6 5 4

The paper in this book is FSC® certified. FSC® promotes environmentally responsible, socially beneficial and economically viable management of the world's forests.

For the Adorables —
you know who you are

LONDON

one

'GoodafternoonNinaspeakinghowmayIhelpyou?' Nina warbled into the phone automatically while trying her best not to stare at Rob, the hotel porter she'd been fantasising about since her first day working on the front desk at the Bickford Hotel. Her mouth went dry as he ambled towards the elevator accompanied by a trolley stacked high with Louis Vuitton suitcases. 'He's so hot, I actually want to lick him,' she thought to herself for approximately the 952,384th time.

'Yeah, hi, this is Tyrone from the Royal Suite,' an American voice said on the other end of the line.

Nina dragged her gaze away from Rob's thighs and forced herself to pay attention. Guests who booked the Royal Suite – which cost five thousand pounds a night – were either A-list celebrities hitting London for their film premiere or sold-out album tour, beyond-rich hedge fund gurus or, in the case of the Saudi family who had booked it for three months the previous summer, international royalty.

'I'm calling to check on the fans,' Tyrone continued. 'Princess Cupcake wants the car to take her to Harvey Nichols in ten minutes, so make sure there's a decent amount of fans in the lobby when she walks through. She wasn't happy with yesterday's crowd.' His tone was slightly ominous.

'Certainly, sir, I *completely* understand,' Nina replied, knowing full well Princess Cupcake's bodyguard wouldn't detect the dripping sarcasm hiding behind her ingratiating tone. 'I'll get it sorted right away.'

She scooted across the foyer to the concierge's desk, where Big Tim had just finished twenty minutes of negotiating with the maître d' of London's hottest restaurant in order to get Mr Rothschild, one of the hotel's regular guests, off the waiting list and onto a VIP table.

'All done, sir, the Wolseley is expecting you at nine pm – just ask for Jean-Marc when you arrive. Thank you, sir, much appreciated; enjoy your dinner tonight,' he said smoothly as Mr Rothschild slipped him a fifty-pound note for his trouble. Nina looked enviously at the pink bill as it went straight into the pocket of Big Tim's waistcoat – she couldn't recall Mr Rothschild tipping her when she'd checked him in and shown him to his room two days ago. Then again, he hadn't exactly been in the mood to tip after realising he hadn't received his free American Express Platinum upgrade. Nina cringed as she remembered explaining that the upgrade was subject to availability and unfortunately the hotel was fully booked. Not that Mr Rothschild had cared — he'd worked himself into a fury, threatening to move to another five-star hotel down the road and to tell his executive assistant to blacklist the Bickford for all future stays. She'd only managed to escape when Rob had arrived to deliver the luggage. Johan, her best friend who also worked on the front desk, had to cover for her while she'd cried in the switchboard office; even though she knew the hotel had more than its fair share of power-tripping guests, having a grown man scream in her face wasn't what she'd file under F for Fun.

'Orright, luv? Whatcha want, eh?' Big Tim asked, lapsing back into his Cockney accent while looking down at Nina from his two-hundred-centimetre height. 'Hurry up, there's a cup of tea in the staff canteen with my name on it.'

'Princess Cupcake wants the car to take her to Harvey Nicks in ten minutes . . .' Nina began to explain.

'. . . So we need to round up her adoring fans and make sure they're in the foyer when she walks through,' Big Tim finished. 'Gawd, Harvey Nicks is only two hundred yards from here — do her legs not work or something?' He rolled his eyes. 'She probably doesn't want to ruin them six-inch Gucci heels. Well, Victor just got back from Gatwick, so he can drive her.'

Princess Cupcake had arrived at the Bickford five days ago with a twenty-strong entourage. An American singer with ten number-one hits and an ego to match, she was renowned for insisting the hotel redecorate the Royal Suite whenever she stayed so that everything was bubblegum pink and all the suite's rooms were overflowing with plush Hello Kitty toys. Nina had no idea why she insisted on booking under a fake name seeing her fans knew she always stayed at the same hotel – they started camping outside days before she was scheduled to fly in to Farnborough on her record label's private jet. To the annoyance of the hotel's reservations manager, Cupcake's management insisted that no other guests could stay on the same floor as the Royal Suite when the singer was in town, meaning the hotel's occupancy rates took a hit. But hosting a celebrity as big as Cupcake was a publicity coup for the hotel, plus the general manager's fifteen-year-old daughter was a massive fan, so what Cupcake wanted, Cupcake got.

As Big Tim called Victor over and instructed him to cherry-pick thirty fans from the gaggle waiting outside the hotel's front door for a glimpse of their idol, Nina realised she'd left the front desk unattended – a pet hate of Mr Farrington-Smyth, the hotel's manager. He had a TV in his office linked to a direct feed from the video camera that was constantly trained on the front desk so he could monitor the reception area.

As she hurried back to her post, her four-inch heels clicking on the marble floor, Nina remembered the first time she'd walked into the hotel for her job interview. God, it felt like forever ago. She'd now spent almost two years dealing with ridiculously rich guests, showing them to their ridiculously overpriced rooms and putting up with their ridiculous hysterics when it dawned on them that their room didn't have a view of Buckingham Palace. It didn't matter that none of the rooms at the hotel had a view of the palace – in the guests' minds, she should be pulling bricks out of the heritage-listed building with her bare hands to create a view especially for them, while simultaneously noting down their newspaper preference and reciting their credit card numbers off by heart. No wonder she had started dreading going to work.

It had been a totally different story when she'd first scored the job. A decidedly unladylike snort escaped as she remembered the feeling of awe that had washed over her when she'd first laid eyes on the doormen in their dove-grey morning suits and peaked caps; the delicate white orchids on the pristine antique reception desk; the gold flocked wallpaper and obese chintz cushions in the guests' rooms, contrasted with state-of-the-art technology. It was five-star luxury on crack.

And then there were the guests themselves – fabulously wealthy and spoilt rotten. At first Nina had loved watching them strut through the lobby from her perch at the reception desk. The women were usually weighed down with the haul of an afternoon spent at Bond Street's designer stores after dropping thousands of pounds in Prada, Dior and McQueen while the men celebrated million-pound business deals with a fat Montecristo or two in the cigar bar. With the ink barely dry on the Australian immigration departure stamp in her passport, Nina had almost gone into anaphylactic shock when she'd spied her first Hermès Birkin bag (bright pink ostrich) hanging off the diamond-encrusted hand of Ms Giuliani, a New York stockbroker who jetted to London every two weeks and always insisted on staying in suite 329. But the novelty soon wore off. These days, Nina sniffed in disdain if she was handed a Gold American Express card, let alone a bog-standard green one. She barely blinked while charging outrageously inflated Wimbledon box-seat tickets to guests' room accounts and she could no longer conjure up an iota of excitement when the reservations department breathlessly briefed her about the latest celebrity to book the Royal Suite. Even the salacious gossip about the guests from the butlers and housekeeping staff didn't seem as juicy – nothing shocked her anymore.

Sitting down behind the reception desk, making sure she was in full view of Mr Farrington-Smyth's video camera, Nina was about to check how many more arrivals were due that afternoon when ninety-five per cent of the oxygen was sucked out of the room – Princess Cupcake was making her grand entrance. The babble of noise from the fans who'd been ushered into the lobby faded to a reverential silence, punctured by muffled squeaks from teenagers unable to control themselves. As Cupcake glided across the floor, dressed in a pink babydoll dress choked with ruffles and lace, she glanced coyly at the crowd from under her two-inch lash extensions. With a beatific smile on her face, she paused intermittently to sign a magazine cover or a CD, or pose with a fan lucky enough to be deemed worthy. Nina could see Tyrone, Princess Cupcake's massive bodyguard, shadowing her every move, eyes flicking in five different directions at once, just in case a deranged fan happened to be in the vicinity. She caught his eye and he gave her a curt nod – Cupcake was happy with the turnout. Despite herself, Nina felt her shoulder muscles unclench. 'Sheeeeeeesh, anyone would think you'd engineered peace in the Middle East,' she chastised herself while watching the singer swan out of the double doors, leaving a cloud of sickly sweet fairy-floss scent behind her. 'Telling the concierge to round up a crowd of fangirls in order to keep a VIP guest happy isn't exactly the stuff of Nobel Peace Prizes.' She looked at the remnants of the adoring posse, still gazing after their idol with glazed eyes, some shaking with emotion, and sighed. 'My brain is turning into polystyrene,' she thought crossly. 'There has to be something better than doing this for the rest of my life.'

There was just one problem – well, two problems actually, if you wanted to get pedantic about it. The first was that Nina had no idea what else to do with her life. The second was that her working-holiday visa was fast running out. She'd got as far as moving to London and had managed to avoid not only the dreaded 'Heathrow injection' weight gain, but also the pedestrian fate of so many Aussies who had gone before her – pulling pints at a dodgy Earls Court pub was definitely not on her agenda, no matter how many guests threw tantrums about their room with no view. 'Just suck it up,' she told herself sternly. 'You used to love talking shop with Johan and Tess. Comparing room rates, occupancy percentages, who had the biggest A-list celebrity booked in to stay, which guest had charged a second room for his mistress to a secret credit card so his wife wouldn't find out . . .'

It was true – when she'd first dipped her toes in hospitality, Nina had obsessed over every single industry detail, endlessly discussing fifty-quid tips, staff meals and industry gossip with her cousin Tess, with whom she shared a shoebox apartment. Tess worked at a small boutique hotel near Piccadilly, one that prided itself on its proximity to Buckingham Palace (although none of its rooms had an actual view of the famous landmark either).

Tess was the reason Nina had packed her bags and booked herself a one-way ticket to London. With less than six months difference in age, they considered themselves sisters. Tess had been living in London for a year longer than Nina, thanks to her college's industry placement program; unlike Nina, who had blagged her way into her front-desk job, Tess was busy carving herself a long-term career in hospitality, clawing her way up the ladder with her eye firmly on the front-office manager prize.

'When are you coming to see me?' Tess had asked during one of their Skype sessions back when they'd been stranded on opposite sides of the world. 'You'd love it here – you haven't lived until you've set foot in Topshop and the bars are ahhh-mazing . . . Oh my God, I've got the BEST idea!' Nina's cousin had screeched suddenly, flapping her hands like she always did when she got excited. 'Why don't you fly over for your birthday?!'

Nina hadn't needed much convincing. After two weeks of worshipping at the altars of Topshop, H&M, Oasis and Warehouse, and stumbling out of too many bars to count,

Be Careful What You Wish For

Nina had been determined to call herself a Londoner as soon as possible. Three months later, her working-holiday visa got stamped by a miserable lump masquerading as a British immigrations officer, then she sardined herself onto the Tube and settled in for the commute to Brixton. She would be sharing a flat with Tess and Camille, a college friend of Tess's who now worked in the food and beverage department of another posh London hotel.

'Nina? Schweedie? What did I just say, hmmm?' asked a singsong voice with a Scandinavian accent. 'The late shift will be here in half an hour, so we need to get handover sorted.' The smell of Marlboro Reds mixed with Coco Mademoiselle and fake tan interrupted Nina's zone-out. She blinked and forced her mind back to the lobby of the Bickford, where Annika, the Swedish reception manager, was busy printing off the daily report of who had yet to check out so the late shift could chase them up.

'Sure, no problem, Annie. Thank God we won't have to deal with all the bump-outs tonight,' Nina said with relief. 'Reservations have done their usual trick of over-booking, so I called Claridge's while you were downstairs on your ciggie break. They have a few rooms available so the late shift can offload the last arrivals to them. I'm thinking the usual "We're terribly sorry, but a water pipe has exploded in your room; it's uninhabitable at the moment, so we've arranged for you to stay down the road in another hotel while we fix the damage" excuse is the way to go?'

Nina and Annika smirked at each other, both feeling smugly happy that they wouldn't have to be the ones to lie through their teeth to the unlucky guests who arrived late at night, desperate to ensconce themselves in their plush rooms and help themselves to the top-shelf mini bar, only to be ambushed at reception and booted out the door to a completely different hotel before they realised what was happening. 'Bumping out' was standard industry practice but no one like doing it, thanks to the risk of the guests smelling a rat and demanding to see the supposedly flooded room.

'I'm just going to the loo – back in a sec,' Nina said hurriedly. She'd spotted Mike, the head doorman, escorting a family of five to the reception desk; the mother was decked out in head-to-toe Chanel while her triplets were dressed in matching Burberry outfits, with the nanny trailing behind. 'Stuff it, Annika can deal with that can of worms,' Nina thought as she pushed open the heavy doors separating the lobby from the hotel's back-of-house area. There was no marble, orchids or thick luxurious carpet here. Utilitarian was the decor du jour – concrete floors, bare walls and the lingering aroma of laundry detergent mixed with chip fat from the staff canteen. She waved to the guys in the security office, as they sat slumped behind bulletproof glass with their eyes locked on the fifteen monitors in front of them. Nothing happened in the public areas of the hotel without them knowing. And thanks to the unstoppable tongues of the butlers and housekeeping staff, the security guys knew most of what happened in the private guest areas too.

Nina entered the female change room and opened her locker. Pawing through the tangle of spare tights, the mandatory oversized pearl necklace she'd forgotten to put on when she'd arrived for her shift, and various bottles of duty-free perfume gifted to her by regular guests, she pulled out her Miu Miu tote (yet another gift) to find her lip gloss. Shoving her hands into the bag, her fingers brushed against a smooth glossy surface and she felt a thrill of anticipation. Somehow she'd forgotten all about the new issues of *Vogue*, *Grazia*, *ELLE* and *Glamour* she'd bought that morning from the newsagent in Green Park Tube station. Suddenly her afternoon was looking better — much better.

Nina was a hopeless magazine addict; she blamed it on having nothing to do while growing up on her family's cattle stud in the Northern Territory. Always a fast reader, once she'd ploughed through her library books she started to devour her grandmother's well-thumbed copies of *Woman's Day* and *New Idea*, then moved on to her mum's collection of *Vogues*. She loved everything about magazines, from the smell of the ink and the feel of the paper stock to the chatty tone of the articles as they spruiked the latest fashion and beauty products. Nina's magazine habit made her feel like she had her finger on the pulse — she loved knowing about the next big thing, whether it was a nail polish colour, up-and-coming celebrity or new social media site. She never missed reading the editor's letters and always looked out for her favourite writers' by-lines. Whenever they disappeared from the staff list at the front of the magazine, she practically went into mourning, until they popped up on the masthead of another glossy. 'Here comes the magazine tragic,' Tess always said when Nina came home with an armful of new issues. Some people went to the gym or to the movies for stress relief or escapism; Nina read magazines. It was an expensive habit, but she had no intention of quitting any time soon.

Forcing herself to ignore the glossy covers that promised perfect hair in sixty seconds, the secret to true happiness and, in *Glamour*'s case, the DIY trick that would stick a rocket up her sex life, Nina reluctantly left the magazines in her bag and checked her phone – only twenty minutes till the late shift arrived to start handover with herself and Annika. 'That's only one thousand, two hundred seconds till you can get out of here,' she told herself. 'Then you can spend the rest of the afternoon reading. Maybe with a cheeky G&T or two. How's that for a deal?' She quickly swiped on her lip gloss, took one last look at the stash of mags, then slammed the locker door shut and headed back to reception.

two

Instead of heading back to the one-bedroom flat she shared with Tess and Camille after clocking off from her shift, Nina found herself traipsing through the back streets of Soho until she was standing outside Freedom on Wardour Street. It was one of the first places Tess had taken her during her two-week London taste-test, and even though the cool crowd had chewed it up and spat it out long ago, Nina still had a soft spot for the cafe/bar. Its bright orange leather banquettes reminded her of massive nights in the downstairs club area and boozy Sunday afternoon sessions with Johan. The service was always terrible and the food beyond ordinary, but there was something about the place that drew Nina to it.

Settling in next to the window overlooking the grimy street, she pulled the stash of magazines out of her bag, while trying to catch the eye of the hipster Brazilian guy who was preening behind the bar. 'Why do I keep coming here?' Nina muttered under her breath, trying unsuccessfully to keep her frustration in check as he refused to acknowledge her. One of the side effects of working in the hospitality industry was that Nina couldn't help judging waitresses, barmen, supermarket cashiers, shop assistants . . . pretty much anyone in a customer service role. Having been trained up to the Bickford's exacting standards, it grated when she stepped outside of the five-star bubble and had to deal with less than attentive service. Then again, comparing one of London's top hotels with a past-its-prime bar wasn't exactly the fairest of contests; Nina doubted the barman had ever been given a designer handbag, a fistful of fifty-pound notes or a pair of limited-edition Nike trainers as a tip for his efforts. Even Tess and Camille couldn't get over how much swag Nina came home with, especially during the summer when the crème de la crème of Dubai, Abu Dhabi and Riyadh descended on London to escape the blistering heat at home.

Having given up waiting for the barman to tire of admiring himself in the reflection of the cocktail shakers, Nina was on the way to the bar when she caught sight of Freedom's magazine rack. 'Is that a new *Marie Claude*? I don't remember seeing that cover . . .' Gravitating towards it like Charlie Sheen to a mountain of cocaine, she picked up the magazine then couldn't help grabbing a few of the celebrity gossip weeklies that were hiding behind it. 'I still haven't read last weekend's *Sunday Times Style* magazine either,' she thought, adding it to the growing pile under her arm. Nina wasn't fussy when it came to magazines – glossy fashion bibles, weekly trash, free newspaper supplements, obscure indie titles: she'd read anything that had a masthead.

Putting her haul down on top of the bar with a heavy thump, she rolled her eyes as the Brazilian pretended he'd only just noticed she existed.

'You want something?' he asked arrogantly.

'No, I've been waiting fifteen minutes in an empty cafe just for shits and giggles, while Pretty Boy behind the bar plays with his hair,' Nina said tersely. 'Can I have a gin – Hendrick's, not Tanqueray – with half tonic, half soda, in a tall glass, with a slice of cucumber . . . please,' she added quickly, before he started to translate her bitchy words in his head.

'Make that two,' said a lightly accented voice behind her. Nina swivelled around, almost sending the magazine stack toppling to the floor.

'Johan! What are you doing here? Did we organise to meet up after my shift and I've forgotten about it?' Nina asked as she hugged her best friend.

'No, I was just walking past after having coffee with Fred at Caffè Nero and spotted a small blonde fluffball raping and pillaging the magazine rack – I figured it had to be the one and only Nina Morey, desperate for her fix after a fun-filled shift at the Bickford, so I thought I'd join you.' He smiled while checking out the Brazilian's butt as he measured out the drinks. 'Mmmm, I see Freedom has recruited some tasty new talent,' he murmured, scooping up the magazines with one massive hand and carrying both glasses in the other as they made their way back to the table.

Nina had met Johan on her third day on the job. She'd been learning the shift-handover ropes when the sound of bouncing footsteps interrupted her training. Sauntering through the lobby from the back-of-house area was one hundred and ninety-five centimetres of Mother Nature's finest work.

'Rob who?' Nina had thought as her eyeballs were taken hostage by shoulders the width of a three-seater couch, the black hair styled just so, striking green Eurasian eyes and huge hands with perfectly groomed fingernails. 'You know what they say about men with big hands,' she couldn't help reminding herself, as her future husband strode towards the front desk, dressed in the hotel's dapper uniform of striped grey trousers, crisp white shirt and matching striped tie topped off with a black morning coat complete with tails. The man was sex on a stick.

'Hey, Johan, how was your weekend?' asked Stéphanie, the French receptionist who was talking Nina through the handover process.

'Precious, I've just come off a three-day bender – don't talk to Daddy now, he can't quite cope just yet. Let him go hide in the back with the reservations girlies for fifteen minutes until the rest of the late shift arrives,' he had replied in a tone that had an unmistakeable tinge of gay.

'Bugger,' Nina muttered, without realising she'd said it aloud.

Stéphanie smiled. 'I know. Don't worry, you wouldn't be the first woman to be disappointed that Johan likes men. His mother is German and his father is Korean, if you're wondering. The girl you replaced spent her first six months here refusing to accept that he wasn't straight and would always ask him out on dates – poor Johan didn't know what to do! He finally kissed Thomas, the butler, in front of her at the Christmas party – I don't think she ever recovered . . .'

When Stéphanie had finished explaining the handover procedure, Nina made her way through the switch room and into the reservations department. She found Johan entertaining the four reservations girls with tales of his weekend antics. When he saw her, he stopped mid-sentence, looked her up and down, then announced, 'You must be the new Orrrrstraaaaaayyyylian,' stretching out the vowels with an exaggerated *Kath and Kim* accent. 'I love me some Orrrrstraaaaaayyyylians. Say fruit cake,' he instructed.

'Uh, sorry, what?'

'Say it!'

Nina felt five pairs of eyes burning into her. 'Um, fruit cake,' she said obediently, only to be greeted with a disappointed look.

'Oh. I guess you must be from a posh bit of Australia. Most of the Aussies I've met say *frooooot kaaayyyyk*.' Johan turned back to his eager audience to continue his story of weekend debauchery.

'Actually I'm not that posh,' Nina interrupted, annoyed that he had tried to embarrass her in front of her new work colleagues. 'And we don't eat a lot of fruit cake in Australia, we actually eat a lot of those green things – you know, like broccoli, zucchini, spinach . . .' she trailed off, hoping he'd fall into her trap, while silently thanking Stéphanie for spilling the beans about his German origins.

'You mean like wegetables?' he'd said witheringly, realising too late that he'd pronounced the v the German way, instead of English. As the reservations girls fell about laughing, Nina and Johan had stared at each other. A glimmer of respect crossed his handsome face, then he stepped forward and wrapped her in a bear hug.

'Well, well, well . . . the blonde fluffball isn't as fluffy as she looks, is she? Something tells me we are going to get along just fine,' he'd whispered in her ear. And he'd been right. Johan had become her closest friend in London – after Tess of course. Behind the disgustingly good-looking, confident exterior was a guy who was desperately concealing the truth about his sexuality from his family in case they rejected him. While he loved a good time and never wasted an opportunity to show off, there were a lot more layers to Johan than most people suspected.

'So give me the update on Cupcake – what have I got to look forward to when I go back to work tomorrow?' Johan said as they slurped on their G&Ts.

Nina screwed up her face. 'Do we have to talk about it? That place is doing my head in. If I have to listen to one more person whinge about their overnight first-class flight from JFK, I can't be held responsible if I pummel them to death with the Sunday Times. As for Cupcake, she's added a new cup of crazy to her repertoire – guess what Thomas told me was on her list of room requests this time?'

'Ummm, unicorns?'

'Almost. She wanted the bathroom in the Royal Suite to be filled with hundreds of white butterflies so they'd flutter around her as she, er, did her business. Thomas spent days calling butterfly breeders around the UK trying to track down the particular species she wanted and finally got his hands on some just in time to release them in the bathroom before her arrival, but then she was eight hours later than expected. By the time she was escorted to her suite, most of them had carked it and there were dead butterflies all over the bathroom floor. Apparently you could hear the shrieking from three floors away . . .'

Johan snorted. 'Sweet baby Jesus, what is she like? Bet housekeeping weren't happy. Next time she'll probably ask for Maltese puppies to wipe her butt with. Another one?' He picked up Nina's empty glass without waiting for her answer. 'I know, I know – half tonic, half soda.'

Nina smiled as she watched him flirt outrageously with the Brazilian barman. Pulling the forgotten pile of magazines towards her, she started flicking through Marie Claude, past the glossy advertisements for three-thousand-pound handbags and two-hundred-and-fifty-pound jars of eye cream, until she reached the page with the letter from the editor. Staring at the picture of the glamorous brunette wearing next season's must-have green silk Chloé dress, Nina felt a prickle of jealousy.

'Imagine what her life must be like,' she thought. 'Designer clothes at her fingertips, celebrity friends on speed dial, free champagne at parties every night . . . I wish I could be a magazine editor.' Lost in the magic of the magazine world, she didn't notice Johan was back from the bar looking very happy with himself until the clink of ice against glass broke into her daydream.

'Couldn't resist, I see. Come on,' he demanded. 'Hand it over.' All Nina's friends knew there was zero chance of having a decent conversation with her when there was an open magazine in the vicinity. 'I need your advice on what to wear for my date with Mr Brazilian Barman this weekend,' he said smugly.

'You didn't! Of course you did. Why am I even surprised?' Nina reluctantly closed the magazine. 'So where are you two going?'

'God knows. I don't really care, as long as his place or my place is where we finish up – Daddy has a scratch that needs to be itched,' he said in his special 'I'm camper than a row of tents' tone. 'Are you on the late or early tomorrow?'

Nina sighed. She was in the middle of working ten days straight while Stéphanie took annual leave to visit her family in France. She was now on day eight and the cracks were beginning to show, thanks to Annika rostering her on a series of punishing 'late-earlies' – a late shift finishing at eleven pm followed by an early shift starting at seven the next morning. The good thing about doing a series of late-earlies was finishing mid-afternoon and not having to start work again till three the following day, but Nina always struggled with less than six hours in her sleep tank.

'I'm on a late tomorrow . . . which means I'll have to deal with Cupcake's departure – kill me now.'

'Oh, girlfriend, listen to you bitch about your first-world problems. If you hate it that much, why don't you quit?' Johan asked bluntly.

'And do what? Go work in another hotel and deal with the same crap? Don't forget I only have a few more months left on my working visa, so unless I decide to stay and get sponsored, I doubt anyone will throw a job in my lap.'

'I know there's no point in leaving to go somewhere where you'll be just as miserable. And having worked at other hotels, I can tell you the Bickford's actually pretty good compared to the others – it pays better, for one. I meant more that you should quit so you can do something you're really interested in, rather than something you fell into, like working in hotels,' Johan explained.

'But that's the problem – I don't really know what I want to do. I'm not one of those people who have known exactly what they want to be since they were five years old. I barely finished my degree because I lost interest halfway through, I'm not particularly good at anything and the thought of going back to studying makes me want to hurl.'

They sat in silence for a bit, staring out the window. Suddenly Johan said, 'I remember someone on TV once saying that the best career advice they'd ever got was if you never want to feel like you've worked a day in your life, you have to do something that you love. Basically, think of something you'd happily do for free, like a hobby, then find a job that'll pay you to do it.'

Nina stared at him, then they both looked at the magazine mountain on the table.

'But I'm not a journalist. And everyone knows it's impossible to get a foot in the door of the magazine industry. I can't just decide I want to work in publishing and walk straight into a job, that's ridiculous,' she protested.

'Well, you'd have to start at the bottom and do work experience or apply for an internship or something,' Johan pointed out. 'Remember my ex, Will? His sister was a fashion assistant at *Grazia* and she once said that the best way to get into the industry was through work experience. It doesn't matter if you have the best journalism degree in the history of the universe – if you don't have work experience or an internship on your CV, you wouldn't even be considered for an interview. Why don't you contact a bunch of mags to find out what they offer? Surely there must be some kind of contact details on the letters page?' He reached over and grabbed the *Marie Claude*, scanning the pages until he found what he was looking for. 'Look, it says here that they offer three-month unpaid internships in the features department!'

Nina yanked the magazine out of his hands so she could see for herself. Printed in tiny text at the bottom of the page were all the details she needed: 'Please be advised that we do not offer weekly work experience placements, only three-month unpaid internships in our features, fashion, art or beauty departments. Interested parties should email interns@marieclaude.co.uk with a cover letter, CV and the department in which they wish to intern. Please note that only shortlisted applicants will be contacted for an interview.'

Feeling deflated, Nina pushed the magazine away. 'There's no way I'll get an interview, let alone an internship. Why would they want someone like me?'

'Why wouldn't they want someone like you?' Johan shot back. 'I've never met anyone who loves magazines as much as you do! I know that's not all they look for, but it's not like you can't string a sentence together. What have you got to lose by applying? You won't hear a knock at the door one day and open it to find a magazine editor offering you a job out of nowhere. You've got to be in it to win it. There's no point bitching and moaning if you're not prepared to put yourself out there.'

'Alright, settle down!' Nina laughed at how fired up he was. 'I'll email them when I get home, okay? I guess if nothing happens, at least I tried. Plus *Marie Claude* isn't my only option – other titles will have some kind of work experience program too, right? So, seeing that you may have found me a new career, I guess I'd better buy you a drink. Same again?'

three

Hauling herself up the stairs at Brixton Tube station with her arms full of magazines, Nina started to regret the bucketload of booze she'd put away with Johan. 'I wonder if the Brazilian started free-pouring that gin after Johan hit on him,' she wondered groggily, blinking in the weak sunlight as she staggered out of the station onto Brixton High Street.

Weaving her way through the crowd of teenagers flirting awkwardly with each other in front of the Tube entrance, Nina waved to the girls in the nail bar on the corner, trying to ignore the smell of weed mixed with acrylic glue, then turned right into Brighton Terrace. She'd moved here with Tess and Camille almost a year ago, much to the horror of Annika, who lived on a posh street in South Kensington and couldn't fathom how Nina could contemplate taking up residence in

South London, let alone in such a notorious area. She'd given up trying to explain that the Brixton riots of the eighties and nineties were practically ancient history and tried not to roll her eyes when people freaked out because of the high African and Caribbean population. As with a lot of the previously dodgy areas of London, Brixton was this close to taking the 'Next Big Thing' title off Dalston. In the short time she'd lived there, Nina had seen wine bars, art galleries and sushi restaurants squeeze themselves in among Brixton landmarks such as the art deco former-Woolworths-now-H&M building on the high street, the markets sprawled around Electric Avenue, and the longstanding Dogstar club on Coldharbour Lane. Every weekend without fail she could hear the crowds making their way up to the Brixton Academy and the Fridge, ready for a massive night out – and if she was on an early shift, she'd often see the same people at six the next morning, gurning away while waiting in McDonald's for a comedown thickshake. Nina loved the energy and authenticity of Brixton; she much preferred it to the snottiness of Chelsea or Fulham, no matter how much Annika tried to convert her.

'Hiya, I'm home', she called out, dumping everything on the couch as she poked her head in the kitchen just in time to catch Tess hurriedly shoving the last of the Jaffa Cakes in her mouth. Nina screwed up her nose. 'You don't need to hide it from me, I don't rate Jaffa Cakes at all. Give me a milk chocolate HobNob any day over those vile things. But you'd better replace the packet before Camille comes home,' she warned, as Tess's frantic chewing slowed its pace.

'Jmmphofffemssssmvolllljchhhmmmlls,' Tess mumbled through a mouthful of Jaffa Cake.

Nina raised an eyebrow. 'Really? Fascinating. I would never have guessed,' she said sarcastically.

Tess tried again. 'Camille has gone to Pete's place; she won't be home for days.' Since Camille had hooked up with Pete, a new chef at her hotel, Nina and Tess hardly saw her anymore. They tried not to take it personally – living in a one-bedroom flat with two other girls wasn't ideal, especially given how tight Nina and Tess were. Even though the three girls often worked different shifts, there were still times when they found themselves getting on top of each other at home, so Nina didn't blame Camille for grabbing some breathing space whenever she could. Especially when it meant she could sleep in a proper bed every night, rather than rotating between the two single beds and a fold-out mattress. Nina might have escaped the typical profession and postcodes of Aussies in London on a working-holiday visa, but she hadn't been as successful in avoiding the housing cliché. 'No wonder I've been single since moving here,' she thought. 'How am I supposed to bring a guy home when I share a bedroom with two other chicks?'

Not that she'd suffered a total man drought, she reminded herself. There'd been Declan, the Irish restaurant manager from the Bickford, who she'd hooked up with a few times before they both came to the conclusion that it wasn't the greatest idea, and she'd even been on a date with Rob, the hotel porter she was in lust with. Admittedly it hadn't been the most successful date, due to the fact that, apart from the hotel, they had absolutely nothing in common. He was into Marilyn Manson; she liked Rihanna. He had a kid from a previous relationship; she was allergic to children. He was perfectly happy delivering bags to people's rooms for a living; she was burning to get out of the hospitality industry. In a word: awkward. As much as she'd tried to talk it up to Tess afterwards, Nina had known there wouldn't be a second date. But even though they were less suited than Kim Kardashian and Kris Humphries, she still found herself drooling over him.

'How come you're home late?' Tess asked, shoving the magazines aside so she could take up residence on the couch. 'Was there a rush of check-ins during handover or did you just happen to fall into H&M after you got off the Tube?'

'Neither. I bumped into Johan after I finished, so we had a drink. But then one drink turned into several, especially after he worked his magic on the barman in Freedom. I swear our G&Ts tripled in strength after they arranged to hook up this weekend . . .' Nina trailed off. She wondered whether she should tell Tess about Johan's idea for her new career. Now that she was home, she felt a bit stupid for thinking she'd have a chance of breaking into the magazine industry. If it was that easy, why didn't everyone do it?

'Good old Johan; he doesn't waste any time, does he?' Tess laughed as she picked up the *Marie Claude* Nina had swiped from the bar and started flicking through it. 'How come this page is tagged?' she asked.

Nina stalled for time by straightening the stack of magazines on the coffee table; she'd forgotten she'd stuck a Post-it note on the page where the internship details were. It was typical of Tess to notice; her cousin rarely missed a trick. While Nina cruised through life, Tess was meticulous in everything she did, even if it was just flicking through a magazine.

'Ummm . . . I'm interested in some info that's on there,' she said vaguely.

Tess looked at the page again. 'What? The tweets about how fab the last issue was? Or the letter of the month from Pamela in Edinburgh about body image?'

'No, not those.' Nina didn't know why she was so reluctant to tell Tess. Maybe it was because her cousin loved working in the hospitality industry and wouldn't understand why Nina wanted a change. Or she'd look at Nina like she was coco bananas for thinking about pursuing a new career when she already had a perfectly good job and she only had a few months left on her working visa. Then she remembered Johan's words – 'What have you got to lose?'

'I'm going to apply for an internship at *Marie Claude*.' The words were out before Nina could change her mind. She pretended to be busy searching for something in her bag as she steeled herself for Tess's reaction.

'An internship? To do what?'

'To work in the features department, so I can get some work experience under my belt and see if I like it,' Nina muttered. Bloody Johan, she should never have listened to him and his crazy ideas.

'What about your job at the hotel?'

'What about it? I've been there for almost two years; they can't stop me from leaving,' Nina said, hating the tinge of defensiveness in her tone.

'So you'd quit? What will you do for money?'

'I don't know, Tess. To be honest, I haven't thought about it,' Nina sighed, trying not to get frustrated by her cousin's practical nature. 'I only just found out this afternoon that the internship exists. I'm sure they have thousands of applicants, so I probably won't even get an interview, but I thought I may as well give it a crack. You've got to be in it to win it,' she said, echoing Johan's earlier encouraging words, more for herself than for Tess.

'Well, I think it's a great idea.'

'Sorry?' Nina raised her head from her bag to stare at her cousin.

'I think it's a great idea,' Tess repeated. 'You haven't been happy at the hotel for ages and the longer you stay in the industry, the harder it'll be to get out. I've always said you're a total magazine tragic, so if you're going to quit your job to try a new career, surely that's the most obvious one. Plus, weren't you the editor of your school magazine back in the day?'

'Technically yes, but I hardly did anything; I was too busy chasing boys!'

'So? The editor of *Marie Claude*, or whoever you have to apply to, doesn't need to know that! It might not be the same as saying you're Anna Wintour's long-lost daughter, but it could give you a point of difference from the other candidates.'

'True . . . and I do need all the points of difference I can get. So you really think it's a good idea?' Nina asked.

'Life's too short to be miserable,' Tess said firmly. 'If the hotel thing isn't rocking your world anymore, then it's time to move on. And if you don't get the *Marie Claude* internship, I'm sure there are others you could apply for. And if none of them work out, it's not going to kill you to keep working at the hotel for another couple of months until your visa expires. Especially with all the tips and presents you guys get,' she added wryly.

'I might need to sell all those presents on eBay if I get this internship, seeing it's unpaid,' Nina pointed out, while reaching under the couch.

'Especially that one,' Tess said dryly, as Nina pulled her iPad out from its pink leopard print Marc Jacobs cover; both were gifts from Herr Schmidt, an Austrian millionaire who regularly stayed at the Bickford and loved to splash his cash around.

Logging into her email, Nina ignored all the magazine e-newsletters she'd signed up for and started to compose her internship application. Having read a ridiculous amount of magazines, she knew it was important to strike the right tone – chatty but not too familiar, informative but not boring. She needed to sell herself to them, so that it didn't matter that there was a gaping hole on her CV where a journalism degree should be, or that she didn't have any other work experience in the industry to her name. 'Everyone has to start somewhere,' she thought determinedly, tapping out sentences then immediately deleting them, rewriting again and again until she was happy. After almost an hour, she looked up. 'Tess, can you read this for me and tell me honestly what you think?' She handed her cousin the iPad. 'Does it sound like I'm begging? Would you at least get me in for an interview if you were the features editor of *Marie Claude*?'

Nina watched intently as Tess's eyes scanned her letter of application. She paused a couple of times, replaced a word here and there, tweaked the opening sentence, then gave the iPad back to Nina.

'It's good. You're not begging, you're just explaining how passionate you are about magazines and how you're willing to schlep around doing the coffee run every morning for three months if it means getting your foot in the door. I reckon they'd have loads of applications from people who think it'll be twenty-four/seven glamour and assume they'll be interviewing celebrities and sitting front row at fashion shows in their first week of interning – I wouldn't be surprised if they're just happy to hear from someone who's frothing over photocopying.'

'Well, hopefully I'll get to do a bit more than just fetching coffee and photocopying if I'm successful, but I get where you're coming from. Okay, so I'm pressing "send". There definitely weren't any spelling mistakes, right? Maybe I should do another spellcheck, just to make sure. I don't know if I'm one hundred per cent happy with the last sentence, maybe I'll change it . . .'

'Oh, for Christ's sake – it's fine. If you're not going to send it, I bloody will.' Tess reached over and tapped 'send' before Nina could stop her. 'There. Now it's winging its way through cyberspace to *Marie Claude*'s features editor and there's nothing you can do about it, so stop stressing. Here, distract yourself with these, seeing you've just bought them.' She dumped the pile of new glossies in Nina's lap. 'You'd better memorise every single word in *Marie Claude* in case they spring a pop quiz on you in the interview.'

'There's no guarantee I'll get an interview,' Nina reminded her. 'They might have a massive backlog of applications from candidates who have been doing work experience for years, so my email will probably be deleted before they get to the second sentence.'

'Yeah, that's the right attitude to have,' Tess said witheringly. 'Talk yourself out of it before anything has even had a chance to happen. There's something to be said for positive thinking, you know. I would have thought you'd be an expert on that, given the endless self-help articles that are in those magazines of yours.'

'Oh shut up. As if you don't read them, too! Go on, give me the *Marie Claude* then; I can't read it when you've got it, can I? Here, you can have the *Grazia* – I know you can't wait to find out about Angelina's secret affair with her nanny . . .'

four

It was after midday when Nina emerged from the bedroom the next day. Tess had taken herself off to bed at a respectable hour, thanks to her alarm being set for five thirty am for the early shift, but Nina had been sucked into the magazine vortex until two in the morning. Or was it closer to two thirty? Her body clock had waved the white flag of surrender a few months after she'd started working shifts, so now she felt like she was permanently jet-lagged.

Opening the fridge, she pulled out a half-full bottle of Diet Coke and swigged the lot, staring blankly at her reflection in the kitchen window. As usual, her mop of hair was all over the place – parched from repeated slatherings of peroxide, it had rebelled by morphing from dead straight to full-on frizz, no matter how many deep-conditioning treatments she fed it. If she was lucky, sometimes it would behave and curl itself into respectable waves, but most of the time it ignored her attempts to control it, giving Johan no reason to stop calling her 'fluffball'. Smoothing her eyebrows, her fingers traced over her forehead, cheeks and chin, checking for any eruptions that might have occurred overnight. Having had bad skin as a teenager, Nina was constantly on high alert for the next breakout, and was always sceptical when people complimented her on what nice skin she had. If she had to choose, her favourite feature was her eyes – actually, her eyelashes to be precise. They were naturally Bambi-esque, but made thicker and darker thanks to the four different mascaras she slathered them in every day.

Satisfied that the pimple fairy hadn't paid an overnight visit, she chucked the empty Diet Coke bottle in the bin and started tidying up the scattered magazines, sorting them into piles of what she'd read and what she had yet to devour. Picking up a cushion, she found her iPad hiding underneath, its battery icon glowing red with less than twenty per cent power remaining. Plugging it into the charger, she left it on the coffee table and headed to the bathroom.

Sitting in the bath as the water from the handheld shower dribbled pathetically over her shoulders, Nina longed for a proper stand-up shower like she'd grown up with back home in Australia. England's obsession with baths didn't impress Nina at all; they made her sleepy instead of waking her up like a powerful burst of hot water did. Plus, she hated having to sit in scummy water full of shampoo suds while waiting for the conditioner to penetrate her frizz. Then there was the problem of the building's antiquated hot-water system – if one of the girls forgot to flick the hot-water switch on before they went to bed, they'd have to suffer through a freezing-cold bath in the morning. Not exactly ideal when it was five thirty am and zero degrees outside.

After drying herself, Nina threw her wet towel over the bedroom door in a futile attempt to dry it in time for tomorrow's shower-slash-bath then pulled on a pair of metallic black skinny jeans and an oversized grey marle t-shirt. Slapping on some moisturiser, she brushed her teeth then began her make-up routine. Liquid foundation mixed with a dab of illuminator, Touche Éclat concealer blended under her eyes and around her nose, a liberal application of bronzer to combat her London 'ghost tan', then a swipe of Topshop silver eyeliner and the requisite application of four different mascaras – one for thickening, one for lengthening, one for curling and the last for separating. Tidying up smudges with a cotton tip, she patted on a tiny amount of pink cream blush, pulled her hair up into a topknot, squirted on some Coco Mademoiselle, then switched off the bathroom light. Winding a chunky chartreuse-coloured scarf around her neck and shoving her feet into zebra-print pony-hair flats, Nina grabbed her bag and leather jacket and left the flat. She was halfway down the stairs when she realised she'd left her phone next to her bed. Pulling a quick one-eighty, she headed back along the hallway, unlocked the door and grabbed it. 'May as well take one of the mags I haven't read yet for the Tube,' she thought, making a beeline for the living room. Next to the stack of magazines was her iPad, with a much more respectable eighty-five per cent battery power, so she crammed it into her bag alongside the new *Glamour* she hadn't got around to cracking open the night before.

She took the Victoria line to Green Park Tube station, where she forced herself to walk up the endless series of escalators so she could kid herself that she'd ticked the 'daily exercise' box. Fighting her way through the crowd of tourists who were desperately trying to work out which exit was the right one for their afternoon tea booking at the Ritz, she sidestepped the guys selling tickets for the endless parade of open-top double-decker sightseeing buses that chugged their way down Piccadilly to Hyde Park Corner, then dived into the nearest Pret A Manger, the ubiquitous English sandwich store, for a late breakfast. 'Maybe if the magazine thing doesn't work out, I can open a chain of Prets in Australia?' she pondered while trying to decide which sandwich her tastebuds felt like. 'Super club . . . Hoisin duck wrap . . . Coronation chicken – bleurgh, no way in hell . . .' she thought, screwing her nose up at the lurid yellow mayonnaise seeping through the slices of bread. Selecting a sweet chilli chicken and coriander baguette and a honey and muesli yoghurt pot, Nina silently thanked the High Priestess of Pret that the lunch rush was over so she didn't have to wait in an endless line to pay.

Be Careful What You Wish For

Pulling up a stool at the window overlooking Piccadilly and Green Park, she dumped her bag on the bench and tore the wrapping off her baguette. Chewing on her first mouthful, she tried to shove her wallet into her bulging handbag, but it refused to swallow it. Pulling her iPad out to make room, Nina decided to check her email to see if her latest ASOS order had been dispatched. Her inbox appeared as the tablet automatically logged on to Pret's wireless internet and started downloading messages. Seeing none of them were from ASOS, she was just about to shut it down, when her eyes locked onto an email from a name she didn't recognise, but with a subject line she definitely did – 'Re: *Marie Claude* features internship'. Her stomach did a clumsy somersault. Steeling herself for a 'thanks, but no thanks' reply, she opened the email.

To: Nina Morey
From: Lizzie Crawford

Dear Nina, thank you for your interest in an internship in the features department of Britain's number-one women's lifestyle magazine, *Marie Claude*. As you may or may not be aware, the three-month internship is unpaid and shortlisted applicants are required to come in for an interview before the final candidate is selected by our features director. We are currently interviewing for our next internship, which starts Monday May 3. Would you be available to meet with Saffron Pickering, *Marie Claude's* features director, this Friday at 10.30 am? You will find our address below. Please confirm you can attend the interview by return email.

Kind regards,
Lizzie
Features assistant
Marie Claude

Nina was reading the email for the third time when she realised her phone was ringing. Grabbing it from the side pocket of her bag, she recognised the number of the front desk at Tess's hotel. She didn't bother to say hello, instead blurting out, 'Oh my God, Tess, guess what, guess what, guess WHAT?!!!?' She knew she was sounding scarily like a fourteen-year-old who'd just found out she'd won a date with Justin Bieber, but she couldn't help it.

'Hi to you too. What?' Tess said in a resigned tone that was code for 'I've been up since five thirty and have been dealing with incessant demands from guests all day, and the last thing I want to do is play guessing games so make this quick'.

'I just got an email from the features assistant of *Marie Claude* – they've asked me to go in on Friday morning for an interview!' Nina squealed, reading the email again just to make sure it wasn't a figment of her imagination.

'That's great! What time? Where do you have to go? What are you going to wear? Did they ask you to bring anything with you, like story ideas or something?' Excitement rose in Tess's voice as she fired off questions.

'It's on Friday at ten thirty at their offices near the London Eye. They don't mention taking anything with me. Shit, I haven't even thought about to what to wear, I only got the email literally a minute before you called. Do you think I should go down the corporate road or wear something more on trend? I don't want to look like I'm going to a fancy-dress party as Lady Gaga, but I need to look like I know the difference between Prada and Primark.'

'At least you've got some time to think about it seeing the interview isn't till the day after tomorrow – are you rostered on that morning?' Tess asked.

'No, thank God. My ten-day stint finishes tomorrow with an early shift, so I'll have time to hit the shops afterwards if I need to buy something. I'll have to workshop it tonight when I get home, sorry.' Nina knew that Tess would probably be tucked up in bed by the time she walked in the door after clocking off at eleven pm, but this was an emergency.

'I'm sure I'll survive; just take everything you want out of the wardrobe and try it on in the living room so I don't have to deal with the light being on.'

'Roger that – I'll be as quiet and as quick as possible, I promise. I'd better go. I need to finish my breakfast and email the *Marie Claude* chick back about the interview before heading to work.'

'All good, there's a new arrival walking in the door right now anyway. Talk later.'

Nina ended the call and did a time check – she had twenty minutes in which to cram the rest of the baguette in her mouth, reply to Lizzie's email and hoof it down to the Bickford, where she had to change into her uniform before making her way through the back-of-house labyrinth to the front desk for handover. Chewing furiously, she hit the 'reply' button and sent a quick email to the features assistant to confirm the interview on Friday. Then she gathered up her things and started walking towards Knightsbridge, while spooning muesli, honey and yoghurt into her mouth. 'Johan will have kittens when I tell him,' she thought. 'Maybe I should keep it quiet and wait to see how the interview goes before I fill him in . . . ? Nah, never going to happen; not when we're about to do an eight-hour shift together.' As she disappeared into the Hyde Park Corner underpass, Nina felt excitement bubbling away in the cauldron of her stomach. Something good was about to happen – she just knew it.

five

Four weeks later, Nina was lurching across the Thames via the Waterloo Bridge, feeling distinctly average. Slurping water from a large bottle, she desperately tried to knock her hangover on its head before rocking up on the doorstep of Marie Claude HQ for the first day of her three-month internship.

'What made me think it was a good idea to go to Freedom for a few drinks last night? Why didn't Tess take me home after the sixth round of G&Ts? Bloody Johan, he was a mission to get me hammered. It's fine for them, they're both rostered on late shifts today,' she bitched to herself as she counted down the seconds till the painkillers would kick in, knowing full well she only had herself to blame. She should have been tucked up in bed by nine o'clock, getting a bucketload of shut-eye to kick-start her new life, but instead she had been ricocheting around Freedom, celebrating the end of her hospitality career a little too enthusiastically. Thankfully she had realised it was time to leave after she'd drunkenly fallen off her chair, ending up with her head in a total stranger's lap. 'Classy, Nina, very classy . . .' she berated herself as she tiptoed gingerly down the steps on the south side of the river and turned left towards the OXO Tower. She walked past the National Theatre and along Southbank, taking the same route as she had four weeks before when she'd fronted up for her internship interview. Lizzie, the stand-offish features assistant, had collected her from the reception area of *Marie Claude*'s editorial office and ushered her into a small meeting room where Saffron, the features director, was already waiting, surrounded by empty takeaway coffee cups. Ignoring her nerves, Nina had pasted on her most confident smile and gripped Saffron's outstretched hand with slightly more force than she'd intended.

'That's quite a handshake you have there,' Saffron had said in an upper-crust 'Daddy, I want a pony' accent, while she checked out Nina's bright pink skater-style Topshop dress teamed with the black YSL Tribute knock-offs she'd bought from Zara the day before. Nina swallowed, about to apologise for her vice-like grip, but Saffron continued, 'I always think you can tell a lot about a person from their handshake; there's nothing worse than feeling like you're holding a dead fish.' She smiled. 'Do they teach everybody to shake hands like that Down Under?'

'Uh, not that I know of. My dad always told me to have a strong handshake; he also thinks that it has a lot to do with first impressions . . .' Nina had trailed off, wondering why on earth she was talking about her dad, of all people.

'Your father sounds like a very sensible man. Now, tell me a bit about yourself, Nina – what makes you get out of bed in the morning?'

'You mean besides coffee?' she had joked, looking pointedly at the collection of cups before she could stop herself.

'Aha, a fellow caffeine addict, are we?' Saffron had nodded approvingly. 'That will come in handy, seeing our features intern does a coffee run for the team at least twice a day, sometimes more. Luckily, there's a Pret just around the corner, so you don't have to go too far. You'll also be required to do the lunch run, if needed, especially when we're on deadline. Transcribing interviews, photocopying, researching, writing call-outs to find talent for stories, following up reader requests, basically helping out with anything the team asks you to do. What you won't be doing is schmoozing with celebrities, going to fabulous parties or playing in the fashion cupboard – I've interviewed too many wannabe interns who think their time here will involve being besties with Alexa Chung.' She sighed wearily. 'Not. Going. To. Happen.'

'I'm not here to suck up to celebs,' Nina had blurted out, the ghost of Cupcake lurking at the back of her mind. 'I'm here because I really, really love magazines. I want to learn what makes the industry tick, how magazines are compiled, how the content is decided and how to write a really great article. I know I won't be doing any actual writing, but quite frankly I'd just be happy to breathe the same air as you guys. I'm willing to run and fetch whatever you want me to – as long as it's not illegal!'

Saffron had raised an impeccably groomed eyebrow as Nina finished her spiel. 'I think you should meet the rest of the features team,' she'd said.

Three hours later, Nina's phone had rung – it was Lizzie, telling her that out of the one hundred and fifty candidates who had applied for the internship, Saffron had chosen Nina. She'd given the Bickford four weeks' notice, turning on the charm offensive during her last weeks so she could make the most of the guests' deep pockets. She became an expert at casually mentioning she was leaving her job just as they reached for their Louis Vuitton wallets, and was pleasantly surprised at how many fifty-pound notes she'd accrued by the end of her shifts. Annika and Johan had organised a farewell party where she'd made endless promises to keep in touch and had gritted her teeth through the constant *Devil Wears Prada* jokes everyone insisted on telling her when they found out why she was leaving. She had called her bank and begged them to increase her overdraft limit and had uploaded most of the freebies she'd been gifted from the hotel's guests onto eBay to boost her savings, which she now had to live off for the next three months. Eeeek . . .

And now the first day of her new salary-free life had arrived – with a vicious hangover along for the ride. She pressed the buzzer and gave her name to the voice at the other end of the *Marie Claude* intercom, while sucking furiously on an extra-strength mint, hoping it would kill off any whiffs of eau de booze that might still be lingering. Pushing the door open, she walked up two flights of stairs, stopping halfway to change out of her ballet flats into a pair of high-heeled red suede ankle boots, before arriving at the frosted-glass doors with the name of the magazine emblazoned in silver. Desperately hoping she looked better than she felt, Nina presented herself at the reception desk. Behind it sat a girl with a full-on Afro, bright orange lips and a dove grey dress that Nina was sure she'd spotted on the catwalk in Victoria Beckham's latest collection.

'Hiya, you're the new features intern, yeah?' the girl said with a strong South London accent. 'Saffy's not in yet, but Lizzie is here – let me give her a buzz. Take a seat while you're waiting.'

Grateful to be told what to do so her throbbing brain didn't have to think for itself, Nina perched on the white leather couch next to the reception desk as the receptionist dialled Lizzie. 'The Australian is here. Yeah, your new intern. Oh. Really? Jaysus, the poor girl. I'm glad it's her and not me! See you in a bit,' she said cheerily, not bothering to lower her voice, despite the fact Nina was sitting less than two metres away. Turning towards Nina, she said, 'Lizzie's coming for you now. I'm Shantaya, but everyone calls me Taya. Welcome to *Marie Claude*.' Her face broke into one of the most stunning smiles Nina had ever seen. Before she had a chance to introduce herself, Lizzie appeared, looking as welcoming as Jennifer Aniston would if Angelina Jolie had crashed her wedding.

'Nina, come with me,' she said abruptly. 'There's been a slight change of plan – you'll still be sitting with the features team, but for the first four weeks of your internship you'll be the acting PA to our editor-in-chief, Charlotte. Her new PA can't start for another month and the temp we'd booked cancelled this morning, so seeing you have some receptionist experience, we figured you'd be a good fill-in. I presume that's okay?' As she spoke, she was leading Nina to the features department, which was positioned just outside what was obviously the editor's office.

Nina wasn't sure if it was okay or not – acting as the editor's assistant didn't exactly sound like her cup of Earl Grey. She remembered all the jokes about *The Devil Wears Prada* at her farewell party and wondered if Charlotte was anything like the book's villain, Miranda Priestley. Oh please God, no . . .

'I forgot to mention that while you're acting as Charlotte's PA, you'll get paid. Not a lot but it's better than nothing, which is what you get paid during the internship. And when Charlotte doesn't need you, you'll help out with the features department. It's the best of both worlds, really,' Lizzie said, somewhat unconvincingly. Nina got the impression that the features assistant was getting a kick out of telling the new intern that she'd be at the mercy of the editor-in-chief's whims for the next month and wondered why she already felt a prickle of animosity between them. 'But Charlotte won't be coming in today, she's in Paris having lunch with Monsieur

Lagerfeld, so you just have to take messages from anyone who calls for her.'

Nina realised she didn't have much of a choice. The situation wasn't exactly ideal, but she wasn't going to be a precious princess about it. There was nothing to be gained from stamping her feet and insisting that she was here for a features internship and nothing else. Four weeks wasn't that long, and at least she'd be getting paid for her efforts. She'd never been a personal assistant before, but how hard could it be? It was just as well she didn't have to deal with Charlotte in person today, though; she could sit and stew in her hangover while fielding phone calls and getting coffee. Maybe she could even read a magazine or two – surely that was considered legitimate work?

'No problem, Lizzie,' she assured the other woman, determined to be nothing but courteous, even though Lizzie was yet to offer her a shadow of a smile. 'Where would you like me to sit? And could someone show me how to work the phone system?' Nina continued to bombard the features assistant with questions, from how to get a computer log-in to where the bathrooms were, and making notes on how to transfer calls, who to put through straight away and, more importantly, who to take a message from after informing them that Charlotte was in a very urgent meeting and couldn't possibly be disturbed, even though she was actually sitting in her office, gossiping with the advertising director while having her weekly in-office manicure.

As the rest of the *Marie Claude* staff trickled in, Nina forced herself to ignore her hangover as the phone began to ring incessantly, and an avalanche of emails started pouring in from publicists desperate to know if the editor-in-chief would be gracing them with her presence at the launch of a new yoghurt/toilet freshener/scrapbooking website later that week (no . . . no . . . let me think about that for a second – no.) Then there was the avalanche of *Marie Claude* staff who all wanted a piece of the Charlotte pie – Nina started to explain to the mob who turned up in front of her desk that she wasn't Charlotte's new PA, she was actually the new features intern, just filling in until the new assistant could start. But no one seemed to care – all they wanted to know was, 'What time are we expecting Charlotte? What do you mean she's in Paris?! When will she be back? Does she have her BlackBerry with her? Why didn't I know about this?! I need her to approve this new model for tomorrow's shoot; the one we had booked has pulled out because her rock star boyfriend overdosed backstage in New York on the weekend. And now the photographer is having a tantrum because we couldn't get his favourite caterers so the shoot is pretty much doomed – you don't know how he can be when he doesn't get his favourite roast beef with Yorkshire pudding just the way he likes it!! This shoot is going to be a complete disaster, I just know it!!! I don't know why I bother sometimes, I really don't!!!!'

Throughout all the histrionics and exclamation marks, Nina nodded and smiled sympathetically as the fashion editor grew increasingly hysterical. She could feel Lizzie's eyes on her from behind her computer screen, no doubt waiting to witness how she'd handle her first potential stumbling block as Charlotte's temporary PA. She took a deep breath, determined not to crumble, although she was quite tempted to remind the fashion editor that there were bigger problems in the world at the moment than a no-show model and a picky photographer. She was on Planet Fashion now, she reminded herself with a shiver of glee, which meant these kind of hiccups had to be taken seriously. 'Why don't you send Charlotte the link to the new model's website and she can look at it on her BlackBerry in Paris?' she suggested, desperately hoping that the editor did indeed have her BlackBerry with her and she hadn't forgotten to charge it before she glided onto the EuroStar that morning. 'And surely the other caterers can whip up roast beef with Yorkshire pudding for the photographer if you ask nicely? You never know, it may even be better than his favourite . . .' The fashion editor looked at her like she'd just blasphemed, then shook her head and stalked off, with Lizzie quickly following.

Nina became aware of an expectant silence behind her. Swivelling around in her chair, she came face to face with Saffron and the rest of the features team — Amelia, the associate features editor; Solange, the senior features writer; Kitty, the commissioning editor — all of whom she'd met briefly four weeks before. After stalking their by-lines in the magazine for so long, it was slightly bizarre to not only put faces to the names but to be sitting right in front of them, ready to help with whatever they needed her to do. But first things first — she could tell by the looks on their faces that they were all gagging for one thing: the same thing she was. Grabbing the nearest pen and scrabbling in the top drawer for a Post-it note, Nina injected a double shot of enthusiasm into her voice and asked in her best 'eager intern' tone, 'Right then, ladies, who wants a coffee?'

six

'I want to hear ALL about it – how many celebrities have you met? What are the girls in the office like? Is the editor a total bitch or is she one of those inspirational Oprah-esque women who everyone adores? And most importantly, what killer outfits have you been busting out?' Johan fired off multiple questions as they walked towards the pub near the *Marie Claude* office. It was Nina's third day on the job and Johan had come to meet her for lunch on his day off, practically foaming at the mouth in anticipation of hearing all the salacious office gossip from the world of women's magazines.

'So far, so good,' Nina replied, 'despite you pouring G&Ts down my throat the night before my first day. Luckily the editor was out of the office having lunch with Karl Lagerfeld in Paris, so me and my raging hangover didn't have to deal with her. I just answered the phone, replied to emails and helped the features team with transcribing. So yesterday was the first time I met Charlotte.'

'She's the editor?'

'Editor-in-chief, actually. Yep, she's been the editor for a couple of years; before *Marie Claude* she was the editor of *Grazia*. What do you want to drink?' she asked.

'Do you even need to ask?' Johan said.

Nina smiled and asked the barmaid, 'Can I get one gin and tonic and a Diet Coke, please?'

'*Diet Coke?*' Johan repeated incredulously.

'Unlike you, I have to go back to work – it wouldn't be a good look if I walked in reeking of booze and slurring my words, would it? Monday was bad enough, so I need to behave myself. Plus I don't think Lizzie, a girl who I have to deal with quite a bit, likes me very much so I don't want to give her any opportunity to spread a rumour about the new intern being an alcoholic,' she half-joked, thinking she wouldn't put it past her. Ignoring Johan's disappointed look, she collected the drinks and led the way to the large communal table in the middle of the room.

'So what's Charlotte like? Is she Miranda Priestley's long-lost sister?'

'She's . . . interesting. Very glamorous and polished, decked out in the most amazing head-to-toe designer gear, but for someone who's very successful and in charge of a magazine brand that is supposed to inspire and empower women by tackling serious issues, she seems to be a bit of a neurotic, spoilt brat.'

'I love it! Tell me more. Does she throw tantrums when her lunch isn't heated up to the right temperature or something?'

'Not that I know of, although she went out for lunch yesterday and today. It could definitely be on the agenda. From what I've heard the staff say, she doesn't have a lot of confidence in her decisions, whether it's who to put on the cover, what to wear in her editor's letter photo or which order the stories should run. It drives the features girls mad because they'll get briefed on an article but then she'll change her mind five times about what angle she wants it to have, whether it should be a first-person point of view or have expert advice mixed with narrative; stuff like that. So the writers can be halfway through a three-thousand-word article and she'll suddenly decide that instead of a serious investigative piece she wants a fluffy, celebrity-filled trend report. And then she also spends the magazine's budget like it's her own bank account – I had to hide her from the managing editor yesterday after a massive invoice arrived from the car company.'

'Why? Had she crashed it or something? And what's the difference between an editor-in-chief and a managing editor?' Johan asked.

'The managing editor mainly deals with all the invoices and budgets, so they're the ones who hold the purse strings. Apparently Charlotte had asked her previous PA to book a car to take her and her boyfriend to Glastonbury, but she wasn't sure how long she wanted to stay. So instead of sending the driver back and booking a time to pick them up again, she got him to wait outside the VIP entrance for the entire time they were there, which ended up being three days – at a rate of seventy-five pounds an hour. You do the maths.'

Johan drained his G&T with an impressed look on his face. 'It sounds like Charlotte could give Cupcake a run for her money. So even though she was going to Glastonbury for personal reasons, she still charged the car to the company account?'

Nina nodded. 'I think there might be something in her contract about using the car service for big events where she needs to be seen, and I guess she figured Glasto was one of them. Although I get the impression that the managing editor had other ideas. Shall we order food?'

While they waited for their meals to arrive, Johan filled her in on all the Bickford gossip. His favourite guest, AJ Armstrong, had arrived for his annual three-month stint in one of the large suites, preferably the one with its own private entrance at the back of the hotel so his visitors could come and go as they pleased. And AJ always had a lot of visitors when he was in London, particularly young male ones. The only son of a disgustingly wealthy landowner in Kent, AJ looked like a well-bred country Englishman from central casting. But you only had to catch the gleam in his eye as he watched Johan faff around the Bickford's front desk to realise that all was not quite as it seemed. It had reminded Nina of a hawk watching its prey, but Johan loved the attention. That wasn't surprising, seeing Johan loved any attention, especially if it was from a good-looking guy in his late thirties who also happened to be stonkingly rich.

'Do you think he'll ever ask me out?' Johan asked, before shovelling a huge portion of bangers and mash into his mouth.

'Would you go if he did? You know staff aren't allowed to fraternise with the guests outside of work,' Nina chided him as she picked at her caesar salad. 'Then again, that never stopped Sofia . . .'

'Exactly! And if she could get flown to Dubai and stay in that plush seven-star hotel, thanks to Sheikh El-Shamed, then why can't I go for a drink with AJ Armstong?'

'Because he hasn't asked you,' Nina said promptly, then followed it up with, 'and Sofia was sacked when Mr Farrington-Smyth found out about her Dubai trip.'

'Hmmm, I guess you're right,' Johan admitted reluctantly. Then he brightened. 'Although if I was AJ's boyfriend, I probably wouldn't need to work anyway so it wouldn't matter if I got fired . . .'

'Alright, princess, don't get too far ahead of yourself. I suspect AJ Armstrong has plenty of guys who'd be happy to go for a drink with him, so take a ticket and get in line. I've got to get back to work. What are you doing for the rest of the afternoon?'

'Going to the gym to work off those bangers, then I might see who's around Soho for a coffee or something. I really should call my mum at some stage too; it's been a while since Mutti heard from me.'

Johan's parents lived in a small town near Munich, blissfully unaware that their youngest son was a champion batter for the other team. They were under the impression that Nina was his girlfriend, a situation that Johan was in no hurry to rectify — after all, technically she *was* his girlfriend, just in a platonic way. Luckily, neither of his parents liked travelling so he didn't have to worry about them turning up in London for a surprise weekend to see him in his natural habitat, although he always remembered to remove the posters of a half-naked David Beckham and hide his gay porn magazines under his mattress before he Skyped them, just in case they caught a glimpse of something suspicious on the webcam.

Five minutes later, Nina was back at her desk in the *Marie Claude* offices, surreptitiously checking for any lettuce remnants lurking in her teeth before dialling her voicemail to see if there were any messages for Charlotte. Just as she finished writing them all down, already knowing full well that Charlotte would never call any of them back, the woman herself made an appearance. So thin she made a chopstick look like it should sign up to Overeaters Anonymous, she was dressed in head-to-toe Gucci, except for the sold-out Céline bag that was draped over her arm. Walking through the office, she called out to Martin, the magazine's long-time art director, who rushed to her side. Nina could hear their conversation get louder as they approached Charlotte's office.

'Martin, darling, I'm not sure about this cover shoot next week. Do you really think Chantelle Sainsbury is the right person for us? I know that talent show she's on is hugely popular and she's married to that footballer, but she's a bit common for *Marie Claude*, don't you think?'

'Charlotte, the shoot has already been confirmed; it's taken us months to secure time with Chantelle. We've already promised her publicist the September cover so if we don't go ahead with it, the PR will blackball us – not only for any future covers with Chantelle, but with all the other celebs on her company's books too.'

'Oh rubbish, that's what they all say,' Charlotte said airily. 'I never listen to their pathetic threats – they know that we're the number-one women's lifestyle magazine in the country; they need us more than we need them.'

'If it was any other celeb, I'd agree with you, but it's Chantelle – she's the nation's sweetheart. Plus it's an exclusive. All the other magazine editors would burn their Prada media discount cards on the spot if it meant they could shoot her for their cover.'

'And perhaps that's exactly why we shouldn't. If everyone else is so desperate for her, maybe it would be better to shoot her for an inside story, but run someone else on the cover. That would show everyone that even though every other rag is desperate to have her on their cover, she's not yet worthy of a prestigious *Marie Claude* cover.'

Nina caught sight of Martin's face as they stopped outside Charlotte's office – it showed a mix of disbelief and frustration. She didn't blame him. Since she'd become part of the *Marie Claude* team, the favourite topic of office gossip was the Chantelle Sainsbury shoot – how it'd taken almost six months of negotiations to get the shoot date locked in, not to mention all the demands that had to be met to keep Ms Sainsbury and her PR company happy. As green as Nina was, even she knew Charlotte was being unreasonable. After all that hard work, it didn't make sense to throw away what would probably be a best-selling cover just because of Charlotte's ego and exaggerated views of where *Marie Claude* sat in the magazine food chain. Despite the magazine's impeccable pedigree, the last circulation audit had reported a double-digit percentage slip in sales. It was still the best-selling magazine in the UK, but only just – its closest competitor was now snapping at its Manolo Blahnik heels. 'Maybe that's why Charlotte is panicking,' thought Nina. 'And when you panic, you make stupid decisions.' Suddenly she realised Charlotte was talking to her.

'Tina, get me an Americano – extra hot – and a plain pretzel. Then grab a camera and dictaphone from the features team and go do some vox pops on what people think of Chantelle Sainsbury. Not just any people – choose women who look like *Marie Claude* readers. Covent Garden is probably the best place, if you can avoid the tourists. Actually, ask them if they read the magazine before you ask them about her; I'm not interested in people who aren't our audience. We need to get an idea of whether she's *Marie Claude* cover material or not.'

'Isn't that what the research department is for?' asked Martin, before Nina could say anything.

'Oh, bugger the research department! They always sit on the fence and never give you a definitive answer when you ask them about the popularity of celebrities. I haven't bothered with the research people for months; I'd rather the interns hit the streets to get our own idea of what the public thinks, so that's what Tina is going do.'

'Uh, it's Nina, actually,' Nina said, hoping she didn't sound too pathetic.

'What?' Charlotte said tetchily. 'Oh, right. Nina. Yes. Well, hurry up, Nina, I won't be impressed if Pret have run out of pretzels by the time you get down there.'

'Of course, Charlotte. I'll be right back.' Grabbing her wallet, Nina waved at Taya as she scooted past the reception desk and clattered down the stairs. Pushing open the doors of the cafe around the corner, she gave Charlotte's order and waited for the coffee to be brewed.

'So how's being Charlotte's slave working out for you?'

Nina immediately recognised the bitchy tone and turned to see *Marie Claude*'s features assistant in the line behind her. 'Oh Lizzie, hi. It's good, thanks. I'm just getting her a coffee and a pretzel, then she's asked me to go to Covent Garden to do some vox pops to see what people think about the cover,' Nina told her.

Lizzie's face lost its smirk and her eyes widened. 'She's asked you to do *what*?' she choked out. 'Vox pops?! That's *my* job. I'm the vox-pop princess of *Marie Claude*! I had to wait three months before she trusted me enough to do them. You've been here for what? Three days? Did she ask you to take me along?'

Nina looked at Lizzie's face, which had become red and blotchy. She was obviously upset, but there wasn't much Nina could do about it – she wasn't going to lie, just because Lizzie was throwing her toys out of the pram.

'Uh no, she didn't. Maybe she figured you're too busy doing other stuff for the features department? She gave me quite detailed instructions so I should be okay by myself, but can I call you if I have any problems?' Nina was trying to leave Lizzie with a scrap of pride, but the features assistant didn't seem to appreciate the gesture.

'Don't bother,' Lizzie snapped. 'If Charlotte thinks you're up to it, let's see how you go. But believe me, if you don't come back with exactly what she's asked for, you'd be better off not coming back at all,' she warned, before stalking off empty-handed. Nina stared after her, wondering what all the fuss was about – after all, it wasn't like Charlotte had proclaimed that Nina would be spending five hours interviewing Chantelle Sainsbury for the cover story; it was just some random vox pops. But Lizzie obviously felt her turf was being stomped all over by the new girl, on top of whatever else she'd done to rub her up the wrong way. As Nina collected Charlotte's coffee from the barista, tucked the pretzel into her bag and headed out the door, she had the horrible feeling she'd just made her very first enemy in the publishing industry.

seven

Looking around the private room of the swanky members club in Shoreditch, Nina nudged Tess. 'Can you believe it's our leaving party? Truth be told, I don't know if I'm ready to go back to Australia . . .'

'I hate to break it to you, but it's not like you have any choice,' Tess reminded her. 'There's the small problem of your visa expiring in a week, so it's time to go, sunshine. But it's not like you're going back to the same old place – it'll be exciting moving to Sydney and starting our new lives there. I don't know about you, but after three years in London, I can't wait to kick back at North Bondi Italian and perve on cute surfer boys with a glass of prosecco in my hand.'

'Yeah, I guess,' Nina said grudgingly. 'I just feel like I'm on a roll here – I've finally found what I want to do with my career and have managed to get a foot in the door of the British magazine industry, and now I have to pack up and start all over again in Sydney, where I don't know anyone and no one knows me.'

'Oh, for God's sake, drink a concrete milkshake and harden the fuck up,' Tess said exasperatedly. 'It's not like you're moving back without any magazine experience on your CV – you scored a coveted internship at a globally recognised magazine, where they absolutely loved you. If that reference from Charlotte doesn't open doors for you, then nothing will.'

Despite throwing herself a pity party, Nina knew Tess was right. Her stint at *Marie Claude* had come to an end the week before; as Nina had told the features team before she walked out the office door for the last time, it had been the best three months of her life. Loving photocopying, transcribing and the endless coffee runs more than any human being should, she'd joked to Johan that she'd found her spiritual home. Even the original hiccup of being Charlotte's assistant for the first month had worked to her advantage – from what Saffy had told her, Charlotte had made an art form of pointedly ignoring all the previous features interns, but seeing Nina had been her acting PA, she had been forced to acknowledge her existence after Josephine, her new assistant, had started. She'd even tried to keep Nina on as her PA, only backing down when the HR department pointed out that Josephine's contract had already been signed and it would mean paying out three months' salary if they reneged on their offer. Of course, Nina had no interest in becoming Charlotte's PA on a permanent basis, but

Be Careful What You Wish For

Charlotte hadn't consulted her before talking to HR – she'd just assumed that what Charlotte wanted, Charlotte got. Even after Nina had gladly done her handover to Josephine and officially started her features internship, Charlotte would still sometimes single out Nina to do her bidding, much to Lizzie's obvious fury. After their run-in during her first week, Nina had watched her back whenever Lizzie was around – she didn't blame her for being peeved after Charlotte had decided Nina was the flavour of the month, seeing Lizzie was the more experienced staff member who'd been there for much longer, but Nina wasn't about to shoot herself in the foot. If the editor had taken a liking to her, for whatever reason, who was she to argue? Especially when Charlotte would come back from breakfast with yet another fashion advertising client, loaded up with gift bags of accessories and clothes which were way too high street for her designer tastes, and dump them on Nina's desk with an offhand 'There you go Nina, just throw them out if you don't want them.' Score!

As Tess got caught up chatting with some of her hotel friends, Nina headed to the bar. Catching sight of herself in the mirrored wall behind the bottles of Tanqueray, Patron and Grey Goose, she untucked the hair behind her ears and smoothed her blow-dry. The spray tan from the secret salon the *Marie Claude* beauty team had booked her into looked flawless, the golden colour contrasting with the black leather peplum top she had teamed with a black sequinned pencil skirt. She'd bought both pieces the day before with the Harvey Nichols vouchers the *Marie Claude* girls had given her as a leaving present, alongside a classic Tiffany & Co. silver heart necklace. She couldn't believe their generosity until Kitty, the commissioning editor, had let slip that Charlotte had donated an extremely large amount to her leaving-present fund. As a joke, they'd also gifted her the custom-designed Versace t-shirt that Nina had flown especially to Milan to pick up from Versace's head office for the Chantelle Sainsbury photo shoot, so they could photograph her wearing it for a huge charity initiative in an upcoming issue. She smiled as she remembered Saffy asking offhandedly, 'Nina, is your passport up to date? The couriers are on strike in Italy, so we need you to go to Milan tomorrow to pick up the sample of the charity t-shirt for the Chantelle shoot, otherwise it won't arrive in time.' Johan was still paying her out about her 'little day trip to Milano to hang out at Versace', as he put it. And being the chosen one hadn't exactly thawed her relationship with Lizzie, but by then Nina had sussed out that the features assistant was a classic power tripper, who was insanely jealous of any junior who got more attention from the senior staff than she did – especially Charlotte, who didn't seem to have any idea who Lizzie was. Of course, the Versace t-shirt sample was miniscule – Nina doubted it would fit a Cabbage Patch Kid – but it was a nice memento of her time at *Marie Claude*.

'There you are! Mwah, mwah, darling!' The glamorous whirlwind that was Taya kissed her on each cheek, then wasted no time in checking out what Nina was wearing. 'Girl, you are looking damn fine!'

'It's all thanks to you guys; I bought the top and skirt yesterday with my Harvey Nicks vouchers. So you approve?'

'Hell yes, I approve! You'll be getting lucky tonight, my friend!'

'Hah, I seriously doubt that. It's been so long, I wouldn't know what to do anymore. I've managed to survive two years of England without getting much bedroom action and I can't see that changing just because it's my last night in the country!'

'So you guys fly out tomorrow afternoon? Are you all packed and ready to go?'

'Just about.'

'You must be so excited to be going home! I've never been to Sydney but my friends say it's ahhh-mazing. I'm so jealous; I'd love to live in Australia.'

'You can come visit! I'm really going to miss you guys, I had the best time working at *Marie Claude*. I learnt so much about the magazine industry and everyone was so lovely. I thought Charlotte would be a total bitch to me, but I think being her PA at the start helped a lot.'

Taya looked at Nina like she wanted to say something but shouldn't, then blurted out, 'It wasn't being Charlotte's PA that made her like you so much, although I guess that might have helped.'

Nina frowned. 'I don't understand; what do you mean?'

Taya looked around to make sure the rest of the *Marie Claude* crew were safely out of earshot. 'Charlotte took a shine to you because you're Australian. She has a soft spot for Aussies because that's where her husband was from.'

'Her husband? But Charlotte has a boyfriend.'

'I know that, stupid. But before him she was married to an Aussie guy for ten years, give or take. From what I've heard, she was a different person back then – totally loved up and much less of a nightmare than she is now.'

'What happened? Did they divorce or something?'

'No,' said Taya, lowering her voice. 'He died unexpectedly, from some sort of cancer. Apparently it was really sudden – one of those cases where you're diagnosed out of the blue and only given weeks to live. She was devastated; it's taken her years to come to terms with it and she's only just started dating again. Anyway, from all accounts, he was more Australian than the lovechild of Crocodile Dundee and Dame Edna Everage, so that's why she has a soft spot for anyone who's from Down Under.'

Nina was stunned. She'd had no idea that Charlotte, the impossibly glamorous editor-in-chief who had the A-list on speed dial, had gone through so much heartbreak. 'It just goes to show that someone can look like they have it all on the outside, but be crumbling on the inside,' Nina thought to herself.

'That's terrible,' she said out loud. 'Poor Charlotte.'

'Shhh, here comes the woman herself,' Taya hissed, before scuttling over to the safety of the *Marie Claude* group in her studded Valentino snakeskin kitten heels.

Nina swivelled to see Charlotte, decked out in an acid yellow Lanvin cocktail dress, making her way through the crowd towards her. She had only invited the editor-in-chief to her leaving party to be polite; she'd never expected her to actually turn up. Suddenly, she was glad that the concierge at Tess's hotel had insisted on booking the private room at the members club on their behalf, rather than having it at the local bland All Bar One, like they'd originally planned.

'Charlotte, how nice of you to come, I really appreciate it,' Nina stammered awkwardly, acutely conscious of what she now knew about the editor's personal life and hoping her face didn't give it away.

'To be honest, I wasn't going to come at all, but it's on my way to Stella's fortieth birthday dinner, so I thought I'd drop in,' Charlotte retorted. 'Can I buy you a drink?' Without waiting for answer, she commanded the attention of the barman and ordered a bottle of Cristal, discreetly pushing her black American Express card across the bar.

'Cheers – here's to your new life in Sydney!' Charlotte smiled tightly at Nina, raising the glass of bubbles. As Nina was wondering if she'd just imagined the tinge of sadness in Charlotte's perfectly made-up eyes when she mentioned the Australian city, the editor-in-chief continued talking. 'Now, the reason I came was to give you this,' she said, handing over a business card. 'An old colleague of mine works in Sydney – she's the publisher at a magazine company there. I've been in touch with her this week and one of her magazines is looking for an editorial assistant. I've already told her about you being a fairly decent intern at *Marie Claude*, so she's expecting you to get in touch when you arrive. I believe she's keeping the job open for you, so don't waste any time. Try not to reflect badly on me, will you, Nina? I don't go out of my way to help people very often, you know,' she said.

Nina was utterly speechless. Ten minutes before, she'd been stressing about having to navigate the waters of the Australian magazine world without her *Marie Claude* safety net, and now she'd just been handed a job on a silver platter – accompanied by a bottle of Cristal to wash it down with!

'Charlotte, I can't thank you enough. Seriously, you don't know what this means to me . . .'

Charlotte glanced at her vintage Rolex then interrupted. 'What nonsense, Nina; all I did was contact an old friend in the industry. Now, I have to dash – the McCartney family has a thing about lateness. Enjoy your last night in London and good luck for Sydney.' She pivoted on her Nicholas Kirkwood spike heels and disappeared into the crowd, leaving Nina staring at the business card in her hand, trying to absorb what had just happened. After a minute or two, she shook her head, seized the ice bucket with the bottle of eye-wateringly expensive champagne that Charlotte had left sitting on the bar, grabbed two more glasses from the barman then made her way over to where Tess was deep in conversation with Johan.

'Well, well, well, who did you have to blow to get that?' demanded Johan, practically salivating as Nina poured them each a glass of bubbles.

'Wow, you're all class tonight, aren't you? I didn't have to blow anyone, but thanks for asking. The editor of *Marie Claude* just bought it for me, actually.'

'Charlotte? Charlotte was here?' Tess asked incredulously, her eyes darting around in hope of catching a glimpse of the high-powered editor.

'She sure was,' Nina said, trying to keep a lid on her excitement. 'She had to go to Stella McCartney's birthday dinner, but before she left, she gave me this.' She showed them the business card.

'It's too dark to see. What is it?' asked Tess, taking a big slurp from her champagne flute.

'It's the business card of a magazine publisher in Sydney who's a friend of hers. There's an editorial position going at one of her titles, which she's holding open until I get there. Guys, I think I've got a JOB!!!' Nina almost screamed.

'Oh my God, that's amazing,' Tess squealed.

'Congratulations!' Johan said.

Nina looked at her two best friends and couldn't help thinking this was the happiest she'd ever felt.

'I guess this calls for a toast,' said Johan, raising his glass. 'Here's to Sydney!'

Nina and Tess smiled at each other and clinked their glasses together with Johan's, as they repeated his words: 'Here's to Sydney!'

SYDNEY

eight

Sitting on the back seat of the ancient station wagon, Nina made the difficult choice between protecting her freshly GHD'd hair or melting into a puddle by rolling the car window the rest of the way down. The humidity slapped her across the face like a warm wet towel and the buzz of cicadas droned loudly in her eardrums. Squinting through her mirrored Ray-Ban aviators as the late afternoon Sydney sun blasted her eyeballs, she sat back and listened to Tess in the front seat, chatting easily to Leo as he drove them home from the airport.

Leo, an old school friend of Tess's, had agreed to let the girls stay at his place while they looked for somewhere to live. Nina had never met the guy before but Tess had told her that he lived with two other guys in a sharehouse in the inner-city hipster suburb of Surry Hills. He was about to take off on a six-month trip around South America and had tried to offload his soon-to-be-vacant room to them, but after having been sardines with Camille for two years, there was no way in hell Tess and Nina were getting sucked into the sharing black hole again. The plan was for Tess to sleep on a mattress on the floor in Leo's room while Nina made herself comfortable on the couch. It wasn't the most glamorous start to their Sydney adventure, but they were hoping it would be a case of days, rather than weeks, before they scored their own place – with two separate bedrooms. Tess, being the more organised of the two, had already done her research on suitable areas and had announced that Potts Point, Darlinghurst and Rushcutters Bay would be their first ports of call. They'd scrapped the idea of Bondi Beach after realising what a bitch it was to commute to via public transport. Besides, why surround themselves with transplanted Poms when they'd just been immersed with the natives in the Motherland?

'So what do you do for a crust, Nina?' Leo asked in his ocker accent, eyeing her in the rear-view mirror. 'You don't work in a bed factory like Tess, do you?' he joked, knowing full well that Tess had only ever worked in exclusive boutique hotels, as opposed to the massive global chains with two-thousand-plus rooms that prided themselves on looking exactly the same, no matter where you were in the world.

'Not anymore – I'm a journalist; I work in women's magazines,' she informed him, trying not to feel like a total fraud. It was true, she told herself fiercely – she might only have three months' experience under her faux Gucci belt, but with her by-line attached to a small Q&A with a next-big-thing DJ on *Marie Claude*'s website, she was now officially a published writer. Ignoring the gnawing feeling she was pretending to be something she wasn't, Nina forced herself to tune back into what Leo was saying.

'. . . Like *Cosmo* and that? Awesome! Me and the boys can provide you with plenty of material if you need it for stories. Let us know if you need any talent for those "man candy" photo shoots before I head overseas, I reckon that'd be ace! Total chick magnet, for sure,' he said, reminding her of Tigger as he practically bounced up and down with enthusiasm.

'Er, I've only worked on one magazine so far,' Nina admitted, 'and it was a bit more high-brow than *Cosmo*, but I have an interview tomorrow with the publisher of *Modern Woman*, so fingers crossed.'

'Yeah? Wow, good luck with that. Here we are, ladies – home, sweet home.'

As the battered car came to a shuddering halt, Nina and Tess looked at each other in dismay. They'd been told Leo's sharehouse wasn't exactly palatial but the lopsided terrace with peeling paint, an overgrown garden and a graffiti-covered front fence looked like it belonged on a council estate back in south-east London, not in one of Sydney's hippest suburbs.

'Christ almighty, Tess better get on the phone to the real estate agents first thing tomorrow,' Nina thought. 'That's if we survive the night and aren't eaten alive by cockroaches and bed bugs.'

As if she could tell what Nina was thinking, Tess mouthed, 'It'll be fine' at her as they peeled themselves off the sticky vinyl seats and clambered out of the car.

Reaching into the boot to wrestle with one of their suitcases, Nina was only vaguely aware of Leo calling out, 'Hey Jez, come and give us a hand, will you?'

Suddenly a strong, hairy arm reached over hers and grabbed the case out of her hands, then picked up another like it was full of marshmallows and swung them both effortlessly onto the nature strip next to the car. Turning around, Nina's brain lapped up the alpha male specimen who was standing in front of her. Her eyes travelled from his thick wavy brown hair and green eyes to shoulders the width of Uluru, right down to tree-trunk thighs encased in board shorts. She swallowed. Or at least tried to.

'Hey, I'm Jeremy, one of Leo's housemates. You're Nina, right?'

'Right,' she croaked, shaking Mr Extremely Tall, Very Dark and Incredibly Handsome's huge outstretched paw, then followed him into the house of horrors. Plonking the suitcases down in the dingy hallway, Jeremy led the way into the living room, where Tess was perched gingerly on a threadbare sofa that was missing one of its arms and pretty much all its cushions. Behind it was a slightly better couch, propped up on blue and orange milk crates.

'How do you like our grandstand seating?' Leo asked proudly, gesturing towards the set-up. Nina had been so busy cataloguing the sticky carpet, the curtains made out of

Be Careful What You Wish For

Sydney Swans AFL flags and the Mount Everest of dirty dishes threatening to topple over any minute in the kitchen sink, that she hadn't noticed what was obviously the boys' pride and joy — a gleaming sixty-inch plasma television and surround sound system, complete with cable TV box, PlayStation, Nintendo Wii and X-Box consoles and a hectic tangle of wires duct-taped to the wall, all positioned directly in front of the couches.

'We have some fully sick nights here with the crew when a big match is on,' Leo continued. 'Everyone brings a slab of beer, we dial in some pizza and chill out watching cricket, rugby, AFL, Premier League, whatever. It can get pretty rowdy though, so the neighbours hate it, don't they, Jez?'

Nina tried not to look at Jeremy as he verified Leo's story, but couldn't help sneaking another glance, just to confirm she still found him as insanely attractive as she had two minutes ago. 'Typical,' she thought, as a swarm of butterflies fluttered to life in her stomach. 'I meet a hot guy within an hour of landing in Sydney, but of course he lives in a Neanderthal cesspit. Not ideal.'

Realising that Jeremy was staring at her staring at him, Nina blurted out, 'C'mon, Tess, let's get the rest of the bags from the car.' She looked at her cousin with what she hoped was an urgent 'we need to talk' expression.

'I can do that,' Jeremy said, oblivious. 'Leo, make yourself useful and get the girls a drink,' he called over his shoulder as he strode down the hallway. As Leo opened the fridge, Nina pretended she hadn't seen the congealed noodles spilling out from crusty takeaway containers or the slimy green sticks that had once called themselves celery crammed in among the bottles of beer. Urrrgh.

'What can I get you? We've got beer . . . um . . . more beer . . . another type of beer . . .' Leo looked at the two girls, waiting expectantly for an answer.

'Don't s'pose you've got any gin?' Nina said hopefully, thinking a frosty cold G&T was just the elixir she needed.

'I think there's some leftover vodka stashed in the freezer from a house party, if you're not beer drinkers,' Jeremy's voice called out as he dumped the last of their stuff in the hallway.

'That'll do, thanks,' Nina squeaked awkwardly, almost breaking out into a sweat as he brushed past her on his way to the kitchen. Tess raised an eyebrow at her, then whispered, 'Are you okay?' as the guys twisted open beers, cracked ice blocks out of their trays and found a random bottle of tonic at the back of the pantry.

'I'm not sure,' she whispered back. 'I feel a bit weird. Not sick or anything, just a bit strange. I'll be fine, it's probably just the heat,' she said quickly, as she saw her cousin's concerned look.

'Why don't you get changed? I think we're moving to the courtyard out the back,' Tess said, gesturing to the guys, who were carrying the drinks, plus a packet of corn chips and a jar of salsa, out the back door.

Nina nodded, collected her suitcase from the hallway and dragged it into the bathroom. 'Right, what should I change into?' she asked herself. Something cool, obviously; the humidity was killing her. It was definitely the moisture in the air that was making her feel spacy — it was nothing, absolutely nothing, to do with Jeremy. She was about to dump a pile of clothes on the floor, then noticed how filthy the tiles were and placed them on top of the washing machine instead. She held up a dress and studied it critically. No, not casual enough. She picked up a top. No, too low-cut — she didn't want him to think she was getting the girls out for him. Was he a legs or a boobs man? she wondered. She was startled by a banging on the door.

'Nina! You've been in here for ages; I thought you'd passed out or something!' Tess exclaimed when Nina unlocked the door.

'Sorry, chook, I was just trying to find something suitable to wear. What do you think between this and this?' she asked, holding up two options. 'Or maybe this?' she added, scooping up another option from the pile. Tess shot her a knowing look.

'Would this agony of indecision have anything to do with Jeremy, by any chance?' she asked sweetly.

'What?! Who? Don't be ridiculous!' Nina tried to bluff, but knew by the look on her cousin's face she was failing miserably. Tess knew her too well. 'Don't you think he's kind of cute?' she asked.

'He's not my type, but I can see what you mean.' Tess's answer was like a double green light — not only did he get her tick of approval, she wasn't interested, which cleared the path for Operation Seduce Jeremy. Sure, he lived in a hovel, but that didn't mean she couldn't have a fling while she was living at said hovel, did it? In fact, it might just make the hovel slightly more bearable . . .

'Hurry up, would you? Just pick an outfit and be done with it – the ice in your vodka tonic has almost melted and I don't know if there's any more in the freezer,' Tess warned, yanking a pair of distressed denim cut-offs and a loose pale pink tank from Nina's hands and shoving them at her. She turned to the door then stopped suddenly and whimpered.

'What? What is it?' Nina spun around to look at where Tess was staring, her expression one of pure revulsion. Damp towels were strewn over the side of the scummy bath and the basin was caked with chunks of dried toothpaste, topped off by spots of grey mould around the taps. 'Men,' Nina thought in disgust, conveniently forgetting that she wasn't exactly the neatest person in the universe. Just then, one of the mould spots moved. Then another. And another. Nina couldn't help herself – she stepped forwards to get a better look, then recoiled.

'Don't tell me that they're what I think they are,' Tess begged her.

'They're slugs,' Nina confirmed, trying not to gag.

'Leo and Jeremy have slugs crawling around their bathroom basin?' Tess asked disbelievingly.

'Yep. This house is an absolute sty. I don't know why the Department of Health hasn't demolished it yet. I don't want to think about how many roaches are probably crawling around that filthy kitchen.' They both shuddered, then, as the full extent of the grossness sank in, Tess started giggling.

'So, are you still keen on getting it on with Jeremy, now you know that he has pet slugs in the bathroom?' she asked.

'Imagine what his bedroom is like – he probably hasn't changed his sheets in two years! Oh my God, I can't believe this. I thought three girls sharing a one-bedroom flat back in London was bad enough, but this place is hideous.'

'You know what guys are like – they just don't have the same standards of cleanliness that girls do,' Nina said, wondering why she was making excuses for them while at the same time making a mental note not to walk on the carpet without wearing her Havaianas. 'It just means we need to find our own place, stat.'

'Totally,' Tess agreed, helping Nina stuff her clothes back into her case. 'See ya, sluggies,' she said as she closed the bathroom door behind them.

They were still giggling as they walked into the courtyard to find Leo and Jeremy chilling out in the sun. Nina couldn't help comparing the guys' bodies – while Leo was tall, he was also skinny and pale, with blond fuzz coating his bony limbs. Jeremy's broad chest was covered in a smattering of dark hair, with strong upper arms emerging from his impossibly wide shoulders. 'Not too big, not too small,' Nina thought. 'As Goldilocks would say, he's just right.'

Taking a long hit of her vodka tonic, she tried unsuccessfully not to splutter when the spirit hit the back of her throat.

'Sorry, I should have warned you – Leo tends to mix drinks a little on the strong side,' Jeremy said, leaning over to whack her on the back.

'I did warn them!' Leo protested. 'Well, I warned Tess anyway. I don't know where Nina was.'

'I was in the bathroom, making friends with the wildlife,' Nina retorted.

'What wildlife?' Jeremy asked, swigging from his long-neck of Coopers Pale Ale.

Nina and Tess looked at each other – maybe the slugs were a brand-new addition to the household that the guys hadn't noticed yet? Maybe they weren't as filthy as they thought?

'I hate to break it to you, but there are slugs crawling around your bathroom sink,' Tess said, clearly expecting the guys to flinch or at least look surprised. But there was neither.

'Oh, those,' Jeremy said, like it was the most normal thing in the world. 'Yeah, they eat the mould,' he explained casually. 'Saves us having to clean as often. I reckon every bathroom should have them. They're more environmentally friendly than using chemical cleaners.'

Nina tried to work out if he was joking, but it seemed he wasn't. She remembered Tess's comment about the last time he changed his sheets and grimaced. He might look like sex on a stick, but even she drew the line at getting it on with someone who thought slugs were a better option than a liberal coating of Jif. She sighed, feeling slightly bereft as she mentally packed up her arsenal of flirtation tricks and put them back in their box for another time. It had been a nice idea while it lasted, but discovering how talented Mr Tall, Dark and Handsome was with his own slug had just been wiped off her 'to do' list.

nine

'Hi, I'm Nina Morey — I have a nine o'clock meeting with Christina Hill from *Modern Woman*,' Nina told the surly-looking receptionist sitting behind the rickety desk in the foyer of Words and Pictures Publishing — aka WaPP — Australia's third-largest magazine publisher. Sinking into the pleather couch while the Incredible Sulk dialled the publisher's PA, Nina hoped she looked more with it than she felt. How much sleep had she got last night? Not much, judging by the burning sensation every time she blinked.

By the time it had become too dark to see each other the night before, the vodka was long gone and the beer supply had been getting dangerously low. Jeremy had made the executive decision to order Thai takeaway and move inside away from the mozzies who were busily treating themselves to an eight-course degustation of Tess. Thankfully, Nina had been sensible enough to stop drinking after dinner, not wanting to make the same mistake of waking up on Struggle Street like she had on her first day of the *Marie Claude* internship. Even so, she wasn't exactly feeling as fresh as a daisy. Although that probably had less to do with her booze consumption and more with making out with Jeremy for most of the past twelve hours instead of getting a decent night's sleep.

Nina's face flushed under her carefully applied make-up as she remembered how the two of them just happened to find themselves sitting next to each other on the pathetic excuse for a couch after polishing off the chicken panang and massaman curry. While Tess and Leo reminisced about their school days, catching up on gossip about people neither Nina nor Jeremy knew, they'd awkwardly started to chat. Or rather, Nina had panicked at the thought of having a one-on-one conversation with a guy she was instantly attracted to, remembering the stilted conversation during her date with Rob back in London, so had switched into journalism mode and started to pummel him with questions. Had he and Leo known each other before they were housemates? Was he Sydney born and bred? What did he do for a job? Was he a cat or dog person? It was only when Jeremy had interrupted her barrage of questions with one of his own – 'So, what's with the interrogation?' – that she'd realised she was being a bit full on dot com, as Johan would say. When he had come back from the kitchen with another beer for him and a soda water for her, she'd expected him to hand over the drink then beat a hasty retreat, but instead he'd sat back down on the couch, this time in even closer proximity to her than before. Not that Nina was complaining. Even though she still had no intention of taking things any further, she wouldn't be worthy of her XY chromosomes if she hadn't appreciated sitting next to the hottest man she'd met in years.

Three hours later, they were still in deep conversation when a pissed-as-a-nit Tess and Leo called it a night, leaving beer carcasses littering the sticky carpet. By this time, Nina had stopped pretending that she wasn't interested in throwing Jeremy around the bedroom and was busily formulating a plan to manoeuvre her way off the couch and into his bed – dirty sheets, be damned. She had an itch that needed to be scratched and by the way he was looking at her, Jeremy seemed like he'd be more than interested in taking care of it. In the end, she didn't have to do a thing – he'd been flicking through the latest issue of *Modern Women*, insisting he wanted to check out the magazine where she'd soon be working, when he stopped at a quiz with an amused look. Nina hoped he hadn't noticed her face could have given a beetroot a run for its money when she saw the headline 'Is He The One?' and played along as Jeremy read the questions and multiple-choice answers aloud so she could choose the most apt one, then added up her score at the end.

'Forty-three out of fifty – congratulations! According to this, he is The One! But only by two points, so you'd better keep an eye on him,' Jeremy joked. Before Nina could make a self-deprecating crack about some of the ridiculous content in women's magazines, Jeremy's arm had snaked around her waist, pulling her up against his chest before he lowered his mouth onto hers. As their tongues met, Nina found her arms had made their way around his neck, one hand buried in his hair while the other held onto his shoulder as if her life depended on it. As his free hand grazed her cheek, she pulled away, hoping he couldn't see how turned on she felt just by one kiss. They'd spent the rest of the night together curled up in his bed, kissing, talking and touching, but as if by unspoken agreement, they didn't go any further. Nina couldn't remember the last time she'd felt so comfortable wrapped in a guy's arms.

'Jesus, listen to yourself – you sound like some nineteenth-century idiot from a Mills and Boon novel,' Nina chastised herself, forcing herself to stop thinking about Jeremy. 'Focus, Nina! You need to knock the socks off the publisher of *Modern Woman*, so stop acting like a smitten kitten and pull yourself together.'

'Nina Morey? I'm Christina Hill, publisher at WaPP – pleasure to meet you.' Her accent was a hybrid of English and Australian, the raspiness giving away a cigarette habit that had crossed the pond with her when she'd emigrated to Australia more than a decade ago. Dressed in shapeless black pants covered in dog hair, with a white shirt that showed off remnants of her morning flat white, the older woman wore no make-up and her hair was pulled back off her face with a couple of bobby pins – and not in an effortlessly chic way, à la Chloë Sevigny. Charlotte she was not.

'Ms Hill, thank you so much for meeting with me, Charlotte speaks very highly of you,' Nina babbled as they waited for the elevator.

'So she should, seeing she has me to thank for her first magazine job,' came the dry response, followed by, 'and call me Christina.'

Trotting behind Christina as she got out on the third floor and led the way to her office, Nina suddenly felt ridiculous in her yellow leather shift dress with the laser-cut geometric pattern, teamed with blue and white polka dot platform heels. Even though she guessed she was on the corporate floor, there wasn't a power suit or killer heel to be seen. Everyone was dressed down – the women in flat sandals and the men without ties. 'Toto, we're not on Planet Fashion anymore,' Nina thought, as she attempted to sit down on the only chair in Christina's office before realising there was a stack of bulging manila folders in her way.

'Uh, is it okay to move these?' she said, looking around for a space to move them to, but failing. Piles of magazines, financial reports, ring-binders and loose pieces of paper covered every horizontal surface.

'Here, give them to me. So Charlotte tells me you've just moved back from London and are looking for a job in the industry?' Without waiting for a response, Christina continued. 'As I think she may have told you, one of my titles, *Modern Woman*, is looking for an editorial assistant. It's a fairly small team, so you'll be doing everything from general office duties and financial stuff to helping out on photo shoots, with some writing thrown in, too. Great place to start, if you ask me. The editor, Clarissa, will be here in a minute to meet you. Now, the salary isn't anything to get excited about, but as I'm sure you're aware, you don't work in editorial for the money – you do it because you love it.' She glanced at the numerous awards that cluttered her bookshelf. Nina realised she was in danger of looking deaf, dumb and mute if she didn't get a word in soon, so jumped in with, 'Oh, I do absolutely love it – the three months I spent at *Marie Claude* in London was the best time of my life; I learnt so much and I know that working in magazines is what I really want to do . . .' Nina trailed off, realising Christina had stopped listening and was eyeballing someone behind her.

'Nina, this is Clarissa, the editor of *Modern Woman*. Clarissa, this is Nina, your new editorial assistant, fresh off the boat after living in London for two years.'

Gripping Clarissa's outstretched hand, Nina clocked the small, bookish woman who was her new boss. Looking at least ten years older than the photo above her editor's letter, she was wearing jeans, Birkenstocks and a black acrylic cardigan over a white t-shirt that had lost its shape several washes ago. 'My, didn't we put a lot of effort into our outfit today?' Nina thought, then promptly flicked her bitch switch off before she accidentally said something out loud. 'Stop comparing everything to London,' she scolded herself. 'Remember, Sydney is on the other side of the world, with a completely different lifestyle, so of course it's going to be more Billabong than Balmain. Although apparently there is a suburb of the same name somewhere around here, so maybe people who live there cut the style mustard a bit more . . .'

'Well, you two go and get acquainted, some of us have work to do around here,' Christina said brusquely, her eyes already fixed on her computer screen. 'Nina, Clarissa will give you a starter pack which has your contract in it – sign both copies, then return one to me and keep the other for your files. And welcome to WaPP.' She smiled for the first time. 'Charlotte sang your praises, so I hope you'll work as well for us as you did for her.'

'Thank you, I promise I will. It was lovely meeting you,' Nina managed to reply before hurrying after Clarissa, who was already halfway down the corridor. 'Surely getting a job shouldn't be that easy?' she thought. 'I know Charlotte put in a good word for me, but I thought she'd at least ask a few interview questions instead of handing it to me on a platter. Not that I'm complaining . . .'

'We'll take the fire stairs, if that's okay with you?' Clarissa asked, peering down at Nina's five-inch heels. 'The editorial office is only three floors up.'

'Sure, not a problem. Just show me the way. So how long have you been the editor of *Modern Woman*?'

'Nine and a half years. I've got five months to go until I can take my long-service leave,' Clarissa replied, not bothering to hide the fact she was counting down the days, much to Nina's surprise.

'And how many people are on the editorial team?' Nina asked, even though she'd already checked out the staff list on the masthead.

'There are five of us now, including you.' It wasn't the answer she was expecting. Five?! Nina remembered seeing at least fifteen names on the masthead, which she had thought was pretty small compared to *Marie Claude*'s forty-plus team. How could only five people produce an entire magazine?

'We use a lot of freelancers, especially when we're on deadline,' Clarissa explained, as if reading her thoughts. 'But most of the time, it's just the five full-timers in the office – you, me, Jenny the art director, Lauren the features editor and Monica, our chief sub. We're a tightknit team.'

Five minutes later, Nina had been introduced to her new colleagues and had stashed her Miu Miu bag behind her desk, which was adjacent to Clarissa's. With no need for separate departments, everyone was crammed into the same small room, its windows looking straight across to another office block. Nina tried not to think about Charlotte's enormous glass-walled office with its white leather Eames chairs, glossy coffee table books and Net-a-Porter delivery boxes stacked almost to the ceiling, or the *Marie Claude* features team's view overlooking the Thames.

Making herself look busy, she opened her starter pack and read through her contract, trying not to eavesdrop on Monica and Lauren's conversation, which revolved around the best time to plant tomato seedlings. While all the *Modern Woman* staff had been perfectly pleasant to her, she got the distinct feeling she wouldn't be bonding with them quite as well as she had with the *Marie Claude* girls. It wasn't just that they were a lot older than Nina – after all, Saffy had been in her mid-thirties and had two kids, not that you'd know by looking at her whippet-thin figure – they seemed to be on a whole different wavelength. Nina doubted they'd have any idea who Anna Wintour was, let alone Carine Roitfeld or Emmanuelle Alt. Obviously there were more important things in life than knowing who the international magazine powerhouses were, but after her *Marie Claude* baptism, Nina had just assumed that everyone who worked on a women's lifestyle magazine would be as obsessed with popular culture and industry gossip as she was. But as Clarissa joined Monica and Lauren's gardening discussion with the same amount of enthusiasm as Taya used to have when dissecting Olivia Palermo's latest outfit, Nina realised she couldn't have been more wrong. Horrified to find the start of tears stinging her eyes, she clamped her tongue to the roof of her mouth to stop herself crying – a trick Annika had taught her after a particularly vicious tongue-lashing from an irate guest at the Bickford – and stared out the window while trying to pull herself together. When the phone on her desk rang, she snatched it up, grateful for the distraction, as everyone in the office jumped in surprise. 'Something tells me the phone doesn't ring a whole lot around here,' she thought to herself while saying in her best professional voice, 'Good morning, *Modern Woman* magazine, Nina speaking.'

'Sorry, who's this?' said the voice on the other end.

'It's Nina. At *Modern Woman* magazine.'

'Oh, sorry, wrong number.' The line went dead and the staff resumed their conversation, having moved on to whether it was best to grow basil in a pot or in the ground. While she waited for them to finish so she could ask for something to do, Nina surreptitiously pulled her iPhone out of her bag to see if Jeremy had texted her, before remembering he didn't have her number. 'I wonder how Tess is getting on at the real estate agent . . . surely it's almost lunchtime?' she thought, as the day stretched endlessly before her. When she checked the time, it took all her willpower not to whimper out loud. It was only nine thirty-three.

ten

When she walked into the Paper Scissors Rock Publishing (PSRP) building in North Sydney, Nina immediately felt like she'd belonged. This was more like it — clusters of people were brainstorming over hits of caffeine in the company's on-site cafe, while fashion interns in strappy heels tottered down the endless hallways on their way back from the courier dock, loaded up with garment bags full of mouth-watering clothes. The breathtaking one-hundred-and-eighty-degree views of a sparkling Sydney Harbour from the reception area on the twenty-fifth floor of the award-winning building almost made Nina drop to her knees and kiss the glossy tiled floor. 'Jeremy will die when I tell him the offices are in a Renzo Piano building,' she thought, as she waited to be collected for her interview with the editor of *Nineteen*.

She could thank her relationship with Jeremy for getting her through the first weeks at *Modern Woman*. She'd tried to grin and bear it, but she couldn't keep a lid on how miserable she had been going to work every day. Not only did she not fit in, she'd quickly realised the magazine was almost on its last legs. Clarissa was obviously hanging on until she could cash in her long-service leave and the three other women clocked on and off without any enthusiasm or excitement for their jobs. Nina felt like she was losing her will to live – bored out of her brain, she'd spent her days writing long emails to Johan, checking Facebook, Twitter, Instagram, Pinterest and her favourite blogs, then counting down the seconds until she could see her new boyfriend again – which was pretty much every night. They couldn't stay away from each other.

After overhearing one of the other editorial assistants in the WaPP mail room talk about a beauty writer role that was up for grabs at *Nineteen*, a popular fortnightly magazine for older teenagers and uni students, Nina was determined to make it hers. Squashing her guilt at betraying Christina and Charlotte, who had gone out of their way to help her onto the first rung of the Australian magazine ladder, she told herself they would have done exactly the same thing. As Johan always said, you had to look out for number one. And as Tess had reassured her, life was too short to be miserable. After all, if Charlotte had any idea what the *Modern Woman* job was actually like, she'd be the first one to tell her to get the hell out of there, stat. And that's exactly what Nina planned to do.

Be Careful What You Wish For

The interview went like a dream. Unlike Clarissa, *Nineteen*'s editor Kat couldn't have been more than five years older than Nina. They clicked immediately, comparing notes on their favourite perfumes and Nina divulging her secret four-mascara strategy after Kat confessed she couldn't let her leave without asking which brand she used. Nina had taken the liberty of fudging her CV slightly, so it looked like she'd been a beauty and features intern at *Marie Claude* – in reality, she'd been too intimidated to go anywhere near the immaculate, fragrant beauty department for the entire three months she'd been there. Lying on her CV was all kinds of wrong, but she was desperate. She knew she could do this job and, what's more, do it bloody well. Luckily, Kat seemed to agree – the day after the interview, she called to offer Nina the job. Then all she had to do was break the news to Christina and Clarissa. Gulp.

Unsurprisingly, Clarissa couldn't have cared less, even though it meant she'd have to recruit another editorial assistant just three weeks after Nina had started. It was telling Christina that Nina was freaking out about – after all, she'd stuck her neck out for her as a favour for Charlotte, even keeping the job open for Nina until she'd arrived in Sydney. She didn't want to be in Christina's bad books – she'd already made one enemy in the publishing industry, albeit on the other side of the world, so she didn't really want to add to her collection. But Christina just nodded silently when Nina told her she didn't feel like she was the best person for the job at *Modern Woman*, and had accepted an offer at PSRP. And as she was still within her three months' probation at WaPP, she would be finishing up at the end of the week. Given it was a Thursday, Nina thought it sounded better than 'I'm leaving tomorrow'. If she'd learnt anything during her hospitality days, it was that it wasn't what you said, it was how you delivered it.

Every day since starting her new job, Nina thanked her lucky stars that she'd bitten the *Modern Woman* bullet. Working at *Nineteen* was so much fun, she sometimes couldn't believe she got paid to do it. With the exception of Kat, the editorial team were all around Nina's age; they lived and breathed celebrities, fashion, gossip and comparing hangover stories after the weekend. When it came to Nina's job description, it was no secret that writing about the latest beauty trends and products wasn't exactly rocket science, but what girl wouldn't like being schmoozed by glamorous beauty publicists, lunching at the hottest restaurants as soon as they popped up on the Sydney scene, sipping French champagne at the unveiling of yet another lip gloss, or – Nina's favourite moment so far – rocking out at the Rihanna concert in a private box with all the other beauty editors, courtesy of the cosmetic company the singer was a spokesmodel for? Then there was the staggering amount of products that landed on her desk every single day. Skincare, haircare, make-up, body products, perfume, brushes and scented candles, not to mention the offers of free treatments – eyelash extensions, haircuts and colour, massages, manicures and pedicures, facials, microdermabrasion, eyebrow shaping . . . Nina literally didn't know where to start. The only thing she considered off-limits was Botox, despite eager publicists assuring her it was better to start as early as possible, and that 'prevention is better than cure'.

She knew her position was the envy of the *Nineteen* office, so decided in her first week to share the love by opening up the beauty cupboard every Friday afternoon to let the team choose a product they'd been lusting over, rather than making them wait for the quarterly beauty sales when they could buy the products she no longer needed with a massive discount. Nina hadn't realised what a big deal it was until a beauty editor at another PSRP title had asked her about it at a breakfast launch at Bills in Darlinghurst.

'Is it true you let the *Nineteen* team loose in your beauty cupboard every week, Nina?' she'd demanded, flicking a balayaged hair extension over her shoulder.

'I wouldn't say I let them loose – they're allowed to choose something they like at the end of each week. Products that haven't hit the counters yet are off-limits, but otherwise they can help themselves,' she'd replied innocently, unaware of all the other beauty editors listening intently. 'We get sent so many products, no one could possibly use them all, so I figured sharing is caring.'

'I really wish you wouldn't,' the other beauty editor had sighed. 'One of the *Nineteen* girls told her friend who works at my magazine and now they all want to know why I don't do the same thing. I mean, seriously, the last thing I want is their sticky paws all over my beauty cupboard. What if they took something I needed for a story?'

Nina had been about to retort, 'I guess you'd just contact the PR and ask her to send you another one – duh . . .' but had held her tongue when she realised the rest of the beauty mafia were agreeing with the shrew who seemed to think the beauty loot sent to the magazine was for her and her alone.

In her short time in Beauty World, Nina had already discovered there was a hierarchy among the beauty editors. The women working on the prestigious haute-fashion titles were perched at the pinnacle, their pearl-encrusted Chanel heels keeping the beauty editors of 'lesser' titles firmly in their place. Next in the pecking order were the girls who worked on the popular monthly women's lifestyle glossies – they had their eye on the fashion title prize, but while they patiently waited for an opening to come up, they spent their time bitching about the beauty bloggers who also attended the product launches. Not that the bloggers cared – they were too busy feeling quietly superior because they were part of the brave new world of online – everyone knew print was dying a slow, painful death. Then there was the random mix of beauty editors from the weekly gossip magazines, teen mags and the cooking mags that had decided to include a couple of beauty pages to attract the lucrative advertising dollars from the cashed-up global beauty companies. These poor girls weren't considered worth talking to by the clique made up of the beauty mafia from haute-fashion and women's lifestyle glossies. Nina fell somewhere in the middle – *Nineteen* was considered better than the teen and weekly trash mags, but because it was fortnightly, and therefore more disposable, she wasn't granted the same status as the monthly glossies. Complicated? Yes. Ridiculous? Most definitely. That was just the way the beauty cookie crumbled.

But Nina wasn't about to let a few bitchy women burst her happiness balloon — she had scored a job where she got paid to road-test beauty products, she had a great inner-city apartment with chic cafes and quirky bars on her doorstep, and she had Jeremy, her big hunk of burning man love, as she'd jokingly referred to him once to Tess, who'd promptly made vomiting noises and had begged her never to call him that again in her presence. Nina had to admit that life in Sydney was pretty damn good.

'So how many invitations to swanky launches landed on your desk today? Let me guess — nine? Ow!' Jeremy yelped as Nina punched him on the arm. They were chilling out in front of the TV after he'd surprised her by turning up on her doorstep with a takeaway container of her favourite salted caramel and white chocolate gelati from Gelato Messina, the ice-cream mecca up the road.

'It was three, actually,' she corrected him, before flopping back down on the couch, practically on top of him. 'One for a skincare launch, one for a new mascara and the other is for a razor. That one sounds pretty good actually — they're flying us up to Whale Beach in a seaplane for lunch at Jonah's.'

'Are you serious? Just to promote a new razor that does exactly what every other razor on the market already does?'

Jeremy asked in disbelief, pulling her closer while switching TV channels.

'Deadly serious,' she replied, threading her fingers through his. 'Hair removal companies seem to have bigger budgets than some small African countries. I'm not going to say no – I haven't been to Jonah's yet, but it's supposed to be lush. Plus the razor brand advertises with *Nineteen*.'

Three months after they'd first met, Nina and Jeremy had their feet planted firmly on the relationship accelerator. They'd become so used to spending every night together during Nina and Tess's ten-day stay at the house of horrors, it'd seemed like a given for Jeremy to sleep over four or five times a week once the girls had moved into their own apartment in Potts Point. Nina had even convinced him to move out of the dump he had shared with Leo and into a new place, after his boss at his up-and-coming architectural firm had decided to give him a substantial promotion. Tess had tried to warn her that they'd gone from zero to one hundred in just a matter of days, but Nina was so ensconced in the love bubble, she didn't care. Her relationship with Jeremy was so easy – there were no awkward silences, no bickering, no worrying about whether he was as into her as she was into him. With Jeremy, what you saw was what you got. He loathed game-playing and could see straight through her whenever she sneakily tried to manipulate him in order to get her own way. Which, admittedly, could be frustrating, but Nina couldn't really complain – especially when he surprised her with her favourite ice-cream like tonight, or an impromptu foot rub when she limped through the door after standing in five-inch heels for two hours at yet another beauty launch. If this was the honeymoon period, Nina never wanted it to end.

'Hey, guess what?' Nina prodded Jeremy, trying to distract him from the episode of *Game of Thrones* he was engrossed in.

'What?' he asked, grabbing both her hands and trapping them in one of his so she couldn't keep poking him.

'Kat told me this morning about a rumour going around that WaPP had decided to close *Modern Woman* – and then our publicity department got a press release confirming it this afternoon. No wonder Christina didn't seem pissed off when I handed in my notice; she probably knew it was on the cards back then.'

'Yeah, you're probably right. Lucky escape for you, Miss Morey. Good thing you jumped to another magazine to work at the coalface of investigative beauty journalism,' he joked, pinning her hands above her head while kissing her neck.

Nina squirmed, pretending to hate the attention. 'Shut up! I don't see you complaining about the hair product I bring home for you, or the posh soap you use whenever you stay here!'

They were getting busy on the couch when Nina heard the key in the front door. Shoving Jeremy aside, she quickly refastened her bra and pulled her top down just before Tess walked into the living room, looking absolutely knackered.

'Hiya, how was your shift?' Nina asked.

'Fine,' came the monotone reply.

'Hi, Tess, feel like some gelato?' Jeremy offered.

'No thanks. Think I might just go to bed.'

'Hey, I was just telling Jeremy that WaPP closed *Modern Woman* today, so that probably explains why Christina couldn't have cared less when I resigned,' Nina told her, expecting her cousin to pounce on the piece of gossip.

'Oh. Yeah, I guess it does,' Tess said listlessly, heading towards the bathroom.

Jeremy looked at Nina, who shrugged. She wasn't sure what was going on with Tess lately, but she figured it was probably just teething problems that came with a new job and moving to a new city. While Nina had hit the jackpot almost straight away, thanks to hooking up with Jeremy and her position at *Nineteen*, Tess had found herself a job as duty manager in a boutique hotel in The Rocks, dealing with the same shit from demanding guests who were under the impression that the bigger their credit card limit, the more they could treat the hotel staff like dirt. Leo had flown out to South America a couple of weeks earlier, so Tess was trying her hardest to make new friends at the hotel, but had quickly found that while the staff were nice enough at work, they had no interest in going for a drink with their manager after they knocked off. Nina had tried to make an effort to include Tess whenever she and Jeremy went to the movies or down the street to one of the hundreds of restaurants on the Potts Point/Kings Cross strip but, apart for a couple of times, Tess always politely declined. Nina knew she didn't want to be a third wheel with her and Jeremy, but she worried about how much time Tess was spending alone, cooped up inside the apartment. 'Then again, she's a big girl who survived

London by herself before I got there, so I'm probably just being paranoid and making a mountain out of a molehill or whatever that stupid saying is,' Nina thought, as Tess emerged from the bathroom in her pyjamas.

'Are you on a late or early tomorrow?' she asked.

'Neither; I have the next two days off,' Tess said.

'Any plans? The weather forecast is looking lush, I wish I had the next two days off,' Nina moaned, wondering if she could convince Jeremy to chuck a sickie with her so they could hit the beach.

'No plans, besides catching up on some sleep,' Tess answered, before disappearing into her bedroom and shutting the door behind her. Nina stared after her, thinking all Tess seemed to do these days was sleep. Or spend her free time watching crap TV with the curtains closed, even when it was a stunningly sunny Sydney day outside. Something seemed to be sucking the life out of her, but Nina had no idea what it could be.

'So . . . where were we?' Jeremy whispered in her ear, as he slid one hand underneath her top and the other in between her thighs. Nina gave him her best sex-kitten smile as she slithered down the couch, pushed his legs wide open and kneeled between them. As she started to undo his belt buckle, while accidentally-on-purpose brushing her hand against his hard-on, her vague concerns about Tess took a back seat. 'She'll be fine,' she reassured herself as her hand reached inside Jeremy's favourite navy blue Calvin Klein boxers. 'I'm sure it's nothing to worry about.'

eleven

When Nina got home from work the next day, she was surprised to find the curtains still closed from the night before. 'Maybe Tess left in a hurry,' she thought, looking guiltily at the couch, hoping her cousin had conked out straight away and not heard what she and Jeremy had got up to last night. Pulling the curtains open to let the last remnants of sunshine into the apartment, she caught sight of her lacy coral bra poking out from underneath the TV where Jeremy had thrown it, and quickly grabbed it. 'Thank God, Tess must not have seen it, otherwise she probably would have hung it on the front door just to taunt me,' she thought, tossing it onto her bed. Heading back out to the living room, Nina stopped when she realised Tess's bedroom door was still closed. They always left their doors open unless they were sleeping. 'Surely she couldn't have been so tired that she's still in bed?' Nina wondered. 'It's past six o'clock! Maybe her window's open and the wind blew the door shut.'

Nina was about to open the door to check if Tess was taking an afternoon nap when she heard a muffled sound. It was the distinct ringtone of Skype, which meant only one thing – Johan. Skidding into the living room, she rummaged through her bag till she found her iPad.

'Darl!' she cried. 'To what do I owe the pleasure?'

'Oh, you know how it is – I woke up this morning and realised it had been far too long since I'd spoken to my favourite Australian fluffball,' Johan replied.

'Er, in case you've forgotten, we spoke the other day,' Nina reminded him. 'Not that I'm complaining, of course. I miss you!'

'Daddy misses you too,' he said. Johan often referred to himself as 'Daddy' in the third person – a habit which Nina always found particularly gay-tastic. 'But you won't have to miss me much longer . . .' he added.

'Oh my God, are you coming to Sydney for a holiday? When? When? When?' Nina screeched in excitement. She couldn't wait to show him the sights of Sydney, and for him to meet Jeremy.

'Well, it's more than a holiday, actually. I've done some investigating and I can get a twelve-month tourist visa, so I've just booked myself a ticket to Orrrrstraaaaaaaaaaaaaylia. Watch out Oxford Street, Daddy's coming!'

'What do you mean, you're coming for twelve months? What about your job at the hotel?' Nina's brain couldn't keep up. She knew Johan was hopeless with money, so how he could afford to book a flight to Australia and not work for a year was not making any sense whatsoever.

'Ah yes, that. Well, you see the thing is . . . I don't have a job anymore.'

'What?' she gasped. 'What do you mean? Did you quit?'

'Not exactly. Mr Farrington-Smyth sacked me after he found out I was having a relationship with AJ.'

'WHAAAAAAT?! You had an affair with AJ Armstrong?! When did this happen? Why didn't you tell me? How did you get busted?' It felt like only yesterday that they had been sitting in the pub near the *Marie Claude* offices, while Nina warned him against going for a drink with the Bickford's VIP guest – if he was ever asked. But as Johan went on to explain, in the months since that conversation AJ Armstrong had asked Johan to do more than just have a drink with him – a lot more.

'Honey, I didn't tell you because I knew you'd tear strips off me. We were busted after one of the butlers saw me sneaking out of AJ's suite at five am when I wasn't rostered on to work. I thought I'd managed to convince him to keep it quiet, but you know what the butlers are like – their mouths are bigger than Perez Hilton's. So soon everyone knew and it was only a matter of time before Farrington-Smyth heard about it. He hauled me into his office three days ago and went ballistic. Seriously, you'd think I'd burnt the hotel down on purpose;

he was carrying on like a pork chop. Anyway, he sacked me for gross misconduct.'

'Gross misconduct? Sheeeeesh . . . What did AJ say when you told him?'

'He laughed. And then he wrote me a cheque for five thousand pounds.'

'He. Did. Not.'

'Yes. He. Did,' Johan responded, mimicking Nina's disbelieving tone. 'He figured it was his fault that I got fired, so he should make it up to me. And was I going to refuse? Hell, no! That man's bank balance makes the Kardashians look like they're on welfare. Five thousand quid is like five pence to him. It wasn't like he was going to ask me to move in with him and be his house pet, so I grabbed the money and I'm about to run – all the way to the other side of the world. I've decided a relaxing stopover in Koh Samui on my way to Australia is just what I need to get over the shock of being unemployed, so I'll be touching down in Sydney two weeks after that. Now, remind me: where are you and Tess living again? How close is it to Oxford Street? My gays in London tell me that's where I need to be. Correct?'

'Correct,' Nina confirmed. 'There's also Newtown, which has a large gay community, but from what I've heard, it's a bit more grungy than Oxford Street.'

'Urrrrrgh . . .' Johan's shudder oscillated down the Skype connection. 'Darling, you know Daddy doesn't do grunge. Lock in Oxford Street – you'd better warn all the best-looking boys that a new gay is about to hit town!'

'Hold on, I'll just add it to the top of my to-do list,' Nina said dryly. 'So I'll pick you up when you fly in from Thailand – email me your itinerary so I know what flight you're on, okay?'

'Will do. And let me know what booze you want me to pick up from the duty-free shop, because we will have some serious celebrating to do when I touch down! I think I arrive early on a Saturday morning, so we'll have to go out that night – after chillaxing on a beach in Koh Samui, I'll be gagging to get laid.'

'Uh, sure,' Nina said, wondering how Jeremy would cope with being dragged up and down the infamous Oxford Street strip on a Saturday night. On second thoughts, maybe it would be better if she went out solo with Johan. That way, they could catch up properly without her worrying if Jeremy felt left out when they reminisced about London and caught up on all the gossip.

'Fabulous, I'll start planning my outfit now. I'm due at the travel agent in fifteen minutes to pay my deposit, so Daddy's gotta run. Can't wait to strut my stuff through Australian customs and see my fluffball waiting for me!'

'Oh my God, I can't believe you're going to be here so soon! Wait till I tell Tess – she'll die. Don't forget to send me your itinerary, okay? Love you!'

Nina cut the Skype connection then looked up in surprise when Tess wandered into the living room in her pyjamas, looking pale and drained.

'Tess! I thought you were out! Sorry, if I'd known you were here, I would have been quieter when I was talking to Johan. Wait till you hear what's happened to him!' She quickly filled her in on the latest developments, finishing with, 'So he's booked on a flight that arrives in three weeks – can you believe it?! It's going to be so great having him here, it'll be just like old times!'

Tess sank slowly down onto the couch, pulling the cushions on top of her like she wanted to disappear.

'Where's he going to stay – with us? How long for?'

'Um, I guess so . . .' Nina realised she'd forgotten to ask Johan about his accommodation plans. 'He'll probably stay with us until he gets his bearings, but I doubt he'll be here the entire time – twelve months is too long for a house guest, even if it is my best friend.'

'Especially if he's bringing home a new guy every night,' Tess muttered. 'He'll be sleeping on the couch, so he'll need to behave himself. I don't really want to get up at five thirty am for work and walk out into the living room to find him shagging some random.'

'Tess! I'm sure he won't do that, he is house-trained. And it's not like he hasn't worked in hospitality before, so I'm sure he'll be sensitive to your early morning shifts.' Nina decided it was time to change the subject, seeing Tess was clearly in one of her moods. 'So how was your day off? Were you sick?'

'Not really. I couldn't sleep last night so I didn't wake up till late, then I just couldn't be bothered getting out of bed.'

'How could you stay in bed when it was such a pearler of a day?'

'Was it? I didn't really notice, to be honest.' Tess stared out the window at the rapidly darkening sky, watching the silhouettes of the bats as they winged their way to dine on the fig trees in Centennial Park.

'Were you too busy reading or something?' Nina asked absentmindedly, her mind already busy planning what she and Johan would do on his first day in Sydney.

'No.' Tess shrugged. 'I just didn't feel like getting up.'

'So you haven't even had a shower yet? Nassssssty! Come on, stop marinating in your own filth and go make yourself look decent, then we can hit up Fratelli Paradiso for some of their calamari. I've been craving it all week.'

'Stop the press! You mean you're not seeing Jeremy the Wonderboy tonight?' Tess said sarcastically. 'How will you ever cope?'

'Very funny. He has a work dinner on tonight – some important clients are in town, so his company pulled out all the stops and booked a table at Quay.'

'Quay? Nice. Wonder if he'll get to sample the snow egg . . .' Tess trailed off wistfully, obviously fantasising about the award-winning restaurant's famous dessert.

'Did I not tell you? I had it the other day when I was at the launch of that new Calvin Klein fragrance. They booked the private room and it was on the tasting menu – but it was a white nectarine variation, not the guava one that everyone was drooling over when it was on that cooking show. It still was delish, though.'

'Oh, poor you – having to put up with white nectarine instead of guava,' Tess mocked, as she headed to the bathroom for a shower. 'Life is so hard, isn't it, Nina?'

'I wasn't complaining, I was just saying!' Nina shouted indignantly, then gave up trying to defend herself. 'Yeah, I know, first-world problems and all that . . .'

Fifteen minutes later, Nina raised an eyebrow when Tess walked out of her bedroom dressed in paint-splattered trackies and a tank top, *sans* bra. 'You're going to Fratelli's dressed like that? Is there some new trend I don't know about?'

'I never said I was going to Fratelli's, you just assumed that. I'm not in the mood for going out. Sorry, you'll have to find another partner in calamari crime.'

'Tessssssssssssss . . . I don't want to go with someone else, I want to go with you. You're never in the mood for going out anymore,' Nina protested, thinking it'd been ages since the two of them had headed out together. 'Come on, it'll be fun. We can wash the calamari down with a bottle of prosecco while we score all the hot Italian waiters out of ten.'

Tess sighed irritably, assuming her previous position on the couch. 'I just don't feel like it, okay? Just because you're a social butterfly extraordinaire doesn't mean I have to be, too,' she said narkily.

'But you haven't left the house all day,' Nina said. 'It'll be good for you to get out. Have you forgotten how to have fun or something?' She immediately regretted her off-the-cuff comment when she saw Tess's face shut down.

'What don't you understand about the words "I don't want to"?' Tess snapped. 'I just want to slob on the couch, okay? I'm tired and, quite frankly, I can't be bothered making conversation with you.'

The two girls stared at each other in silence for a minute, then Nina grabbed her iPad, stalked into her bedroom and slammed the door. She had no idea what was wrong with Tess, but whatever it was, she didn't like it. There was no need for her to lash out like that; she'd only been trying to help. Scrolling furiously through her Facebook news feed, Nina stabbed at the red notification icon that informed her that Johan had recently commented on one of her photos. As the image loaded on screen, she was suddenly aware of a lump in her throat. It was a shot of herself and Tess at their London leaving party. Grinning widely into the camera, the cousins had their arms wrapped around each other, oblivious to a tipsy Johan making bunny ears with his fingers behind both their heads. 'Three weeks till we're reunited, schweedies!!! Mwah!' Johan had commented underneath the picture. Nina smiled sadly; if only he could see them now. 'This is ridiculous,' she told herself. 'Stop being childish and just apologise for whatever you did that upset her.'

Quietly opening the bedroom door, she snuck into the now-darkened living room, ready to make amends. But as her eyes adjusted to the dim light, the words shrivelled up and died on her tongue. Tess was lying utterly still on the couch, staring blankly at the ceiling. If it wasn't for the tears leaking slowly from the corners of her eyes, Nina could have thought she was dead.

twelve

While the crowd of people pushed and shoved around her, Nina tried not to spill the overpriced, under-flavoured skim flat white down her brand-new white Zimmermann sundress. 'Why is airport coffee always so bad?' she wondered, craning her neck to see if she could spot Johan waltzing down the ramp after being spat out by the airport's international quarantine area.

Given it was so early on a Saturday morning, Nina couldn't believe how many people there were, breathlessly waiting for a glimpse of their newly arrived loved ones. 'He totally owes me for getting out of bed to pick him up at this hour,' she bitched to herself, wishing she was still snuggled up to Jeremy's warm body. But she couldn't wipe the smile off her face when she eventually saw a familiar figure strutting towards her, pulling a monogrammed Louis Vuitton suitcase behind him.

'Look how tanned you are!' she screeched, practically jumping on top of him.

'That's what chillaxing on an island for two weeks does for you, Miss Bitch!' Johan retorted, picking her up and almost squeezing the life out of her.

'Oh my God, your hair! I can't believe you've shaved it all off!'

'It's my new butch look – what do you think? I got rid of it just before I left; I figured it would be cooler now that I'm living in the tropics. Plus it was an "eff you" to all those years of having to conform to the short-back-and-sides hospitality brigade. I was tempted to bleach it too, but AJ talked me out of it.'

'So you did see your sugar daddy again after he wrote you that big fat cheque?' Nina asked, knowing Johan wouldn't be offended. She looked pointedly at his suitcase. 'Is that his farewell present you're dragging behind you?'

'Oh God, no – this is one of Bangkok's finest. I think it cost me less than twenty quid at the markets. It's plastic fantastic, darl!'

Instead of going straight back to the apartment in Potts Point, Nina took Johan on the scenic route, driving Leo's shabby car along Campbell Parade so he could see the famous stretch of Bondi Beach, then back into the city and down Macquarie Street to check out the double whammy that was the Opera House and Sydney Harbour Bridge. By the time she parked outside her apartment building, her houseguest had almost nodded off.

'Wake up, sunshine, we're home. Tess is on an early shift so you won't see her till this afternoon, but I thought we could go get some brunch once we've carted all your stuff upstairs.'

'Sounds good,' Johan said sleepily. 'I might need a nap afterwards though. I bought some crazy cheap sleeping pills in Thailand, plus some Xanax to take the edge off the eight-hour flight. Best stuff ever,' he declared, hauling his second suitcase up the stairs while Nina carried the faux Vuitton.

'What else did you get up to in Thailand, besides buying cheap meds and fake designer bags?'

He batted his eyelashes at her, before replying saucily, 'What or who?'

'Oh please, I'm sure I've heard it all before,' Nina said before he could start regaling her with tales of his holiday conquests. 'Okay, so you'll be sleeping on the couch while you're staying with us. I'd be happy for you to share my bed but there's not really room for three.'

'Oh yes, when do I get to meet the famous Jeremy, hmmm? Does he happen to have any good-looking brothers who have a taste for German-Korean sausage?'

Nina rolled her eyes. 'Put the double entendres back in the smutty box they came from. You may have landed in the city with the second-largest gay community in the world, but unfortunately there are still some Aussie blokes who aren't comfortable with blatant homosexuality, so you need to behave yourself.'

Johan pouted, then smirked. 'Orrrroyte, cobber, I'll just crack a tinnie and throw another shrimp on the barbie,' he growled. 'Speaking of food, did you mention brunch?'

Walking around Rushcutters Bay Park after stuffing themselves full of Sydney's favourite breakfast – corn fritters with rocket, bacon and tomato relish – they found a prime patch of grass and stretched out in the sun.

'So I've been meaning to ask you,' Nina spoke up after a few minutes of easy silence, 'what did your parents say when you told them you'd been sacked from the Bickford and were moving to Australia?'

'First of all, I didn't tell them I was sacked because I obviously didn't want to explain why. Letting the cat out of the bag, and all that . . . I just said I'd decided to leave and that I wanted to go travelling.'

'Did they ask why you wanted to come all the way here?'

'Yep – I told them my Australian girlfriend had moved to Sydney because her visa had expired, and I wanted to follow her because I missed her. I think they were so excited that our "relationship" is still going strong, they didn't question it too closely.'

'Aw, Johan, I'm honoured. I didn't think you were the long-term type.'

'Speaking of types, I think I love Sydney already,' he announced, eyes glued to the pumped-up physique of a guy jogging along the water's edge, his tanned bare chest slick with sweat.

'Yeah, you don't see that in London much,' Nina admitted. 'So what's on your list of things to see? Do you want to go to Taronga Zoo? Catch a ferry over to Manly Beach? Climb the Harbour Bridge? Explore The Rocks?'

Johan flopped back onto the grass and waved a hand dismissively, not bothering to pretend he was even remotely interested in any of Sydney's prime tourist destinations.

'Plenty of time for that, my fluffball. I'll tell you what's first on my list — after witnessing that impressive specimen of the Australian male species, I think we need to hit the town tonight. And by "town", I mean Oxford Street.'

'I would never have guessed,' Nina said dryly. 'So here's what I'm thinking — we start with drinks at the Green Park, a gay-friendly pub in Darlinghurst, then we'll get something to eat at Una's, then bar-hop our way up Oxford Street until we get to Arq — it's the biggest gay club in Sydney,' she explained.

'Sounds perfect. Tess will be joining us, yes?'

'Um, I'm not sure,' Nina replied, thinking of her cousin's recent mood swings and lack of interest in doing anything remotely social. The image of Tess crying on the couch, misery clearly etched on her face even in the darkness, had bothered Nina every day since that night. She'd been trying to find a suitable time to sit her down and ask if everything was okay, but Tess seemed to be avoiding her. She was trying not to take it personally, especially seeing Tess seemed to be avoiding everyone. 'To be honest, Tess has been acting kinda weird lately. I guess it depends on how tired she is after her early shift.'

'It's my first night in Sydney! She has to come out and celebrate! I'll drag her out by her hair if I have to,' Johan protested.

'I know, honeybunch. Don't worry, I'm sure she'll be up for it,' Nina assured him, mentally crossing her fingers.

The next morning, Nina gingerly cracked open an eyelid as she groped for the painkillers on her bedside table. Popping two out of the packet required major effort and she almost admitted defeat when she realised there wasn't any water left in the bottle she'd somehow had the good sense to grab from the fridge when she'd stumbled through the door. Battling through the fog of her hangover, she hauled herself out of bed and made a beeline for the kitchen sink. The sooner the painkillers were swallowed, the sooner they could stop the jackhammering that was going on inside her head.

Steadying herself against the kitchen bench, she tried to remember how she'd ended up in this sorry state. It was all Johan's fault, of course. He'd insisted on buying bottle after bottle of French champagne in the succession of bars they'd visited on Oxford Street. And that was after numerous beers and three bottles of wine over dinner. A somewhat subdued Tess had joined them for drinks at the Green Park and Una's famous schnitzel, then made her excuses when it was obvious Johan was itching to pop his Oxford Street cherry, leaving the two of them to hit up the Colombian, Stonewall, Midnight Shift and Nevermind, before queuing up for Arq. Johan had been in his element, checking out the talent and loving the attention from the locals, who were always on the hunt for fresh meat. Nina had never felt so superfluous in her life – even when she'd been out on the gay scene with Johan in London, she'd always found someone to talk to while he was burning up the dance floor to his favourite cheesy house tunes. But here, she was practically invisible. Which was why she'd found herself necking multiple glasses of bubbles while he flitted from one group of new friends to another, his iPhone contacts list multiplying by the millisecond.

Peering over her shoulder to see if Johan was also on Struggle Street, Nina panicked when she saw that the sofa bed she'd made up the night before was empty, its sheets and pillows untouched. Where the hell was he? Surely she hadn't lost her best friend on his first night in town?

'Shit, where did I last see him? I'm sure it was at Arq, but maybe we went back to the Midnight Shift afterwards and I don't remember . . .' she thought, frantically wracking her dehydrated brain. 'I don't think he has our address written down anywhere, so maybe he's wandering the streets of Potts Point trying to find his way home.' Berating herself for leaving him to fend for himself in a strange city in the early hours of the morning when they were both liquored up to their eyeballs, Nina searched for her phone, desperately hoping he'd texted to say he was okay and not lying in a gutter somewhere. Eventually she found it in the fridge, where she usually kept her water bottle. She felt sick at the sight of the blank screen – no missed calls, no text messages. With shaking hands, she dialled his number but it went straight to voicemail.

'Johan, it's me. I've just woken up and you're not here. I'm so sorry for ditching you last night, I don't really remember anything after waiting in line at Arq. I don't think you have our address, so I'll text it to you in case you got lost trying to get home. Or maybe you're still partying . . . I don't know. Please call me and let me know you're okay.'

Nina was tapping out their address in a text message when her phone buzzed. But instead of it being Johan, it was the other man in her life whose name started with J – Jeremy.

'Jez, I'm the worst friend ever – I've lost Johan. We had a massive night on the sauce and the last thing I remember was queuing up to get into a club and I've just woken up and he's not here and his bed hasn't been slept in,' she said breathlessly.

'Settle down, I'm sure he's fine. From what you've told me, he's a big boy who can take care of himself. Maybe he got lucky and picked up?'

'But it was his first night in Sydney – he doesn't know the city and I left him by himself . . . Maybe he tried to walk home and got lost? What if he's been bashed and is in hospital? Or arrested for buying drugs? I've just tried to call him but it went straight to voicemail. I don't know what to do . . .' she wailed.

'Okay, calm down, honey – does he have your address?'

'I don't think so – I was in the middle of texting it to him when you called. And he doesn't have keys either, because I forgot to get a spare cut. So he could have come home later than me but not been able to get in because I was passed out and didn't hear him knock.'

'Okay, I'll get off the phone so you can send him the address and make my way over to yours, so you're not sitting there freaking out by yourself. Sound like a plan?'

'I guess,' Nina mumbled, secretly grateful to be told what to do. Sometimes she really didn't know what she'd do without Jeremy. Whether he was gently deflating her drama queen bubble, effortlessly fixing the pipes in their bathroom when they'd burst in the middle of the night, or whisking her off on a surprise trip to the Hunter Valley for a weekend of wine tasting, Nina sometimes thought that if Jake Gyllenhaal and MacGyver had a love child, Jeremy would be it.

Fifteen minutes later, Jeremy had arrived with a frosty cold Diet Coke and two McDonald's hash browns – her favourite hangover cure. Nina nibbled at some of the deep-fried potato goodness, then pushed them away, feeling too sick to eat. She still hadn't heard a peep from Johan and was now convinced he was lying in the morgue of St Vincent's Hospital up the road. Just as Jeremy was trying to talk her out of calling the emergency room, there was a loud knock on the front door.

'Daddy's home!'

As Nina flung open the door, fully expecting there to be policemen on the other side, Johan made his grand entrance, looking somewhat dishevelled in his Saturday night outfit of black leather trousers and white sleeveless T-shirt, a deep V slashed into the neckline to show off his Thailand tan. Nina had never been happier to see anyone in her life, even though he was obviously as high as a kite.

'Where have you been? Did you not get my voicemail or text? Why didn't you call me? I've been freaking out, thinking you were lost or injured or something horrific had happened to you! I'm so sorry I left you all alone, I must have been really drunk and gone home without you. Are you okay?'

'Honey, slow down! I'm fiiiiiiiiiiiiiine! So you don't remember last night? Hang on, who do we have here? And why is he sitting on my bed?' Johan had spotted Jeremy, who was perched on the sofa bed.

'Johan, this is Jeremy. Jeremy, Johan. It's not exactly how I pictured you two meeting, but I'm just glad you're alive.' Nina looked nervously at the two most important men in her life, hoping they'd play nice.

'G'day, mate, great to meet you.' Johan tried his best to give a macho Australian greeting, much to Jeremy's amusement, as they shook hands.

'And you. Nina's told me a lot about you – mostly good, don't worry. So you two had a big night last night, I hear . . .'

'My first night in Sydney was never going to be small. But madam here got stuck into the bubbles and was quite the inebriated young lady by the time we got past the door at Arq. I'd already made some new friends, so I put her in a taxi and sent her home – quite frankly, I didn't want her to cramp my style.'

Nina cringed; she must have been pissed as a nit if she didn't remember Johan sending her home.

'But where have you been all morning? How come you didn't text me? Didn't you get my voicemail? I've been worried sick!'

'Sorry, my phone died. After the club closed at six am, we decided to continue the party at Ed's place. I'm just going to have a shower and get changed, then I'm meeting him at a place called the Beresford — apparently it's the place to be on a sunny Sunday afternoon in Sydney.'

'Ed? Who's Ed?'

'Edward. I don't know what his last name is. We met him last night at Stonewall when I was dancing on the bar, and then I hung out with him afterwards. Older guy? Looks a bit like George Clooney? Was wearing a pink-and-navy-striped Paul Smith shirt?'

Nina shook her head; she had no recollection of Ed whatsoever. Then again, Johan had met so many people last night, she'd given up trying to remember their names after the twentieth introduction — especially when it was obvious it was Johan they wanted to talk to, not her.

'So how do I get to the Beresford from here? Can I walk?' Johan emerged from the bathroom, smelling of Issey Miyake Homme and decked out in a preppy outfit of Gap chino shorts and a red Ralph Lauren polo shirt.

'You can, but it'll take you a while. What time are you meeting Ed there?' Nina asked, trying not to feel peeved that he'd prefer to hang out with a random he'd just met rather than spend time with her and get to know Jeremy better. With directions typed into his recharged phone, he was halfway out the door before she called out, 'What time do you think you'll be home?', and immediately hated how she sounded like an overprotective mother hen.

He shrugged. 'Who knows? But don't wait up, children. Daddy hears there's a lot of fun to be had at the Beresford.' With an over-the-top wink, he was gone, the door slamming behind him. Nina sighed. Cyclone Johan had well and truly arrived.

thirteen

'Nina, darling, schweedie! So happy you could make it; it wouldn't have been the same without you! Trust me, the show is going to be AMAZE – wait till you see what Nathan, our style director, has done with the models' hair. Loving your frock – Camilla and Marc?' the fawning beauty publicist asked, kissing her on both cheeks while blatantly looking over her shoulder to check if any of the more important beauty editors had arrived at the runway show that was kicking off Australian Fashion Week for another year.

'ASOS, actually,' Nina replied, getting a kick out of the surprised look on the publicist's face. She didn't see the point in pretending she'd spent seven hundred dollars on a dress when it had actually cost seventy. Nina knew plenty of beauty editors who blew every single cent of their pay packets on

Be Careful What You Wish For

designer gear, as demonstrated by the latest Marc Jacobs and Alexander Wang bags swinging from their perfectly manicured fingers, but she'd refused to succumb to the competition that was rampant among the beauty mafia. She didn't want to be one of those girls who crammed canapé after canapé into their mouths at evening launches because they couldn't afford dinner, thanks to investing in Prada's electric blue fur tote that resembled Cookie Monster's cut-offs and would be out of date three minutes after they carried it out of the Prada boutique.

It was almost one year into Nina's beauty job, and as much as she hated to admit it, the gloss was beginning to wear off. Her bathroom cupboards were bulging with the latest and greatest moisturisers, fragrances and styling products; she'd been flown business class to Kuala Lumpur for the opening of the newest Sephora store; had more degustation dinners in Sydney's three-hat restaurants than the *Sydney Morning Herald* restaurant reviewer; and her desk groaned under the weight of Jo Malone candles, Missoni homewares and multiple GHD hair straighteners. She was spoilt rotten, but she was bored. If she had to write one more word about mascara, her brain would morph into concrete – sacrilege really, considering how much Nina loved her mascara. As she flashed a fake smile at the beauty publicist and took her seat in the front row, she knew she had to talk to Kat about it soon. It wasn't fair to all the other wannabe beauty editors who were snapping at her heels if she stayed in her job just because it was dead easy. And there were certainly plenty of girls who would take her place in the blink of a false eyelash – to an outsider, Nina's job looked like the best job in the world. 'And it is,' she told herself. 'Just not for me.' She thought of all the endless boardroom product showings where they'd have to go into raptures about a new range of whitening toothpaste, or put up with the crude sexist comments from a beauty company CEO whom no one dared to complain about because it could jeopardise advertising dollars for their title.

As the lights dimmed, Nina smiled and waved to the group of beauty bloggers who were on the other side of the catwalk, sitting in the social death that was the fourth row — some beauty brands understood the importance of bloggers and didn't treat them like second-class beauty citizens, but this wasn't one of them.

In the darkness, music began blaring and models with chopstick legs started strutting down the catwalk, spotlights trained on the miserable looks on their childlike faces. Nina almost snorted as the first model posed in front of the photographers' pit at the end of the catwalk — the entire back of her head was shaved, with the designer's logo stencilled into the spiky regrowth. Thinking it was maybe just the first model who had gone through the indignity of being shorn and branded, she trained her eyes on the next model, then the next, and the next. All of them had suffered the same fate, making them unemployable by any other designer until their hair had grown out. 'Wait till you see what Nathan's done, indeed,' Nina thought, remembering what the publicist had said before the show. 'I reckon the wigmakers of Sydney will be getting some urgent phone calls from Sydney's model bookers this afternoon.'

As the lights came up, Nina grabbed the goodie bag from under her chair and headed for the door. She couldn't face the battle to go backstage and congratulate the designer on his 'incredible' show, or bother getting a sound bite from the hair and make-up directors about how they got the inspiration for the catwalk looks. 'The less printed about that horrific hair, the better,' she thought, feeling sorry for the models who were probably too young and naïve to put up a fight when Nathan had come at them with his clippers.

Waiting for a taxi, Nina tried not to listen to the sycophantic chatter from the fashion pack, who looked Nina up and down as she took her place at the end of the line, clocked that she wasn't wearing anything by Céline or Christopher Kane, sniffed in disgust, then went straight back to dissecting the show, referring to the designer as a 'visionary' and making noises about shaving their own heads when they got home.

'Kill me now,' Nina thought, pulling out her iPad and checking her Twitter feed to stop her brain from atrophying.

'Hi, Nina. Are you going back to the office? Want to share a taxi?'

Nina stifled a sigh when she saw Ellie, the beauty assistant of *Femme*, the luxury fashion title owned by PSRP, standing next to her in the taxi queue. The younger girl was new on the beauty scene and was starstruck by pretty much everything – the mammoth bunch of flowers that arrived with a press release for a new deodorant; the personalised stationery sent with a range of new eyebrow pencils; the French champagne that flowed like tap water at launches. Taking the beauty world way too seriously, she was also one of the girls who thought the discovery of Botox was up there with a cure for cancer.

'Sure. So, what did you think of the show? Reckon there's a stencil of the designer's label in the goodie bag so we can all shave our heads at home?' Nina joked.

Ellie looked at her, eyes wide with excitement. 'Oh, I hope so! That would make my life. I just loved what Nathan did with the girls' hair, I thought it was genius. So post-modern, don't you think?'

Nina gritted her teeth. It was going to be a long ride back to the office.

When she got back to Nineteen's headquarters, Nina dumped her bags on her desk and was logging on to her computer when she realised something wasn't quite right. Her normally rowdy colleagues were unusually quiet, slumped behind their desks looking like they'd been punched in the stomach, while Kat's office door had been stripped of its numerous posters of her number-one celeb crush, Robert Pattinson. Peering inside as she pretended to pick something up from the photocopier, Nina realised it wasn't just Kat's door that had been stripped – it was her entire office. Empty, except for her computer, desk and file copies of Nineteen dating back the last three years. Nina tiptoed back to her desk then dived into the fashion cupboard to find Steph, Nineteen's long-time fashion editor.

'Steph! What the hell happened while I was out? Where's Kat?'

'Gone,' Steph replied flatly, adding a sequinned jacket to the outfit she was styling and looking at it critically.

'Gone? What do you mean? She's been sacked?' Nina squeaked.

'Nope. She got walked. She came back from a meeting with the publisher and told us that she'd accepted a job at Lulu. Because it's published by one of our competitors, the publisher decided it was a conflict of interest, so instead of letting her work out her notice he had security walk her out of the building to make sure she didn't take any of Nineteen's intellectual property with her.'

'Oh my God. I can't believe it. Is she okay?'

'Of course she's okay! She's getting paid to sit at home and do nothing for a month before starting a new job as editor of one of this country's most iconic magazines, which is a huge step up from Nineteen. Why wouldn't she be okay?!' Steph stared at her as if she had the IQ of an ice block.

'When you put it like that, I guess you're right. It's just so sudden, that's all.'

'For us, yes. But remember that Kat would have known all along that this might happen when she resigned. PSRP doesn't muck around when it comes to staff defections, so if she'd had any sense, she would have already smuggled out whatever she wanted to take with her before she handed in her notice.'

'Wow. It's great for Kat, but who's going to be our new editor?' Nina wondered aloud, before asking, 'Hang on, why weren't you at the opening show for Fashion Week?'

'Didn't get an invite,' Steph said with a shrug. 'You probably scored one through the publicist for the hair or make-up sponsor, but I have to rely on the PR agency for the designer, and sometimes they decide *Nineteen* isn't their cup of chai. Not that I'm particularly bothered – when you've been in the industry as long as I have, it's actually a relief not to have to show my face. Plus, most of the shows are streamed on the internet these days anyway, so I watched it from the comfort of my desk rather than tottering around Circular Quay with all the other fashion tragics.'

Nina went back to her desk, trying to digest the news about Kat. While they didn't socialise together outside of work, they'd become fast friends in the office, often swapping stories about their weekend antics in beauty meetings that ran way over their allotted time. Nina was going to miss her but she knew it was an opportunity Kat couldn't refuse – Lulu was one of Australia's best-loved magazines, targeting the twenty-something chick who loved her sun, sand, sex and half-naked guys. It was as Aussie as Tim Tams and Vegemite, but way more fun, and ridiculously more fashionable. It'd be hard to find an Australian woman who hadn't bought a copy of Lulu at least once in her life.

Glancing at the emails clogging up her inbox, Nina ignored the press releases plugging the nail polish strips featured in that morning's catwalk show, the brand of the spray tan worn by a local celeb at Fashion Week and the arrival of yet another eyelash extension salon. In between all the beauty-related noise, she spied an email that had been sent an hour ago, from Kat. The subject line didn't mince words: 'Call me on my mobile as soon as you get this.'

Nina guessed Kat wanted to tell her the news of her departure herself, forgetting how fast news travels in a building full of mostly female journalists. She grabbed her phone and headed outside, not wanting the rest of the office to overhear their conversation – while she and the editor were tight, she was sure a couple of the *Nineteen* staff would be quietly happy to see the back of Kat, not least the deputy editor who had made no secret of her desire to have her name at the top of the masthead, despite everyone else knowing she wasn't really editor material. That was the funny thing about being an editor – you either had it in you, or you didn't. It wasn't enough just to look the part, you also had to be an ideas machine, have a flair for producing snappy headlines and coverlines, know immediately why a layout wasn't working, be able to find your way around a financial report and profit-and-loss statement, come up with creative concepts for advertising clients and, lastly, be a gun at managing numerous staff members who all had their own personalities and agendas. Despite what some people assumed, being an editor wasn't all French bubbles and blow-dries. Nina had started to realise that it was a title she wanted to add to her CV one day in the future. Her ambition had taken a while to uncurl itself, but it was starting to beat its wings. While she could thank luck for a good portion of her magazine career success to date, luck would only get her so far. She knew she still had a lot to learn before claiming the editor prize, but there was no harm in having goals.

Nina perched on one of the benches in the park overlooking the harbour and dialled Kat's number. During Sydney's sun-drenched summers, the park was packed with PSRP employees soaking up some rays every lunchtime, but seeing it was yet to hit eleven am, it was deserted.

'Hi, Kat, it's Nina. Congratulations! You're going to make such a great editor of Lulu!'

'Dammit, so you've heard already? I really wanted to tell you myself but I couldn't wait till you got back from Fashion Week, because it was the only time I could get a meeting with the publisher. I tried to take my time packing up all my stuff to see if I could catch you, but the security guys were having none of it — I think I was escorted out of the building in less than ten minutes!'

'Are you pissed at the publisher for walking you, or were you expecting it?'

'Nah, he's just protecting his own arse. And it means I'm on gardening leave for the next four weeks — gotta be happy with that!' Kat laughed. 'But listen, I didn't ask you to call me just to talk about my new job at Lulu. You don't have to answer this if you don't want to, but how happy are you at Nineteen? Remember, I'm not your boss anymore, so you can be completely honest.'

'Uh, well . . .' Nina stammered, wondering where this was going. It was as if Kat had been reading her mind earlier that morning. 'I've had a great time, the mag is definitely more me than Modern Woman and I really loved working with you, but I'm kind of getting over the whole beauty thing. It's a great job, but not for me. It sounds ridiculous, because everyone knows that beauty editors are spoilt rotten, but I'm getting to the stage where I'd rather eat my own vomit than go to another fragrance launch.'

Kat snorted down the phone. 'So if you're sick of beauty, what do you want to do instead?'

'In an ideal world? I'd really like to use my brain more and I think I'm pretty good at stringing a sentence together, so moving into the features department would be next on my wishlist.'

'Features, huh? I thought as much – your copy is always great and you definitely have a natural tone that's perfect for women's magazines. A few times your story ideas were better than the ideas from the actual features team! And whenever you stepped in for the features girls when they were on holidays and wrote some stories, they've been bang on the money. So I think you've definitely got what it takes,' Kat said firmly. 'I think you'd be perfect for the brand and will help me shake things up a bit.'

Nina was confused – as nice as it was to be complimented by someone she looked up to, Kat seemed to be having a different conversation.

'Sorry, Kat – what are you talking about? Perfect for what brand?'

'For Lulu,' Kat replied impatiently. 'Nina, I want you to come work with me, heading up the features department. What do you think?'

fourteen

'So did you end up interviewing Nicolette Rivera the other week? If I remember correctly, you were terribly excited about it the last time we spoke.'

Nina tried to ignore the tinge of condescension in Johan's voice on the other end of the phone. Yes, she had been excited about the phone interview for *Lulu*'s cover story, and who could blame her? Nicolette Rivera was the Hollywood celebrity who put the A in A-list, thanks to her famous musician father, her posse of headline-grabbing friends, and a clever stylist who guaranteed she was papped in the hottest designer pieces every time she left her palatial Hollywood Hills mansion. Throw in a wild child past, a former drug problem and a string of famous boyfriends and Nicolette had the public eating out of her Balenciaga-toting hand.

'God, don't ask. It was a nightmare,' she admitted, as she walked home from the office. Immediately, Johan's attitude morphed from bored to enthralled – he loved nothing more than hearing inside dirt on celebs.

'Oooh, go on, tell Daddy what happened,' he begged.

'So our phoner was scheduled for six on a Monday morning, after I'd hounded her publicist for three weeks to lock in a time. I schlepped into the office before the sun had even come up then waited by the phone for half an hour, watching the seconds tick past, praying that her assistant hadn't forgotten to tell her about it. Finally, my phone rang . . . but it wasn't Nicolette.'

'Was it her publicist?'

'Nope. It was the assistant, calling to say that Nicolette was too busy to do the interview and asking me to email through the questions. When I told her the issue was going to print at the end of the week, she said she'd make sure Nicolette sent her replies back to me by then.'

'Oh. So you didn't interview her?' Nina could sense Johan's interest dissipating as he realised she hadn't swapped style tips with Nicolette.

'Well I did – kind of. I basically begged her to reschedule the phone interview because it's always better to talk to the celeb on the phone; you can prompt them to elaborate and ask spin-off questions rather than sticking to the list of questions that's been previously vetted by the publicist. Anyway, her assistant insisted she was too busy, even though it had been confirmed just the day before, and that the only way Nicolette would do the interview was over email. So I sent the questions off and started praying to the Celebrity Gods that she'd get back to me in time for our print deadline.'

'And did she?'

'Just. I'm surprised her assistant didn't slap me with a restraining order, the amount of times I stalked her. The publicist finally sent through her answers on the morning the cover story was due at the printer.'

'Phewf – all's well that ends well, then?' Johan said.

'Sort of – out of the thirty questions I sent, guess how many Nicolette bothered to answer?'

'Um, seventeen?'

'I wish. Try nine. And none of her answers were what you'd call scintillating – they were no more than five words long. I had a fifteen-hundred-word cover story to write in less than three hours, with exactly forty-five words to play with.'

'Ouch. Did the publicist explain why Nicolette didn't bother to answer all of the questions?'

'Sure did – apparently it was all my fault because they were "too gossipy", quote unquote. Obviously she was expecting questions about the economic future of the euro and her take on the political situation in Libya. Because, you know, Nicolette is renowned for her intellectual prowess, not just for her impressive collection of Alexander McQueen skull-print scarves,' Nina said.

'Oh doll, how annoying,' Johan sighed. 'So did you fill the rest of the interview with the usual background fluff and some nice big pictures?'

Nina smirked down the phone. 'Not exactly. Her publicist had already given us approval to run the cover shot without seeing the copy for the cover story, so I decided it was time that our readers were told the truth about what dealing with celebrities can be like. So I wrote about exactly what happened – how long it had taken to set up the interview, how I came into work early only for it to be pulled half an hour after the scheduled interview time, the number of emails I had to send to Nicolette's assistant in the lead-up to our print deadline to remind her about the answers, and then after all that, ending up with only forty-five words to work with and how her publicist said it was my fault because the questions weren't suitable. I even included a sample of the questions she refused to answer, so our readers could see that it was a complete overreaction and it wasn't like they were up there with WikiLeaks.'

'Oooh, someone had a big bowl of bitchflakes for breakfast that day!' Johan said admiringly. 'Think of it as payback for all the crap we had to put up with at the Bickford every time a celebrity came to stay. What did your editor say when you filed the story?'

'She loved it,' Nina replied, not bothering to hide the satisfaction in her voice. 'I think she may have toned it down a bit in the editing process because I was quite scathing about a few things but she's already planning to send it to one of the Sunday papers the day before the issue goes on sale, which should score us some PR coverage – something along the lines of 'Lulu tells the truth about celebrity journalism'. Anyway, that's enough about me and my new frenemy Nicolette – what have you been up to?'

'*Moi?* Oh, the usual – pumping iron at the gym, topping up my tan on Ed's rooftop deck, flitting around the bars of Darlinghurst almost every night . . .'

'How are things with you and Ed?' Nina forced herself to ask – after meeting Ed a few times since he'd hooked up with Johan, she wouldn't be voted in as president of the Edward Butler Fan Club any time soon. Older than them by at least a decade, he only seemed interested in showing off how wealthy and connected he was in Sydney's gay community. The one double date they'd organised had been a disaster, with Ed not bothering to make any effort once he realised she and Jeremy had no important social connections he could leverage, and making disparaging comments about 'breeders', his derogatory term for straight couples, throughout the night. Nina found him arrogant, condescending and obsessed with status symbols – he lived in a penthouse overlooking Darling Point, drove a Lotus during the week and a Range Rover on the weekends, and had replaced Johan's faux Louis Vuitton with the real thing as soon as Johan had moved in with him – which had taken all of two weeks. Of course, Johan wasn't complaining, but Nina hated how Ed treated her friend like he was his plaything.

'Things are great, doll – we're planning a little trip to some plush resort on Hamilton Island in a couple of weeks. I think the name starts with Q?'

'You mean Qualia? Verrrry nice,' Nina said.

'Yep, that's the one. Ed's booked out the whole place and we're going with the guys – Ben, Alister, Matt, Jeff, Christian, Gareth and all that crew. It's going to be amazeballs.'

'Ugh, can you please not use that word? It's my number-one pet hate,' Nina snarked. 'So if Ed's Qualia extravaganza isn't for another couple of weeks, when are we going to catch up properly? We haven't seen each other in ages.' Nina crossed her fingers and silently hoped it would be better than the last time she'd met up with her best friend, when Johan had spent the whole time talking about how 'fucked up' he'd got at a famous film director's party, then showed off photos of the latest designer presents Ed had given him and hadn't asked her one single question about Jeremy, Tess or what was happening in her life.

'I know, I know – Daddy's too busy loving life as a kept woman! Let me check what Ed has on and I'll let you know when I'm free, okay? I'm meeting him for dinner now at Rockpool, so I've gotta go. Mwah, schweedie, later!'

'Later . . .' Nina muttered at the dead phone line. She had the distinct feeling that she wouldn't hear from Johan again until he was back from Qualia and then all he would want to do was rave about what a great time he'd had with his favourite new circle of scene queens. Ever since Ed had sponsored Johan through his own business so he could stay in Sydney after his twelve-month visa had expired, Johan had bowed to Ed's every wish. Although when that wish was a trip to a thousand-dollar-a-night resort, she couldn't really blame him. She knew she was probably being irrational, but she was tired of being the one who made all the effort.

Walking into her apartment, the bitter taste from the puddle of frustration sitting in the bottom of her stomach crawled its way up her throat. Jeremy had flown in from a work trip to Melbourne a few hours beforehand and had obviously made himself at home while she and Tess were at work. His bag was half unpacked in the hallway, its contents dribbling their way over the living room floor, including a delightful pair of dirty boxer shorts and a few crusty socks. Her lovely boyfriend was crashed out on the couch, snoring his head off, with an extended family of empty beer bottles beside him. He'd obviously fixed himself a snack because the kitchen was littered with crumbs, condiment bottles and several smears of God-knew-what while a frying pan covered in congealed bacon fat sat on the stove top.

'Welcome home, honey,' Nina said sarcastically, hoping it would be loud enough to wake Sleeping Beauty on the couch. No such luck. As she tidied everything up, she tried to talk herself down off the ledge of irritation that she'd found herself perched on after her conversation with Johan. Yes, it was Jeremy's mess, so he should clean it up – especially seeing it wasn't his house, and she'd been at work till late. But they had agreed he'd stay at hers tonight seeing he'd been in Melbourne for most of the week, and she knew he'd had an early start that morning, so he was probably shattered. 'Still,' the frustrated voice in her head rebutted, 'he doesn't have to treat my place like a hotel. I'm not his fricking mother. I haven't seen him all week and this is what I come home to.'

Stomping around, she accidentally-on-purpose clanked the empty beer bottles together right next to his ear as she picked them up, prompting a bleary eye to creak open before he attempted to pull her in for a cuddle. Nina was having none of it.

'Can you not? I'm trying to clean up all the mess you so nicely left for me,' she said in her narkiest tone, shooting him a filthy look. She knew she was spoiling for a fight, but she was too far past the point of no return to care.

'Sorry, babe, I meant to fix it up after I finished eating, but I guess I fell asleep,' Jeremy said apologetically.

'Yeah, I guess you did.' Nina glared at him. 'I'm presuming you also fell asleep before you had a chance to pick up your dirty socks and jocks from my living room floor. How about I do that for you, too? Oh, that's right, I already have.'

Jeremy struggled off the couch and belatedly attempted to clear up the mess in the kitchen, which just infuriated Nina even more.

'Just leave it,' she snapped. 'I've already done most of it, I may as well finish. You never wipe the benches down properly anyway. You might have been happy living in filth at your old house, but I am not,' she said.

'Jeez, settle down, Nina. What's wrong with you? I'm sorry, okay? You can't bitch about my mess and then not let me help you clean it up.'

'I just have,' she retorted, stacking his plates in the dishwasher and slamming it shut. As quickly as it had arrived, the angry red mist dissipated, leaving an empty shell of regret huddling in its place. Remembering all the sweet, thoughtful things Jeremy regularly did for her – giving her flowers for no reason, sharing a bottle of bubbles over dinner even though he'd prefer to have a beer, delivering a skim flat white to her bedside every Saturday morning – she felt bad for being such a bitch. She sniffled, then forced herself to turn around to face him.

'Okay, I overreacted. I'm sorry. I just . . . I don't know what's wrong with me. I've had a big week at work and I spoke to Johan on the way home which put me in a bad mood, and I guess I took it out on you.'

'You don't say,' Jeremy joked lamely as he wrapped his arms around her. 'So what did Johan say that pissed you off?'

Nina wavered; she normally tried to steer clear of involving Jeremy in her problems with Johan, but maybe he'd have some good advice on how she should handle it.

'It's not what he said, really; it's just his attitude. It's all about Ed, Ed, Ed and all the presents he gives him, and the fabulous restaurants they go to, and which celebrity party they were at. He's turned into a total scene queen and it makes me feel like I'm not good enough to be his friend anymore. Do you know what he told me today? Ed has hired out all of Qualia and is flying their whole group of friends there in a couple of weeks' time – I mean, how can I compete with that?'

'Nina, I have no idea what Qualia is, but I do know that you don't have to compete with it. Stop reading so much into it – I'm sure Johan still values your friendship just as much as he always has. He is allowed to have other friends besides you, you know,' he said dismissively. 'Did you really think he'd move to Sydney and not hang out with anyone besides you and Tess?'

Nina sighed – Jeremy just didn't get it. He might spoil her rotten, but to him, everything was black and white; there were no shades of grey. She found herself wishing he didn't have to be so pragmatic and logical all the time. Most of the time, she loved how he was so laidback he was practically horizontal, and how he never sweated the small stuff. But that didn't mean he couldn't be sympathetic when *she* wanted to sweat the small stuff. Why couldn't he just try to understand that she was upset about the distance growing between her and Johan, and help her deal with it, rather than telling her she was overreacting? Which she probably was, but he could at least acknowledge she was upset and indulge her for a bit. Sometimes, she just wanted him to listen, instead of being a typical guy with a chronic allergy to emotions.

'I'm going to bed,' Mr Black and White announced, completely oblivious to the cacophony of emotions churning inside her head. Nina stared at the bedroom door as it closed behind him, then felt the hot sensation of tears prickling her eyeballs. Squeezing her eyes shut to stop them breaking their banks, she felt like the two guys who mattered most in her life had shifted away slightly and were now just beyond her reach – she could see them, but she couldn't seem to touch them.

fifteen

'Okay, girlies, what have you got for me this month?' Kat ripped open the giant share pack of peanut butter M&Ms she'd brought back from her trip to New York Fashion Week and poured them onto the middle of the table in the features department. It was time for Lulu's monthly features brainstorm to pitch ideas for upcoming issues – if the International Olympic Committee ever decided to introduce feature brainstorming as a competitive event, Nina would be a shoo-in for the gold medal, even if she did say so herself.

'I'll go first,' she volunteered. 'I think we should do a story on guys who are perfect in every way, except for one problem: they're emotionally unavailable. I don't mean like they're cold or humourless – they're easygoing, laidback guys who are in loving relationships, but if you try to scratch the surface, or ask for emotional support when you need it, they just disconnect. It's like the SNAG has lost the sensitive part of himself and now he's just a NAG — a New Age Guy who looks and plays the part, but when the going gets tough, he isn't comfortable discussing any kind of emotion — either his or yours.'

It wasn't the first time Nina had drawn inspiration from her own life when pitching feature ideas, and she was pretty sure it wouldn't be the last. Sometimes she felt guilty about plundering her friendships and relationships for material, but then she figured that if it was an issue she was going through, surely there'd be plenty of other women who were experiencing the same thing. So, in a way, she was performing a community service. Straws? Clutching? Maybe. But it was for a good cause, she told herself. And no one needed to know that her idea had been partly inspired by Jeremy — even though he'd apologised the next day for being blasé about her problems with Johan, blaming it on being exhausted after his work trip, she felt like something had shifted slightly in their relationship but she wasn't sure how to get it back on track.

'From SNAG to NAG — there's a coverline right there. Add it to the list for the next issue,' Kat said, popping her seventeenth M&M into her mouth. 'Anything else?'

After Nina finished pitching a real-life read about an American woman who had sued her ex for giving her an STI and won $1.5 million, a career feature on young, successful twenty-somethings who were franchisees, and a celebrity charity campaign, she reached the next story on her list and started smirking.

'So this one is a bit nuts. But I figured sometimes the crazy ideas are the ones that get everyone talking about the mag, so I'll put it out there.' Nina took a deep breath and hoped she wasn't about to destroy her own credibility. 'You know how there are some women who can't stand chest hair on a guy, and then there are others who love it? But when you meet a guy in a bar, most of the time you have no idea what's hiding under his shirt. I thought we could do a photo shoot with a group of guys who have varying degrees of hirsuteness. In the first pic, they're fully clothed so you have no idea who's hairy and who's not, and you have to guess who is the werewolf and who's the Ken doll. Then you turn the page and there are pics of them topless, showing off their rugs or lack of . . . because it's not always the ones you expect . . .' Nina trailed off sheepishly as the features team cracked up and started talking over one another.

'Ken Doll or Werewolf — I love it!'

'I know a guy who would be perfect for this — he's just an ordinary Aussie guy but he takes his top off and there's a carpet covering his chest, shoulders and arms. You'd never guess just by looking at him!'

'We could rate their topless pictures — the art team could design werewolf and Ken doll stamps! Love me a baby-smooth chest!'

'Euuuwww, no way — a light-to-medium sprinkling is the way to go!'

Be Careful What You Wish For

As Kat added it to her list, Nina poked fun at her idea with a self-deprecating: 'Obviously, that idea is totally going to win me a Walkley Award!'. She knew that some of their more intelligent readers would think it was a waste of space, but having a bit of fun was part of Lulu's DNA. People bought magazines for entertainment and escapism as well as information, so sometimes you had to plant your tongue firmly in your cheek and do something a bit out of the ordinary. It was usually those stories that had the valuable 'pass-around factor' that every editor hungered after – the idea was for a reader to say to her friends, 'Oh my God, did you see that 'Ken Doll or Werewolf' story in this month's Lulu?', which would make her friends run to the nearest newsagent and pick up copies for themselves. Because at the end of the day, the aim of the game was to sell the mag – the more copies, the better.

As the rest of the features team took turns pitching their ideas, Nina played with the small pile of M&Ms in front of her and kept an eye on Romy, the deputy features editor – as usual, she had been the only one to not comment on any of Nina's ideas, instead looking beyond bored whenever Nina had opened her mouth. There was something about Romy that Nina wasn't quite sure about. She'd been at Lulu for a few years before Kat and Nina had landed there, starting off in the advertising department then swapping over to editorial, and had made it quite clear that she thought she should be sitting in the features editor chair. 'Tough luck, treacle,' Nina thought to herself. 'In this industry, sometimes it's not what you know, it's who you know. It's called networking – maybe you should try it sometime.'

It didn't help that word had got back to Nina that Romy had tried to start a smear campaign against her before she'd even started at Lulu, telling anyone who'd listen that she'd only got the job because she had dirt on Kat, and had blackmailed her boss into giving her the job. Nina could totally understand why some people were surprised when her appointment as features editor had been announced, seeing as she'd been camped out on the beauty side of *Nineteen*, but she also knew that Kat wouldn't have given her job if she didn't think Nina could do it – and do it well. It just meant she had been head down, butt up ever since she'd plonked herself down in the features editor's chair, determined to prove her critics wrong. If she cultivated a reputation for being an A-plus features editor, the next logical step would be associate or deputy editor, and then she'd only be one step away from the editor's hot seat. She just had to remember to watch her back whenever Romy was around. Sometimes you couldn't pull all the knives out by yourself.

As the meeting wound up, Nina grabbed her notebook and started heading for her desk – she had a phone interview with a psychologist scheduled in fifteen minutes and needed to go over her questions to make sure she hadn't missed anything.

'Hey, Neenski, have you got a minute?' Kat called after her.

'Sure, but only fifteen of them – I have an interview to do at four thirty,' she replied, ignoring the scowl on Romy's face as she digested Kat's nickname for her.

'Won't take long – come in and shut the door behind you.'

Nina's stomach curdled. Kat usually operated an open-door policy, so whenever she asked for the door to be shut, it usually meant bad news was about to be delivered. Maybe she hadn't been doing as good a job as she'd thought? Maybe Kat was about to give her a verbal warning for something and she didn't want the rest of the office to overhear? Quickly flicking through her mental Rolodex of recent events, Nina tried to figure out what she'd done wrong.

'So, how many months have you got left on your passport?' Kat asked.

Nina looked at her, perplexed – what did her passport expiry date have to do with anything?

'Uh . . . I think it still has twelve months on it. Why?'

'You know how Global Bus Travel is one of our biggest advertisers?'

Nina nodded, mentally scrambling for a clue as to where this was going.

'They're organising an Eastern Europe media trip and want to send a journalist from Lulu. They originally asked me, but the dates fall over print deadline and I need to be here. So I thought I'd send you instead. Interested?' Kat grinned as Nina's mouth fell open.

'Are you serious? A trip to Eastern Europe? When? For how long? Why me?'

'Yes, I'm serious. Yes, a junket to Eastern Europe – starting in Vienna, finishing in Warsaw. Next month. I think it's for eight days. And I'm asking you because I need someone senior to go, who's not involved in print deadline.'

'Romy's not going to happy,' Nina blurted out. 'I haven't even been here for six months yet and already I'm running off to Europe on a press trip.'

'Don't worry about Romy – she went on a South American tour just before you started here, so she's had her fair share of the press-trip pie recently. Plus, I have a feeling she might not be here when you get back.'

Nina raised an eyebrow.

'Don't look at me like that – I may be wrong though, so that's all I'm going to say. You'd better go do your interview – I'll reply to the email from the Global Bus Travel publicist and cc you, so the two of you can organise flights and all that stuff. They'll need a scan of your passport, so remember to bring it in tomorrow. In return, you'll need to write a one-page travel story when you get back, so don't get so hammered on cheap vodka that you can't remember anything – from what I've heard, Global Bus's tours are legendary in the liquid department.'

Walking back to her desk, Nina tried to act normal – she didn't want to rub her good news in everyone's face, but she could tell they were dying to know what had happened behind the closed door, wondering if she'd had strips torn off her. 'Keep guessing, bitches,' she thought. 'It's not what you think.'

Glancing over her interview questions, she picked up the phone to dial the psychologist's number then noticed the red flashing light that announced the presence of a voicemail – or possibly seven. Already one minute late for the interview, she decided the messages could wait, and tapped out the number.

'Dr Clements? Hi, it's Nina Morey here, features editor of Lulu — we set up an interview via email about the body image article I'm writing. Is now still a good time?'

Half an hour later, Nina hung up the phone, turned off her digital recorder and quickly played it back to make sure it had taped the interview properly — like pretty much every other journalist on the face of the planet, she'd been caught out before by accidentally inserting the sound jack into the wrong plug, not realising her mistake until she started to transcribe the interview the next day only to listen to dead silence.

Satisfied she'd got it right this time, it was time for a loo break. While washing her hands, the press trip cleared its virtual throat and tapped her on the shoulder. OMG she was going back to Europe! She hadn't made it to the eastern side of the continent when she'd lived there — France, Spain and Italy, yes. But Austria, Poland and all the countries sandwiched in between? Nuh-uh. She wondered if she'd have time to do a side trip to London to catch up with Camille, the Bickford crew and the girls at *Marie Claude*. Not to mention doing some serious retail damage on Oxford Street.

Back at her desk, she quickly texted Tess: 'A press trip with Global Bus Tours to Eastern Europe next month? Don't mind if I do!' She'd just hit send when it dawned on her that maybe it wasn't the best idea to rub Tess's nose in her good fortune, seeing the black cloud that hovered over her cousin's head didn't seem to be going anywhere soon. She wished she could get the old Tess back, the one who used to love nothing more than getting all her friends together to go to all of the indie music festivals to see her favourite DJs, but then who'd ruin her street cred whenever she belted out Bonnie Tyler's cheesy 'Total Eclipse of the Heart' at karaoke – which used to be often. Nina could remember loads of times when Tess would end up in a karaoke bar with a bunch of her hotel friends after finishing a late shift back in London. These days, she doubted Tess would be able to name one karaoke bar in Sydney without having to resort to Google.

Sighing, she opened Kat's email to the publicist explaining that unfortunately, due to their print deadline, she wouldn't be able to go herself but would love to send *Lulu*'s features editor in her place, then scrolled down to the itinerary the publicist had proposed. Fly to London, then straight to Vienna, where she'd have a free day before meeting up with the rest of the travellers on the bus tour. Then they'd head east to Budapest for two nights, up through Slovakia to the Czech Republic for a couple of nights of partying in Prague, then on to Krakow in Poland, before finishing in Warsaw. 'Bloody hell, that's a lot of time to spend on a bus with a bunch of strangers,' Nina thought, then immediately pulled herself up. 'Hello? You're getting a free trip to Europe. A lot of people spend years saving up for trips like this, so get off your spoilt high horse.'

She quickly composed an email to the publicist, gushing about how excited she was and promising to send her passport details the next day. Halfway through, a text from Tess arrived: 'I hate you ;)'

When she'd sent the email she picked up the phone to call Jeremy, then remembered he was locked away at a crisis meeting, battling to save his company's biggest client from defecting to their main competitor. Working sixteen-hour days had become standard practice, so Nina had barely seen him over the past few weeks – and when she did, he was snoring on the couch by nine pm, while she buried her head in the pile of magazines she brought home from work. 'When his work crisis is over, maybe we should head to Byron for a long weekend of R&R,' she mused, hitting the red flashing voicemail button and keying in her passcode. She took a large swig of water from the bottle on her desk, then almost spat it all over her keyboard when a furious American voice blasted down the phone.

'This is Hayley Zelman, Nicolette Rivera's publicist. I'm calling about the disgusting cover story you wrote about my client. I suggest you call me back IMMEDIATELY, otherwise I will blackball you and your nasty magazine to every single celebrity publicist in the States and Europe, and you will never get approval to run a celebrity on your cover again!'

sixteen

Before Nina could even get her key in the lock, the door of the apartment swung open and Tess greeted her with four words: 'You need a drink.' She pushed her back down the stairs and practically carried her up the road until they were parked at a table at the Old Fitzroy, a pub in the back streets of Woolloomooloo that was big on atmosphere and low on attitude. It wasn't till after Tess put a double gin with half tonic, half soda in front of her and made her drink most of it that she was allowed to speak.

'I thought I was being so clever and flipping the bird to the celebrity publicity machine, you know? Why didn't I think of the consequences? How on earth did I think I'd get away with it? I could have destroyed my career.' Nina shuddered as she imagined no longer working in the industry she absolutely loved. Magazines were more than just a hobby now; they were her life.

Tess patted her arm sympathetically and waited while Nina rallied.

'It pisses me off, to be honest. I only wrote what happened; it's not like I made anything up. I did spend ages setting up the interview, only for it to be cancelled *after* it was scheduled to happen, and then I had to chase Nicolette's assistant for the answers, which only arrived just in time and there were barely any of them. So it's not as if I lied. I guess they're not used to journalists telling the truth, which is ironic when you think about it, seeing everyone reckons we're full of bullshit.' Nina smiled grimly and sucked down the rest of her drink, then dropped her head onto the table with a thud. Without a word, Tess got up and came back with another drink.

'So do you know how she found out about it? Lulu isn't sold in the States, is it?'

'Not the actual magazine, but anyone can download the digital version on a tablet — which I completely forgot about when I wrote it,' she admitted.

'But even if you had remembered, would it have made any difference?'

'Probably not. I was hell-bent on exposing what it's really like to wrangle celebrity interviews and deal with the nightmare that is the publicists. And you know what? When the issue came out, we had so many emails from our readers thanking us for not sticking to the "she's so stylish, she's a total inspiration" line like other mags do, and telling it like it really was. Too bad it's now bitten us on the butt,' Nina said miserably.

'So what happened after you got the voicemail?'

'You mean after I almost threw up in my mouth? I bolted into Kat's office; she was on the phone, but she could tell something was majorly wrong, so she cut it short. Then I broke the good news that we were about to be blackballed by Nicolette's publicist, thanks to my cover story.'

'And this was just after Kat had offered you the press trip to Europe?'

'Less than an hour later. The timing couldn't have been better,' Nina's tone dripped with sarcasm, as Tess put her hands over her mouth in horror.

'So did you call the publicist back? Christ, that's one phone call I don't envy you having to make.'

'Kat and I discussed a strategy first – after I apologised three bazillion times, obviously. I actually wish she had been mad with me – it would have been easier to deal with, but after she got over the shock, she insisted that it was her fault too, because she had approved the text. But I feel like I've totally let her down, after she took a massive gamble on hiring me for the features editor role.'

'Stop beating yourself up – she's right, you know. Yes, it was your idea to write the truth, and that may have not been the best idea in hindsight, but she's the editor and has the final say on what makes the cut.'

'That's probably why she decided she should be the one to call Hayley back, instead of me. Plus it would have made Hayley feel more important that the editor took her threats seriously enough to deal with the problem herself, rather than letting a minion do it. I wasn't in her office when she made the call, but she told me afterwards that Hayley screamed down the phone for a full five minutes without drawing breath, and said she'd already composed an email to all the celebrity publicity firms which she was about to send out, explaining to them what we did and telling them never to work with Lulu again. I don't know what voodoo trick she pulled, but Kat managed to calm her down. It turned out the thing Hayley was most cut up about was how we'd included her quote on our questions being "too gossipy".'

'Seriously? You did a hatchet job on her client – sorry,' Tess apologised when she saw Nina's grimace, 'who pays her good money to make sure she's promoted favourably in the press, but all she could think about was how she had been included in the article?'

'I'm sure she did care about how we portrayed Nicolette, but I don't think including her comments helped,' Nina explained. 'Kat did enough grovelling for Hayley to take her finger off the send button and we had to promise to run a glowing story about Nicolette's style commandments in the next three months as compensation, which Hayley has to approve before it goes to print.'

'So you won't be writing any more warts-and-all celebrity cover interviews in the near future, then?'

'Hah, I think I've done my dash with them for a while. Romy is welcome to have a crack at them. Kat might decide to write them herself from now on!'

'So have you lost the title of Kat's pet?'

'Shut up. I'm not her pet; we just get on well and like working with each other. I'm guessing I'm not exactly her favourite person right now, but I think she knows I'm punishing myself enough for both of us. I offered to resign but she wouldn't let me, so then I told her I didn't think I should be the one to go on the Eastern Europe junket after the debacle and she should send one of the other girls, but she told me I was being ridiculous and insisted I still go – which just makes me feel even worse about the whole thing. It's like she's killing me with kindness. Actually, that reminds me, I need to find my passport tonight. Another drink?' Without waiting for an answer, Nina headed to the bar.

'What'll you have?' asked the barman, his dark auburn hair falling over his brown eyes as he polished glasses.

'One G&T and one gin with half tonic, half soda, please,' Nina told him, while thinking, 'Hmmm, cute. Don't mind me a bit of brown-eyed redhead – I'd totally go there.'

With a start she realised it was the first time she'd consciously checked out another guy since hooking up with Jeremy. Ever since that first night at the House of Horrors, it was like she'd been wearing a pair of blinkers whenever there was another man in the vicinity, but now those vaguely male-shaped blurs in her periphery were sharpening up and she could no longer ignore them – what's more, she didn't want to. 'Hey, there's nothing wrong with a bit of window shopping,' she reassured herself, smiling at the barman as she collected her change. 'As long as you don't touch the merchandise.'

Halfway back to the table, Nina realised Mr Brown-eyed Redhead wasn't the only cute guy in the pub. There was another one sitting in her seat, trying his best to chat up Tess, who looked like she was about to sprint out of the door and keep running until she reached Antarctica. Her breathing was shallow, beads of sweat were forming around her hairline and she was swallowing repeatedly. Taking a closer look at the guy, Nina couldn't work out why – he was exactly Tess's type. Shaved head? Tick. Blue eyes? Tick. Nice hands? Tick. A couple of arty tattoos? Tick, tick, tick! It wasn't like Tess had set the Sydney dating scene on fire, so she should have been loving the attention from a guy who, based on looks, you could package up and put in a box marked 'Tess's Perfect Man'. She was probably just nervous.

'Here's your drink, Tess. Hi, I'm Nina, Tess's cousin.' Sticking her hand out, she gave him an approving glance as he stood up, returned her handshake with a strong one of his own, then held out her chair.

'I'm Jack. Nice to meet you. Sorry, did I take your seat? I was just talking to your cousin about the book I saw in her bag – it's one of my favourites.'

Nina glanced at Tess, who was staring off into the distance with her fists clenched, doing her best to ignore the conversation. It seemed Nina would just have to do the hard work for her.

'I see – so are you a local, Jack? We live up the road in Potts Point, but I've had a shocker of a day at work, so Tess dragged me here so I could vent while numbing myself with gin.'

'That sucks about your work. I'm friends with some of the guys who work behind the bar, so I'm here quite a bit.' He glanced at Tess hopefully. 'Maybe you'd be interested in joining me for trivia next week?'

Before Nina could accept on her behalf, Tess emerged from her comatose state, looked at him blankly then shut him down with, 'Sorry, I'm working all next week. And the next. And the one after that.'

Jack knew when to wave the white flag of surrender. He shrugged, then said, 'No problem, I get it. Well, if you ever change your mind, you know where I am. Have a good night, ladies.'

Nina made sure he was out of hearing range before hissing, 'What's wrong with you? He was totally your type and you just shot him down in flames! It wouldn't have killed you to meet him for trivia!'

Tess glared at her. Her breathing was slowly returning to normal; as she uncurled her fingers, Nina saw the marks where her fingernails had dug into her palms. 'I didn't want to, okay? Just because you think I should do something doesn't mean I have to do it, you know.'

'Yes, I do realise that, Tess,' Nina said patiently. 'However, when a perfectly cute guy who doesn't seem like an axe murderer makes an effort to have a chat and wants to meet up again, I don't see why you wouldn't agree. Don't take this the wrong way, Tess, but it's not like you've had guys bashing down the door since we moved to Sydney.'

'How do you know?'

'Uh, because I live with you, remember?'

'And I spend a lot of time at the hotel where I work. So how do you know that I haven't met someone there? Isn't there some study that says the majority of couples meet each other in the workplace?'

'Oh my God, have you met someone? Who is he? When can I meet him?'

'I'm not saying I have met someone there, Nina. I'm just saying that you don't know everything about me,' Tess explained, like she was talking to a three-year-old.

'Oh. Sorry. You're right, you're right.' Nina toyed with her straw, then couldn't resist asking, 'So you're definitely not seeing anyone?'

'Bloody hell, what is this – a scene from *Sex and the City*? Okay, yes, I am seeing someone! It's very new and I'm not sure how it's going to go, so I'd rather not analyse it to death, if you don't mind.' She squirmed in her seat. 'If and when I'm ready, then I'll tell you about it, okay?'

While Tess went bright red in the face and looked like she was already regretting her revelation, Nina nodded, smiled, did an internal happy dance and mentally started to plan their first double date.

seventeen

'Hi, my name is Nina; I'm from Sydney, Australia; my traffic light is red and here's my joke – why can't Robbie ride a bike?'

The forty-nine other travellers on the Global Bus Eastern Europe trip looked at her expectantly, except for the obnoxious South African guy on the back seat who was busy telling anyone who'd listen about his Viennese conquests from the previous night.

'Because Robbie's a fish.'

As the crowd groaned, Nina said, 'Hey, I didn't say it would be a *good* joke!' then handed the microphone to the tour guide, and found her way back to her seat as the bus cruised through the Austrian countryside. She smiled at Adam, the Canadian guy who'd sat next to her that morning when they'd all piled into the bus for the drive from Vienna to Budapest. As he made his way to the front to announce his name, country and what his relationship status was using the required traffic light colours, she wondered if he'd go the joke option or choose to tell two facts and a lie about himself — they'd been told they had to guess which of the three was the lie. As a way of breaking the ice between the motley crew of travellers who had decided an Eastern European tour was right up their alley, Nina could think of worse things. She wondered how many lame jokes Annie, their disgustingly perky English tour guide, had heard before.

'Hey, guys, my name is Adam; I'm from Vancouver, Canada; my traffic light is green, and here are three things you don't know about me — I have a twin brother, I live for ice hockey and I still believe in the tooth fairy.' A chorus of boos followed him up the aisle as he returned to his seat.

'Phewf, it's a tough crowd out there,' he complained good-naturedly.

'Tell me about it! Then again, we weren't as bad as some of the others, even if I do say so myself. So, you're into ice hockey, huh? I'm guessing that bit was actually true?'

'Yup, I'm an only child.' He looked at her, straight-faced, before cracking a smile that showed off perfectly straight, whiter-than-white teeth. She could almost see her reflection in them.

'No wonder you still believe in the tooth fairy with teeth like that,' she joked.

'Okay, okay, you got me. I was kidding about the tooth fairy. My parents spent a fortune on them when my brother and I were kids. Which might explain my obsession with ice hockey – I wasn't allowed to play it, thanks to said money being spent on my teeth.'

'The Canucks?'

'Dude, of course! I can't believe you had to ask! Is there any other team? Hang on, how do you know about the Canucks? I didn't think they had ice hockey in Australia.'

'They don't – I'm just one of those people who knows a little about a lot.' Nina neglected to tell Adam that Jeremy used to spend his hungover weekends watching ice hockey games with Leo before his friend left for South America.

For the rest of the bus trip, Nina and Adam chatted about travelling, the similarities between Sydney and Vancouver, and his work as an advertising art director. They swapped war stories from the media industry and compared notes on how things worked differently in each country. Confessing that she would be writing an article about the trip when she got back to work, she made him promise not to tell any of the others in case they felt like they had to be on their best behaviour whenever she was around. It wasn't like she was an investigative journalist who would splash an exposé across the major newspapers in Australia, but she was acutely aware that some people thought journalists were on par with used car salesmen and real estate agents when it came to trustworthiness.

As they drove through the outskirts of Budapest, she also discovered that Adam's twin brother was gay, and found herself confessing her problems with Johan – how he was heavily immersed in Sydney's gay scene and didn't seem interested in their friendship anymore. She actually couldn't remember the last time they'd spoken, let alone caught up in person.

'God, sorry!' she apologised after he'd finished giving her some advice on how he dealt with it when a similar thing happened between him and his brother. 'I haven't even known you for twenty-four hours and I'm already treating you like you're my therapist!'

Adam looked at her with his deep green eyes, smiled his killer smile, and said simply, 'Happy to help.'

Later that night, Nina was walking along the Danube River with some of the other girls after spending the afternoon checking out Heroes Square, followed by a river cruise. They were en route to a bar that Annie had promised was currently the hottest place in Buda. Predictably, talk moved from where the nearest Zara store was to the guys in their group.

'That Gerrard is a bit of a fox; pity he seems like such a dick,' Ash, an Irish brunette, announced.

'Is that the Saffa who was bragging about his supposed conquests from last night while everyone was introducing themselves on the bus?' asked Michaela, a feisty Kiwi whose wardrobe seemed to consist solely of All Blacks merchandise.

'Yes, unfortunately,' sighed Ash. 'I'm sure he'll try to hit on all of us before the tour finishes. If I get liquored tonight and any of you see me talking to him, please promise you'll come and save me – I don't trust myself around arrogant good-looking men when I've being doing Jägerbombs.'

'Mmm, I could totally go a Jägerbomb right now – how far away is this goddamn bar?' demanded Lorena, a gorgeous Puerto Rican from LA. 'You're welcome to Gerrard, honey: I have my eye on Adam, the Ryan Gosling lookalike – he's even Canadian like Ryan!'

Suddenly, Nina was glad it was dark. She had no idea why, but she could tell she was blushing.

'You'll have to fight Nina for him!' Michaela squawked loudly. 'I was sitting behind them on bus and I don't think their banter stopped for the whole three hours!'

'What are you talking about?' Nina protested. 'We just happened to sit next to each other and got on well. He's all yours, Lorena, I promise. Plus, I'm taken, remember? Red traffic light and all that?'

'Hey, what happens on Global Bus tours stays on Global Bus tours!' Ash chimed in.

At the bar, Nina made a concerted effort to steer clear of Adam. She didn't need to add fuel to any rumours, plus she wanted to get to know the other travellers in the group, to find out who they were and why they were here. After a few hours of flitting from one group to another, deflecting any questions about what she did back in Sydney and why her boyfriend wasn't with her, she found herself doing tequila shots with Gerrard and his posse. Ash was sprawled on his lap, having ignored the warnings Michaela and Lorena had dutifully delivered. Nina was wondering if there was any point in reminding her of their earlier pact when she slowly became aware — thanks to the butterflies that had taken up residence in her stomach — that Adam was now standing beside her.

'Been avoiding me, huh?' He smiled, checking out her navy bodycon dress with bright orange stitching. 'Nice dress.'

'Thanks. And I wasn't avoiding you. Just thought I should get to know the others better, seeing you hogged all my time on the bus,' she tried to joke, hoping the three tequila shots weren't slurring her words.

'Can I get you a drink — to apologise for monopolising you?' he said, with a wink that somehow seemed charming, not cheesy.

Without waiting for an answer, Adam grabbed her hand and led her to the packed bar. She stood awkwardly next to him, wishing she hadn't worn such high heels. She kept forgetting that most men weren't as tall as Jeremy — with her five-inch stilts, she was only marginally shorter than Adam. 'Just the right height so that I wouldn't have to crane my neck if we kissed,' she thought, then reprimanded herself. 'Don't be ridiculous, Nina. As if you're going to kiss him — you've obviously had too many shots. Pull yourself together, for Christ's sake.'

She stared at the cluster of white blond hairs on the back on Adam's hand — the hand that was still holding hers. Yanking it away, she pretended to fumble in her bag for her wallet, only to find a glass of champagne staring at her when she looked up.

'I got you a glass of Veuve — is that okay?' Adam shouted in her ear.

Nina nodded and took a sip. Suddenly she was boiling hot. 'Let's find somewhere to sit down.'

Perched on a red velvet banquette, Nina watched the Global Bus party rage around them. Adam was talking to her, but she wasn't really listening. She was vaguely aware of the words coming out of his mouth, but she was too busy trying to make sense of what was going on inside her head to process them.

'C'mon, Nina, enough with the butterflies and acting like a teenager,' she scolded herself. 'You've had too much to drink. Jeremy might be on the other side of the world, but that doesn't mean he doesn't exist. Don't be sucked into the Global Bus tour trap of getting it on with a complete random. Yes, he's very nice. Yes, he's very cute. Yes, he gets you, and the industry you work in, which Jeremy sometimes doesn't. But you've known him for approximately eighteen hours, so let's just act like adults, shall we?'

Halfway through her pep talk, she realised Adam had just repeated a question.

'Sorry, say that again? It's a bit loud in here,' she said, hoping he hadn't realised she'd been in a completely different world. A world where she had a long-term boyfriend whom she adored, she reminded herself sternly.

'I said, if I ask you something, will you tell me the truth?' He was looking at her intently.

'Um, sure. Although it depends what it is – if you want to know how many pairs of shoes I have, I might not tell you the truth,' she joked, looking hurriedly away as she caught Lorena staring at them from across the bar.

'You know earlier today, when everyone had to get up at the front of the bus and describe their relationship status as a traffic light colour?'

'Ye-e-es . . .'

'You said red – which obviously means you're taken. But . . .' He paused, then continued in a rush, 'did you just say that because you're here for work and you don't want anyone hitting on you?'

Nina stared at Adam. She knew what she should say – that it wasn't an excuse and she actually wasn't available – but despite the talking-to she'd just given herself, she wasn't sure if she wanted to.

eighteen

The Eastern European techno music felt like it was piercing Nina's brain. She realised Adam was holding her hand while he looked at her hopefully. She took a swig of champagne to give herself time to think, but it didn't help. 'What's wrong with you, you idiot?' she asked herself. 'Remember Jeremy, the big red traffic light sitting at home? Just tell Adam and be done with it.' Still, she hesitated. The DJ cued up a hardcore remix of Rihanna's 'We Found Love' and the dancefloor exploded. Before she could find the words, Adam pulled his hand away. 'Forget I said anything,' he said, giving her an apologetic smile. 'I don't know why I assumed you weren't telling the truth . . . maybe it was just what I wanted to hear.'

'No! Sorry, I mean . . . I don't know what I mean,' she finally confessed, almost melting over his emotional vulnerability. 'It's complicated, and not just because I'm here for work. There is someone at home, but things have been a bit wobbly lately which I haven't really admitted to myself until now. So it wouldn't be fair on either of us, right?' Nina asked, trying to sound assertive but coming nowhere near it. As Rihanna belted out the chorus, they sat and stared at each other.

'I seriously don't think my liver can take anymore,' Michaela groaned as she sat down next to Nina. It was the second-last day of the tour and everyone was feeling the effects of too many late nights followed by too many early starts. Not to mention the copious amounts of alcohol they were consuming each night — everything from beer and wine to vodka shots and the obligatory Jägerbombs — which had been a recipe for multiple hook-ups in the group over the past week.

True to Ash's prediction, Gerrard had attempted to make a move on every female on the tour — even the ones who had their partners travelling with them. So it was no surprise when he'd crawled onto the bus the morning they were due to drive from Prague to Krakow sporting a pearler of a black eye and looking very sorry for himself. The whole bus soon found out that Jim, a Texan who was on the tour with his fiancée, Sally, hadn't taken kindly to Gerrard's attempts to feel Sally up under the table at the restaurant they'd been to the previous night, and had decided to take matters into his own hands — literally.

Things hadn't got any better for Gerrard when the bus stopped at the border of Poland and the Czech Republic and passport control guards stepped on board to check everyone's paperwork. They had eventually reached Gerrard, who was scrabbling around in his bag, desperately looking for his passport. The whole tour had glared at him in annoyance as Annie and the bus driver started pulling everyone's luggage out from underneath the bus in an effort to locate Gerrard's backpack, which hopefully contained his passport, while border security stood over them. Reeking of booze and looking like he'd recently been in a cage fight, he had eventually found his toothpaste-smeared passport stuffed in his toiletries bag, then started arguing with the guards as they flicked through it repeatedly. Watching from the bus window, the whole tour had been transfixed as Annie did her best to translate, while the officers shook their heads sternly and pointed in the direction the bus had just come from. After half an hour of negotiating, Gerrard had admitted defeat, hauled his backpack onto his hungover shoulders and trudged off to the security office with his newfound friends. Annie and the driver got back on board and soon they were driving through the border control into Poland – *sans* the South African.

'What just happened there shows you how important it is to get the right visas,' Annie had explained to the wide-eyed crowd over the PA system. 'Gerrard's travel agent should have told him that he needed a visa for Poland, but obviously didn't, so Polish border control won't let him in.' A few people had started clapping — Gerrard wasn't exactly the most popular person on the tour.

'What's he going to do?' someone had asked.

'He has to go back to Prague and apply for a visa at the Polish embassy. If he gets it, he'll pay for a flight to Krakow and meet us for the last bit of the tour. I can't tell you how many times this has happened to South Africans on tours like this, so if you have any Saffa friends who are planning to travel through Eastern Europe, please warn them that they need to get the right visas, otherwise they'll be refused entry.'

Nina now looked at Michaela, who was draining the last drops of her bottle of Black Doctor, aka Coca-Cola. 'I contacted my cousin in Sydney after the second night and asked her to call the hospital and put me on the list for a liver transplant for when I get back,' she joked. She tried to surreptitiously check where Adam was sitting — and with whom — without giving herself away to her new Kiwi friend. She needn't have worried — Michaela had spied Nina's iPad sticking out of her bag and was now busy logging on to her favourite rugby website to check for news about 'her boys', aka the All Blacks.

Craning her neck, Nina guiltily peered out of the corner of her eye to see if Adam was up the back of the bus, but after a few minutes of searching, she couldn't see any sign of his blond head. It had been the same routine ever since that first night — Nina hating herself for it but always needing to know where he was, who he was with, what he was doing. It was like she had regressed to being an infatuated sixteen-year-old who constantly drives past her ex-boyfriend's house to see if he's at home. Not that Adam was her boyfriend, ex or otherwise, she quickly reminded herself.

Turning back to ask Michaela what Dan Carter had been up to since she had last checked, the words shrivelled on her tongue as she saw Adam board the bus, a giggling Lorena right behind him.

'He didn't,' one half of her brain said, outraged.

'Maybe he did sleep with her, maybe he didn't,' the other half sniped back. 'What's it to you, anyway? He can shag whoever he wants, remember? He's probably shagged every green-light girl on the tour, and probably some of the amber ones, too. And you can't blame him for hooking up with Lorena – most of the guys on this tour are panting after her.'

'But he's supposed to like me,' the first half whined plaintively.

'He does like you. But you knocked him back. So what's a straight, red-blooded man supposed to do?'

'But I also told him that although I was in a relationship, I was beginning to feel conflicted about a few things and wasn't sure what would happen when I got back home.'

'And he was a perfect gentleman who said that he didn't want to be responsible for making you do anything you'd regret, so he'd leave you to it, but you knew where he was if you changed your mind.'

'What if I do want to change my mind?' half her brain whispered.

'Then you'd better hurry up and get on with it,' the other half said sharply. 'It's the last night of the tour, so it's now or never. But you'd better be prepared for the consequences. Because what happens on Global Bus tours doesn't always stay on Global Bus Tours . . .'

Watching Lorena follow Adam down the aisle of the bus, Nina's eyes flicked between the two of them, trying to work out if it was sheer coincidence that they'd boarded the bus together, or if they'd come direct from having a long, hot shower after shagging each other senseless all night. Suddenly, she caught Adam's gaze – he was looking straight at her and making no secret of it. Like Bambi in the headlights, she felt powerless to pull her eyes away. Without a word, they had what felt like an entire conversation as they stared at each other, before Lorena pushed him into the seat opposite Nina and Michaela's, collapsing on top of him with a high-pitched giggle. Nina rested her head against the window, feeling like she was about to throw up.

After the bus trip into central Warsaw from the outer-suburban hotel they were staying in, Annie escorted them through the Old Town, then some groups splintered off to walk around the remains of the Warsaw Ghetto while others wandered down the Royal Route, and some of the girls took the opportunity to do a last-minute smash and grab in one of the many H&Ms dotted around the city.

Several hours later, they all met up at a traditional Polish restaurant for their 'last supper'. As Nina strolled in, the first thing she saw was Adam standing at the bar, ordering a drink. Lorena was nowhere to be seen. 'It's now or never,' she thought, making her way over to him, not bothering to say hello to anyone else.

'Hey, stranger,' she said, poking him in the ribs. He swung around, nearly covering her in beer.

'Oops, that was close,' he grinned, making no secret of how pleased he was to see her. He leant down and whispered urgently, 'I've missed you.'

Although her heart was racing, Nina was determined to keep things light. 'So, what does a girl have to do to get a drink around here?' she asked innocently.

A few minutes later, when Nina was clutching her own overflowing glass of Tyskie, they went to find a seat at the huge table that belonged to the Global Bus group. Already rowdy, the crew got looser as the beers kept on coming, together with the heaped platters of kielbasa sausages and pierogi dumplings. As they toasted Annie and their driver with endless rounds of vodka, the crowd reminisced about the trip, promising to keep in touch when they'd returned home to all four corners of the globe. Underneath the table, Adam's hand found Nina's; he threaded his fingers through hers and held on tight.

After they staggered out of the restaurant, it was time to hit Warsaw's bar scene. Following the crowd in front of them, Nina and Adam walked along the cobblestones hand in hand. Heading downstairs to an underground bar, they found a series of tiny rooms, filled with people drinking and dancing. Getting separated as others in the tour group stopped to talk to them,

Nina found herself chatting with Annie, the tour leader, as well as Ash, Michaela and Carly, a quiet Aussie girl who Nina had barely noticed before — she'd always been on the first bus back to their hotel after the group dinners and hadn't really made a lot of friends on the tour. After half an hour, with yet more vodka shots under her belt, Nina was wondering how to press the eject button on the conversation so she could hunt down Adam, when Annie put her inebriated foot in it.

'So, Nina, can you send me a copy when the article comes out?'

Nina frowned and quickly shook her head as a warning, hoping the others hadn't heard. She had thought Annie didn't know she was a journalist, but figured the Global Bus PR manager must have told her without informing Nina.

'What article?' Carly piped up.

Before Nina could stop her, Annie blurted out, 'Nina's writing an article on the tour for a magazine back in Australia. We're going to be famous! So, do you know which issue it'll be in?'

Nina felt three pairs of eyes staring at her. 'Uh, no, not yet.'

'You're a journalist?' Ash said. 'I thought you said you were a project manager?'

'I kinda am, in a way — but on a magazine. I'm the features editor of Lulu, a women's lifestyle title back in Sydney,' she admitted.

'Cool,' said Ash, swaying slightly. 'Does anyone know where the bathroom is?'

As Michaela escorted Ash to the bathroom, Nina was left to face a ropeable Carly.

'So all this time you've been pretending to be something you're not, while sneaking around and making notes on all of us to print in your magazine?' she accused drunkenly.

Nina took a step back – it seemed vodka had helped shy, quiet Carly to find her voice and she wasn't afraid to use it.

'It's not like that, Carly,' Nina explained. 'The article is more about the tour itself, not the people on it.' Carly would need to be a whole lot more interesting if she wanted to be included in the travel feature, she thought to herself.

'How do we know that? We should have been told there was a bloody journalist on this tour,' she told Annie indignantly, her voice getting louder and louder. 'We should have been able to choose whether we wanted to go on a tour with a journo present instead of it being kept a secret from us until it was too late! This is un-fucking-believable! If I see my name or photo printed anywhere in that piece of shit you call a magazine, I will sue your arse to high heaven.' She stalked off.

'I'm so sorry,' Annie apologised. 'I had no idea they didn't know.'

'It's okay,' Nina reassured her, trying to hide how shaken she felt. 'I thought it was best to keep it on the downlow in case people didn't feel they could be themselves around me. But I guess that backfired.'

'I can go talk to her if you like?'

'It's okay, don't worry about it. It's not your fault she has her knickers in a knot. She probably won't remember it tomorrow anyway.'

As Annie gave her a hug, Nina fought back tears. She hadn't been yelled at so aggressively since her days at the Bickford. 'I'm out of practice,' she thought, as she wiped her nose on the back of her hand.

'Well, that's just charming,' a Canadian accent murmured in her ear. 'Don't they teach you manners Down Under?' Adam's smile quickly disappeared as he noticed her watery eyes.

'Aw, honey, what happened?' he asked, pulling her into a hug.

'It's nothing,' Nina sniffled. 'Annie accidentally let slip that I'm writing a story about the tour in front of some of the girls, and one of them went absolutely ballistic about it. She acted like I was some sort of psychopath who's a danger to society,' she choked out.

'Which one was it? I'll go talk to her,' he said, rubbing her back.

'It was Carly — another Australian chick. It's probably my fault; I should have been upfront with everyone from the start.'

'Carly?' Adam said incredulously. 'The girl who's barely said a word to anyone for the entire time? What the hell is she worried about? That you'll tell your readers how boring she is?'

Nina managed a wobbly smile. 'Don't be nasty,' she chided, even though she'd thought the exact same thing. 'I guess she has a thing against journalists.'

'Or she's jealous — maybe she's a frustrated writer who is desperate to get into magazines?'

'Maybe.' Nina shrugged, feeling deflated. 'It doesn't really matter. It was just a bit of a shock because I didn't see it coming. Especially from her.'

'Come on, let's get out of here,' Adam said suddenly, leading her out of the bar and back up the stairs to street level.

'Where are we going?' she asked, as he led the way along Warsaw's streets with his arm firmly around her shoulders.

'Here,' he said, rounding a corner and leading her up the stairs of an ornate building and into the lobby. 'It's the Polonia Palace, a famous Warsaw hotel that somehow managed to escape any damage in the Second World War,' he explained. 'I've heard it has a decent jazz bar that has views of the Palace of Culture and Science.'

Seated at the bar with extra dirty martinis in front of them, Nina and Adam chatted about everything and nothing – everything, except the fact it was their last night together and Nina would be flying back home to her long-term boyfriend the next day. When Adam leant over, hesitated slightly, then kissed her, Nina didn't try to stop him. Her brain was marinated in a hefty amount of booze, and all thoughts of Jeremy were buried way down below the layers of beer and vodka. All she could process was how good it felt to finally be kissing Adam. She'd thought about what it would be like constantly since the first night in Budapest, but it was better than she'd expected – *so* much better. After the kiss broke off and they were left staring at each other, she could feel electric currents of pure lust uncurling themselves deep in her stomach. Nina bit her lip as she realised she wanted more — much more.

'Are you thinking what I'm thinking?' he whispered.

Nina looked at him silently, not trusting herself to speak.

'I want you so badly,' Adam continued. 'I have since the very first day we met. It's been torture having to stay away from you, Nina, but I promised myself I'd give you space after what you told me in the bar in Budapest. But you're here, I'm here and it's our last night together. Babe, I need to know — have you changed your mind?'

Like a puppet controlled by unseen hands, Nina found herself nodding. Adam was now brushing his fingers lightly up and down her inner thigh, driving her crazy, while he pulled her in for another kiss. 'Let's get a room,' Adam whispered urgently in her ear, pulling her off her bar stool.

In a lust-fuelled trance, Nina followed him to the reception desk, where he quickly registered for a one-night stay. As soon as the door to their hotel room closed, he pinned her to the wall, kissing her so deeply it was like she was his only source of oxygen. She could feel exactly how turned on he was as he grabbed her butt and pulled her up against him. Biting his earlobe as he kissed her neck, they fell onto the bed in a tangle of limbs. Soon Nina had stripped down to her underwear and Adam was shedding the rest of his clothes at a speed that would make Road Runner jealous.

Nina was about to unhook her bra and pounce on him, when she caught sight of his boxer shorts. Navy blue Calvin Kleins — exactly the same as Jeremy's favourites. In an instant, the lust in her stomach dissipated and nausea prickled at the back of her throat. What the hell was she doing in a random hotel room in Warsaw about to have sex with a guy she'd known for less than two weeks? As Adam reached for the waistband of his shorts, Nina felt like she'd had a bucket of cold water thrown over her.

'Adam, stop,' she whispered. His hands paused as he looked up. She couldn't meet his gaze, so stared at the floor, hating herself for ending up in this situation. 'I'm sorry,' she choked out. 'I thought I could do this, but I can't.' As disbelief registered on his face, Nina scrambled for her clothes then fled into the bathroom and locked the door behind her before she could change her mind.

nineteen

To: Nina Morey
From: Adam Johnston
Subject: Please read this . . .

I can't stop thinking about you. I've tried calling you on Skype but you won't answer. You won't return my emails. I don't even know if you're reading them or deleting them without opening them. But I have to keep trying. I don't want to let you go without a fight. Every morning I wake up and the first thing I think about is you. You're the last thing I think about at night. Have you even considered my offer to come to Vancouver? Just for a visit — you don't have to stay with me, we can just see how things go. No pressure. Just promise me you'll think about it, okay? I'll wait for however long it takes.

Nina sighed heavily, hit the delete button and then started clicking on the different menu options on Facebook. Getting frustrated when she couldn't find what she was looking for, she blurted out, 'Tess, do you know where the "block user" option is on Facebook? I can't find the bloody thing.'

'I'm pretty sure it's under the privacy settings, but I could be wrong. Why? Who do you want to block?'

It had been three weeks since Nina had returned from her Eastern Europe press trip, and the guilt over what had almost happened with Adam had been gnawing away at her. It didn't help that he'd been bombarding her with pleading emails, begging her to visit him in Canada, stopping just short of declaring his undying love for her. Now that she was home, she realised how close she'd come to making a huge mistake – but as much as she tried to shove it to the back of her mind, she couldn't help but wonder why she had let herself get in the messy situation in the first place. Was she bored with Jeremy, but just didn't want to admit it? Had their relationship run its course and they just hadn't realised it yet? Would they end up being one of those long-term couples who stayed together because it was easier than breaking up?

She'd tried to act as normal as possible around Jeremy, but when she was lying next to him as he slept, she couldn't stop the slideshow of flashbacks that played on a loop in her head as she stared at the ceiling. While she desperately tried to convince herself that cheating was only a relationship crime when there was actual sex involved, Nina ran hot and cold whenever Jeremy was around. One minute she'd be overcompensating by smothering him with adoring attention, the next minute she couldn't bear for him to touch her. Sometimes she was convinced he must have guessed what had happened and was tempted to confess every sordid detail, if only to put a stop to her internal agonising, but at other times she wondered if he even remembered she'd been away. She was exhausted from the constant stressing, analysing and wondering, which was why, when Tess asked who she wanted to block on Facebook, she made a snap decision. After weeks of battling it out alone inside her head, she needed to tell someone, otherwise she'd drive herself crazy trying to decide what she should do. To confess or keep quiet? That was the million-dollar question, and she only had herself to blame for it.

'Uh, I just want to block a random guy who I met on the Global Bus tour.'

Tess looked at her closely. 'Just a random guy, huh? So riddle me this — why is your face bright pink after telling me that?'

Nina took a deep breath, then said in a rush, 'If I tell you, will you promise never to tell anyone?'

'Of course,' Tess said immediately. 'You know your deepest, darkest secrets are in the vault with me.'

'Okay . . . well . . . I met a guy on the trip who I was really attracted to. Like, REALLY attracted. A Canadian. He works in the publishing industry, too. Anyway, nothing happened.' Nina paused, watching Tess's face for any kind of reaction, but got nothing. She ploughed on. 'Until the last night of the tour.' Tess raised an eyebrow. 'It wasn't like I lied and said I was single – he knew I had a boyfriend. But one minute we were with the rest of the group, the next we were in a hotel bar by ourselves and things started getting intense. One thing led to another and . . .' Nina hesitated, wondering if she was wrong to share her misdemeanour with Tess, but decided she was too far gone to stop now. 'We got a room,' she admitted.

'And then what happened?' Tess asked, her voice neutral.

'Nothing,' Nina said, hating how defensive she sounded. 'Okay, I won't lie – we were about to do the deed, but at the last minute, I bottled it. I just couldn't go ahead with it. It was so weird, Tess – until that final moment, I'd completely forgotten about Jeremy; it was like I'd convinced myself he didn't exist, or was part of a different life. But then something reminded me of him and thankfully I came to my senses before it was too late. Now Adam – the Canadian – keeps sending me messages on Facebook, begging me to go visit him in Vancouver.'

'Are you going to go?' Tess asked quietly.

'What? NO! Don't be ridiculous. He's a great guy, but I just got carried away – my relationship with Jeremy is the longest I've ever had, and I guess it was flattering that this super-cute guy was into me. Maybe I wanted to prove that I could still hook up if I wanted to. But now I'm back and I'm consumed with guilt, twenty-four/seven. I know some people would argue that I didn't cheat because I didn't actually sleep with him, but I came damn close. I hate myself. And I don't know whether I should tell Jeremy or not. It's doing my head in and making me act weird around him.'

'Do you think he has any idea?'

'I don't know,' Nina said miserably. 'Sometimes I think he knows something's not right, but doesn't know what, then at other times I feel like I have "cheater" emblazoned on my forehead and he doesn't even notice.'

'Do you want to tell him?'

'Some days I do, just to put myself out of my own misery. But then I think about how much it'll hurt him, and I really don't know if I could forgive myself for causing him that much pain. Do you think I should?' Nina looked at Tess beseechingly, desperate for answers.

'No, I don't think you should,' her cousin said firmly. 'You were on the other side of the world and got caught up in the moment. You're never going to see this guy again and you're obviously remorseful. Yes, it was wrong to get involved with him in the first place, but you stopped yourself just before the crucial moment. It was a huge mistake — but at least you realise that. You're only human, Nina; we all do stuff that we're ashamed of or regret, but in my opinion, sometimes you have to weigh up whether the relief of confessing will be cancelled out by the hurt you'll cause. Because it will hurt Jeremy — a lot. He adores you. And I don't know if you guys will ever get back on track. It's up to you, obviously, but in my opinion, you know what you did was wrong, you're not planning to do it ever again and, hopefully, you've learnt your lesson. Now you just have to discover what's lacking in your relationship that made you almost cheat in the first place and fix it, so things can get back to normal between the two of you.'

Nina stared at Tess, stunned by her shrewd assessment of the relationship issues which Nina had been agonising over for weeks. 'Thanks, Tess. I guess you're right. Jeremy doesn't need to know, but I do need to have a good hard think about why it happened in the first place. I'm sorry to offload all my crap onto you, but I've been driving myself insane ever since that night. You have no idea how tortured I've been.' After giving Tess a huge hug, she attempted to lighten the mood by asking, 'So where did you learn to analyse problems so quickly, Ms Relationship Therapist?' To her astonishment, it was Tess's turn to go bright pink.

'Um . . . well, seeing this seems to be confession time, I guess it's my turn to share something,' Tess said uncertainly. 'Do you remember when we were at that pub in Woolloomooloo, after you had the run-in with Nicolette Rivera's publicist?'

'How could I forget . . .' Nina muttered.

'You got angry at me because I wouldn't go on a date with that guy who tried to chat me up, and I told you it was because I'd just started seeing someone.'

Nina's eyes widened. Maybe Tess was finally ready to tell her all about her new relationship? 'Typical,' she thought. 'Tess finds love just as my love life is crumbling around my ears.'

'Well, I kind of stretched the truth a bit,' Tess continued. 'I had just started seeing someone, but it wasn't a boyfriend.'

'Whaaaaa? What do you mean? Who was it then?'

'It was my therapist. A clinical psychologist, to be precise.'

Nina was confused. 'I don't understand – why would you need to see a clinical psychologist?'

'Because I've been diagnosed with depression and anxiety,' Tess said bluntly. 'I'm on antidepressants and I'm having cognitive behavioural therapy to help me sort through my feelings and try to deal with my panic attacks. I actually had one in the pub that day, when the guy was talking to me. It had been a while since I'd had that kind of attention, and I guess I freaked out.'

Tears welled up in Nina's eyes as she absorbed the news. Her cousin, her best friend, one of the most important people in her life, had been going through hell and she hadn't even realised. Too wrapped up in her own problems, she'd completely missed the pieces of the depression jigsaw – Tess's reluctance to socialise, her tendency to stay in bed all day, her lack of interest in life in general. Nina had assumed that she was just struggling to find her feet in Sydney after living in London, but it obviously went deeper than that. Way deeper.

'Oh my God, Tess. I had no idea. Are you okay? I mean, of course you're not okay, but is therapy helping? I'm so sorry – I should have realised. I should have been there for you, instead of trying to drag you out to bars and restaurants when it was the last thing you felt like doing. I remember thinking you looked really uncomfortable in the pub that day, but I just assumed you were being stand-offish. I had no idea you were having a panic attack. I'm such a selfish bitch, I can't believe I didn't put two and two together . . .' Nina began to sob.

'It's not your fault, Nina,' Tess assured her. 'It's nobody's fault – it's my problem and I need to deal with it. For a long time, I didn't want to admit there was a problem, because on the face of it, there's nothing wrong with my life. I mean, what do I have to be depressed about? But as my therapist said, depression isn't picky; it doesn't care who you are or what you do. For a while I was making excuses for myself – telling myself it was normal that I didn't feel like going out, or just wanted to stay in bed all day. I felt like my life was in a holding pattern, and I couldn't get excited about anything anymore. I just didn't see the point in anything and getting through the day was such an effort. After a while, you get used to feeling blah and you don't realise that it's actually because something's not right. But when I started having panic attacks, I realised that it wasn't natural to feel like this.'

Nina stared at her mutely, tears running down her face, as Tess calmly explained how she'd gone to the doctor, told him what she was going through and got a referral to a psychologist, who had started her on a course of antidepressants, accompanied by weekly therapy sessions.

'Do the pills make you feel magically better? How long will you take them for? What's the cognitive behaviour stuff you mentioned before? How come you didn't tell me?' Nina asked in a small voice.

'Because I wasn't ready,' Tess admitted. 'I don't have to tell you everything, you know,' she said, with a flash of defiance. 'I don't know how long I'll take the drugs for – as long as it takes, I guess. They're not instant happy pills, they just stabilise my serotonin levels and stop me spiralling back down into the big black hole. They take the edge off everything, so I feel like a bit of a zombie, but it's better than feeling the way I did before. Cognitive behaviour therapy helps with the depression and panic attacks; it teaches me to recognise the signs and learn certain coping mechanisms to avoid following the same patterns. So far, so good, but it's early days yet,' she said matter-of-factly.

'Is there anything I can do to help?' Nina asked hopefully, eager to make up for being oblivious to her cousin's emotional struggle.

'Not really – unless you feel like cooking butternut pumpkin and spinach risotto for dinner?' Then, seeing Nina's puzzled face, she explained, 'The doctor gave me a list of foods that have high levels of tryptophan, which the body converts into serotonin. The more serotonin in my body, the better.'

'Right then, risotto it is,' Nina said brightly, jumping up to check the kitchen cupboard for ingredients. 'One problem – we don't have any arborio rice. I'll nip down to the shop and grab some.' She grabbed her wallet and gave her cousin a quick, hard hug before disappearing out the door.

Once outside, Nina slumped against the wall of their apartment building, feeling like she had been punched in the stomach. The combination of spilling the secret of her indiscretion with Adam and dealing with Tess's revelation had left her shattered. She closed her eyes and couldn't help thinking that somewhere along the way, their lives taken a wrong turn — she had come so close to cheating on her boyfriend, and Tess was battling serious mental demons. It wasn't supposed to be like this.

twenty

'So I got an interesting email today,' Nina began, watching Jeremy closely for his reaction. They were having dinner at mod-Asian restaurant Ms. G's, chowing down on the famous mini bánh mì and, Nina's favourite, corn cobs with shaved parmesan and lime.

'Oh yeah?' Jeremy took a swig from his bottle of Asahi after demolishing the last of his crispy pork belly roll. 'What about?'

'About a role that's come up at ABM – Australian Boutique Magazines,' she explained when he looked at her blankly. 'They publish a lot of smaller niche titles, mainly sports-based ones but also a couple of finance and business magazines. Plus they just bought *Candy*, a monthly women's mag, which is a bit like *Lulu* but not as successful.'

'Uh-huh,' Jeremy said, obviously more interested in the parmesan-smothered corn cob on the plate in front of him. Nina sighed, wishing he'd pay more attention to what she was saying. Couldn't he tell that she was leading up to something, that she had big news to share? She'd been jumping out of her skin ever since she'd got home from the office and had suggested going out for dinner so she didn't have to compete with the TV for his attention when she told him about the email. She unclenched her jaw and battled on.

'They're looking for a new editor for Candy,' she continued, hardly able to contain her excitement. 'Kat used to work with the publisher and says he isn't happy with the current editor, who they inherited when they bought the magazine; he thinks it needs a fresh pair of eyes. Its circulation has taken a massive hit over the past three audits, so they want to shake things up a bit.' Nina took a deep breath. 'I've decided I'm going to apply for it.'

'I didn't think you'd be ready to be an editor,' Jeremy remarked offhandedly while signalling at the waitress for another beer.

Nina stared at him, gobsmacked. This was the biggest opportunity in her career so far and her oh-so-supportive boyfriend immediately assumed she wasn't up for the challenge.

'What would you know?' she demanded furiously. 'You don't see me at work, you barely have any idea what I do! Do you think Kat poached me to go to Lulu with her just because I have a great collection of shoes? It's because I'm bloody good at my job, thank you very much. I know it's not exactly discovering a cure for cancer, but that doesn't mean working in magazines doesn't have merit. I have good ideas and I'm a hard worker. Kat's already told me that the deputy editor role is all mine, just as soon as she can get rid of the girl who's currently doing the job – that's if I don't get another job offer beforehand.' Nina paused for oxygen, then continued, 'But I don't want to be a deputy editor if I can help it – why settle for silver if gold is up for grabs? No one remembers who comes second. Editorships don't become available very often, so I need to put myself out there. It'll be good experience to interview for it and even if the publisher decides I'm not right for this job, at least he'll know who I am for any future opportunities. The last time I checked, ambition wasn't a dirty word, Jeremy. I thought you'd be happy for me,' she finished stroppily, vaguely aware that the table next to them had fallen quiet and were hanging off every word she said. Not that she cared – she was almost foaming at the mouth with indignation.

'I *am* happy for you, Nina,' Jeremy said. 'Jesus, take a chill pill or something. I didn't say you weren't good at your job or that there's anything wrong with being ambitious, I was just asking if you thought you were ready to take on the editorship of a magazine that sounds like it's on its last legs. Everyone knows the print industry is struggling at the moment, so it might not be the best idea to jump into something just because you get to sit in the editor's chair, then find yourself out of a job six months later when they decide to close the magazine.

Maybe you'd be better off staying at Lulu and waiting for the deputy editor to leave, and work your way up at a slower pace.'

'But what if she never leaves? Christ, she's been there for six years already, which is a lifetime in the magazine industry. I could be stuck in the same spot for who knows how long, wishing I hadn't played it safe while someone else becomes the new editor of Candy and does amazing things with it. And I'll have to suck it up, knowing it could have been me, if only I'd been brave enough to take a risk. You don't regret the things you did, Jeremy, you only regret what you *didn't* do.'

'Is that what some expert psychologist told you in an interview for one of your pseudo self-help articles?' he smirked.

Nina's blood boiled. She had hoped he'd be excited for her or at least supportive, but all he could do was tear her down. 'Adam would have understood,' a small voice whispered in her mind. She shook her head, refusing to listen. She'd made a conscious effort to put all thoughts of Adam out of her head since confessing her misdemeanour to Tess all those weeks ago and had been trying to close the gap she felt between herself and Jeremy by spending more time together. She'd thought things had been getting back on track – until now.

'This is a big deal for me, Jeremy, so it would be really nice if you could stop making fun of my job and actually be supportive, for once. You'd think my boyfriend would take an interest in my life and be my biggest cheerleader, but I guess I was wrong. Anyway, I've already sent in my topline application and the email I got today was confirming an interview with the publisher at eight tomorrow morning.

Be Careful What You Wish For

Nothing may come of it, but it's really nice to know that you have my back,' she said, her words dripping with sarcasm as she pushed her chair back and stalked out of the restaurant.

Expecting him to come chasing after her, Nina waited outside, trying to calm down so she could accept his apology graciously. After five minutes, there was no sign of him, so she whipped herself into another lather of indignation and stormed home.

The next morning, Nina presented herself to the receptionist at ABM, determined to blow *Candy*'s publisher out of the water with her brilliant ideas and vision for how the struggling magazine could be turned around. Decked out in a digital print Josh Goot dress that she'd snapped up the last time *Lulu*'s fashion editors had cleared out the fashion cupboard, her shoulder-length blonde hair slicked back from her face and her most recent acquisition – a daffodil-yellow Alexander Wang Rocco bag – swinging from her arm, Nina felt like she was going into battle. She'd had to use triple the amount of Yves Saint Laurent Touche Éclat to hide the dark circles under her eyes after she'd tossed and turned all night, waiting to hear Jeremy's key turn in the front door. By two am, she'd realised he must have gone back to his own place, which had just pissed her off even more.

As she followed the executive assistant down the hallway to the publisher's office, Nina forced herself to forget about the previous night's incident and concentrate on killing it in the interview.

'Hello, Nina. I'm Michael, the publisher of *Candy*. Kat's told me a lot of good things about you.' The short, forty-something salt-and-pepper-haired man rose from his black leather Eames chair, shook her hand, then offered her a seat at the meeting table in his office.

Glancing around, Nina was quietly impressed. Vintage movie posters hung on the walls, and there was a special display case showing off the multiple awards won by ABM's titles. Built-in shelves were stacked neatly with magazines the company published. Okay, they weren't as well-known as *Lulu* or most of the magazines in PSRP's large stable, but for a boutique publishing company, ABM more than held its own.

'So I won't waste any time,' Michael said, once they were both seated. 'As I explained in my email, we recently purchased *Candy* and, to be blunt, I think it could be doing a lot better than it currently is. You probably know that it's taken a hit in the circulation stakes, but there's also the problem of advertising dollars – it doesn't seem to be on clients' radar when they're booking their print schedules. So I'm quietly on the hunt for a new editor – someone who can shake things up, who can inject some personality back into the title. I think it's a magazine with a lot of potential, but the current editor just isn't up to scratch. I'm after someone with a clear vision not only of where the magazine is going wrong but, more importantly, how to fix it – fast.'

Nina smiled at the publisher while reaching into her Wang.

'I totally understand where you're coming from, Michael. Obviously I read *Candy* as part of my job, but when I heard this job was up for grabs, I bought the latest copy and went through it with a fine-toothed comb. I've tagged up the pages that I think could be improved, with an explanation of why they're not working as they currently are and some suggestions for the changes that could be made.' She absorbed his impressed expression as she slid the magazine, littered with Post-it notes, across the table. 'I've also prepared a short summary of where *Candy* sits as a brand at the moment and where I think it should be. I agree that the title could be doing a lot better than it is, and I'd love to be a part of its reinvention.'

'Well, you've certainly done a great deal of preparation,' the publisher said, not bothering to hide the admiration in his voice.

'Oh, my mother taught me to always do my homework,' Nina said playfully, guessing Michael was the type of guy who didn't mind a joke. He didn't need to know that she'd bought the magazine from one of the numerous convenience stores on the Kings Cross strip on her way home from the disastrous dinner with Jeremy, and had then stayed up till after midnight flipping through the pages and working on her analysis until she had it just right.

'Well, I'm not going to lie to you, Nina – this is very impressive,' the publisher said after he'd scanned her brand positioning statement and looked through the tagged copy of the magazine. 'I've learnt a lot just from the brief glance through your so-called homework, so I look forward to reading it in more depth later. One question – does Kat know you're here?'

'No,' Nina confessed. 'I thought about telling her, seeing I know you two used to work together. However she is my boss first and foremost, and I don't want to worry her unnecessarily, so I decided I'd wait to see how our meeting went before letting her know that I've been in contact with you.'

'I see,' Michael said in a completely neutral tone, making Nina wonder if she'd given the right answer. 'So, the problem I have at the moment is that there is another candidate for this role who has a lot more experience than you. She's been with ABM for a while, so we know what she's capable of – a known entity, if you like. But I think you make up for your lack of experience with your ideas and your vision for what *Candy* could be.'

Nina held her breath, wondering where this was going. Surely he wasn't about to offer her the job on the spot? Should she interject or just let him continue? Before she could decide, Michael continued, 'When I received your application, I made a few enquiries about you – most of my contacts agreed that Nina Morey is one to watch in the magazine industry. And I quite like the idea of this company poaching an up-and-coming talent from a much bigger publishing house,' he mused. Suddenly, he leant forward and looked at her appraisingly. 'Obviously you get on very well with your current boss, otherwise she wouldn't have talked you up so much last time I ran into her at an advertising function, but if you do end up as the new editor of Candy, how would you feel about having an editorial director above you?'

'That wouldn't be a problem at all,' Nina replied confidently. 'I totally understand that I'm lacking experience in some areas, so to have an editorial director to advise me would be really helpful. Plus, I've always liked the idea of having a mentor, and when it comes to the creative process, the more brains the better, in my opinion.' She did a mental fist pump as Michael nodded in agreement.

'Great,' Michael said, as they both stood up and shook hands again. 'I'll be in touch when I've had a chance to take a proper look at your analysis and ideas. It'll be sooner rather than later, as I want to get Candy back on its feet ASAP. Thank you, Nina, it's been an absolute pleasure.'

'No, thank you for considering me for the position, I really appreciate it,' Nina replied. 'I look forward to hearing from you.'

On her way back to reception, she passed the women's bathroom. Ducking inside, Nina stared at herself in the mirror, then put her bag down on the bench and stuffed her fist in her mouth to muffle her scream of excitement. The job was so close to being hers, she could almost lick it.

twenty-one

Four weeks later, Nina was back in Michael's office. The same vintage movie posters hung on the walls, the stack of magazines on the shelves were the same and, if her suspicions were correct, the publisher was even wearing the same suit as when she'd last seen him. But one thing was different – this time she was here because it was her first day as the new editor of *Candy*.

True to his word, Michael hadn't wasted any time in making his decision – the day after her interview, he'd called to offer Nina the job. Kat had been devastated when she'd handed in her resignation, but was also one hundred and ten per cent supportive, joking that she only had herself to blame for Nina's defection seeing as she'd raved about her to Michael. The Lulu team was so excited for her, although she had detected one or two jealous glances when Kat had announced the news. But Nina didn't care — although she couldn't help feeling disappointed that her former nemesis Romy hadn't been there to hear the news. Kat's prediction had almost been correct — while the deputy features editor had still been working at *Lulu* when Nina returned from Eastern Europe, it hadn't been long before she was packing up her desk under the steely supervision of the company's security guards, who then escorted her out of the building; she'd been busted stealing luxury products from the beauty cupboard and selling them on eBay.

Tess, who still had good days and bad days with her depression and panic attacks, happened to be having a good day when Nina broke the news that she had scored herself an editorship, so she'd insisted on going out to celebrate. Bar-hopping their way down Darlinghurst's Victoria Street, they'd ended up in the Beresford sinking espresso martinis, then blaming each other when they were still wide awake at two am. Obviously the only solution had been to burn off their excess caffeine intake with a drunken duet of 'Total Eclipse of the Heart' at Ding Dong Dang, the late-night karaoke bar in Surry Hills.

Even Johan had called her, to her surprise, having heard the news on the gay grapevine, thanks to one of Ed's friends who worked in the advertising industry. It had been a slightly stilted conversation, seeing they hadn't spoken in months, but they'd promised each other they'd catch up soon and Nina had really meant it. There was a Johan-shaped hole in her life and they'd been through so much together that she didn't want to let the friendship go without a fight.

That just left Jeremy. She hadn't particularly looked forward to telling him about her new role at *Candy*; she was still angry at him for his lack of encouragement and didn't want him to rain on her parade, so she'd been stunned to find him waiting with a bottle of Veuve Clicquot and a massive bunch of peonies, her favourite flower, when she'd got home on the day ABM had released the news to the industry. Although he hadn't said as much, Nina guessed it was his way of trying to make up for what had happened at Ms. G's. Hopefully, it signalled that their relationship was starting to turn a corner.

'Can I get you a coffee?' Michael's assistant asked Nina, as she sat waiting for her new publisher to get off the phone.

'That would be great, thank you – a skim flat white, please,' Nina requested, as she thumbed through the latest issue of *Candy*. The previous editor had left as soon as the news of Nina's appointment had been announced, with a fat severance cheque in her pocket to make up for the swift derailment of her career. It meant the *Candy* team had been without an editor while they closed the issue that Nina was now perusing and, quite frankly, it showed. The design layouts were all over the place, the story headlines were uninspiring and the picture choices were cheesier than a quattro formaggi pizza from Paddington's Love Supreme. Nina couldn't wait to roll up her sleeves and show *Candy*'s readers – what was left of them – how good the magazine could really be. And if she was as successful as she hoped to be, who knew where her career could take her? Turning around the declining circulation of a struggling magazine was no small task, but if she pulled it off, she could become the golden child of the Australian publishing industry. After she'd worked her magic at *Candy*, there'd be job offers galore – in a few years' time she could even end up back where she started, at *Marie Claude* in London, but this time in the editor's chair. Practically purring with self-satisfaction, Nina sipped on her skim flat white and looked at Michael confidently as he finished his call.

'Nina, welcome! It's great to have you on board officially. We certainly got some people talking when we announced your new appointment, didn't we? Don't listen to all the haters on the media industry blogs; they're just jealous that you're moving up the ladder so quickly. I have the utmost faith in your ability to make *Candy* a success – especially with the help of Elizabeth, who'll be your editorial director. Do you know Elizabeth at all?'

Nina shook her head. 'No, I don't believe so.'

'She's fantastic. She's been with us for a few years, ever since she moved out here from London, and now oversees quite a few of our titles. Mostly the business and finance ones, but from memory she did start out on a women's lifestyle magazine back in the day. Anyway, she should be here to meet you any minute. She'll be invaluable when it comes to covers, content, the look and feel of the magazine, all those kind of things.'

'Great! I can't wait to get—' Nina began, but Michael interrupted her.

'Elizabeth! I must be psychic; I was just telling Nina you'd be here any minute, and here you are. Elizabeth, meet Nina, the new editor of *Candy*. Nina, this is Elizabeth, your editorial director.'

Nina swivelled around, her most dazzling smile faltering as she clocked the woman standing in front of her. Her first thought was that there must be some mistake. But then she remembered Michael's words from less than two minutes ago – Elizabeth had emigrated from the UK, and had started out on a women's magazine in London. There was no doubt about it – her new editorial director was none other than Lizzie, the former features assistant from *Marie Claude*, who'd hated her guts when she was interning there.

Nina swallowed hard, then rallied – she'd told Michael in the interview that she didn't have a problem with having an editorial director overseeing her, so she just had to deal with it. Perhaps Lizzie had mellowed over the years? Perhaps she wouldn't even remember Nina, despite her constant bitching to everyone about how Charlotte used to favour her? But as Lizzie looked at her coldly, taking in the vintage cream leather studded shift dress Nina had paid a fortune for on eBay and the insanely high gold Prada pointy stilettos that she'd bought herself as a celebration present when Michael had offered her the job, Nina knew her hopes were futile. She remembered, alright. There was only one thing for it – to fake pleasant surprise.

'Lizzie! Oh my God, hiiiiiiiiiiii! How great to see you – I had no idea you'd moved to Sydney until Michael just mentioned it! What a lovely surprise!' Nina exclaimed, hoping her gritted teeth weren't noticeable. Seriously, what were the chances?

'Hello, Nina. I know we knew each other a long time ago, but it's Elizabeth now, not Lizzie,' the editorial director said sharply. 'We worked together briefly back in London,' she explained to Michael, who was looking somewhat confused. Turning her attention back to Nina, she barked, 'I hope you're ready to get your hands dirty – there's a lot of work to be done, so I suggest you finish your coffee so we can get started. I'll introduce you to the *Candy* team, then we can get together and discuss the plan of action.'

'Sounds like you two have everything sorted, so I'll leave you to it!' Michael said chirpily, completely oblivious to the tension that was already simmering between the two women.

Waiting for the elevator, Nina and Elizabeth stood in awkward silence. Elizabeth turned her back on Nina, not bothering to make small talk, while a million thoughts chased themselves around Nina's head. Slightly rattled by this unwelcome development, she tried to keep a lid on her panic. 'It'll be fine,' she told herself. 'We're both professionals, we're both here to do a good job and, at the end of the day, I'm the one who'll be in charge of the day-to-day running of the magazine. Michael said she oversees quite a few titles, so chances are I'll barely hear from her.'

As they entered the *Candy* office, Nina couldn't help noticing that the editorial team stiffened as soon as they saw Elizabeth. All chatter stopped, Facebook, Twitter and Pinterest screens were quickly minimised and the music volume dived. 'Look out, the fun police have arrived,' Nina thought, as Elizabeth clapped her hands together like she was a kindergarten teacher trying to get her charges' attention.

'Team, I'd like to introduce you to your new editor, Nina. As you know, Nina has come from *Lulu*, where she was the features editor, so this is a very big step up for her. Even though she doesn't have a huge amount of experience, I'm sure she's up to the job,' Elizabeth announced, accentuating Nina's shortcomings while pretending to talk her up. She obviously wanted to make it crystal clear that she had no confidence in Nina whatsoever.

Nina fumed quietly, behind her beatific smile. 'Thank you, Lizzie – sorry, I mean Elizabeth,' she replied, in a voice that was sweeter than a barrel of maple syrup. She turned her attention to the assortment of people in front of her. 'I'm so excited to be here, and I'm really looking forward to working with you all,' she said sincerely. 'Once I get settled in, I'll book individual meetings with everyone so I can get to know you better – who you are, what you do and, most importantly, what you think of *Candy* as it is now and how you think it can be improved. I'll be asking how procedures work around here and I'll also explain how I like to work when it comes to brainstorming feature ideas, choosing photos, approving layouts and all that, so we're all on the same page. If you've got any questions, my door is always open.' Nina made sure to make eye contact with each member of the team as she spoke, wanting them to feel like she was talking *to* them, not *at* them.

'Right then, everybody back to work,' Elizabeth said briskly, cutting Nina off. 'Nina and I will be in meetings for most of the day as I try to get her up to speed, so I'm sure you all have something to keep you busy. Felicity, fill my water bottle up and make me a cup of tea.' The command was directed at a girl who Nina guessed was *Candy's* editorial assistant, a pretty redhead who looked like she hadn't yet hit her twenty-first birthday, but was decked out in head-to-toe Ksubi. 'Gotta love those sample sales,' Nina thought as Felicity scurried to the kitchen. The lifeline of all cash-strapped editorial employees, barely a week went by without an email announcing yet another warehouse sale from a designer who was offloading last season's stock at rock-bottom prices. If you were lucky, you could scavenge through the endless racks to find one-off samples that had appeared on the catwalk at Fashion Week, but had never made it into production – the only hitch was that to fit into them, you had to give an Italian greyhound a run for its money in the skinny stakes.

Entering her new office, Nina was desperate to have a moment to herself to appreciate the first few minutes of sitting in her very own editor's chair, to collect her thoughts and plan her first move. No such luck with Elizabeth around. Plonking herself down at the meeting table, her frenemy muttered an ungracious thanks to Felicity as her water and tea were promptly delivered, before embarking on a diatribe.

'I don't know what Michael has told you, but we need to turn this magazine around fast. The board was iffy about ABM buying the title in the first place, so we need to pull out all stops to get *Candy* back on track. I've booked in meetings with the national advertising manager, the marketing director, the circulation team and the finance analyst, so you can get the full picture – but believe me, it's not pretty. I was in charge of the most recent issue, seeing you hadn't started yet, but now that you are here, I still need to be across absolutely everything, do you understand? Michael trusts me to deliver, so nothing happens without my knowing about it. That means you send me every story idea, every photo selection, every headline and every layout. And you do not move forward until I'm happy with it. The cover is the most important part of the jigsaw – I don't know how it works where you've come from, but organisation is absolutely key. I want to see three different options for each cover, and you should have them well in advance. None of this "we go to print this week and I don't have a cover" malarkey.'

Nina stared at her, astounded. 'That explains why the current issue is as crap as Lindsay Lohan's career revival,' she realised. 'Because Lizzie had her grubby paws all over it.' God help her. It just showed how horrendously out of touch Elizabeth was. And as for her demands for the cover, did she not remember what it was like to work on a magazine where you were at the mercy of the whims of the celebrity publicists who, loving their power trips something sick, could take weeks to decide whether to grant permission to put their talent on the cover or not? Not to mention that approval was usually only considered when celebrities had something to promote – a new movie, an album, or a tour. Even a DVD release wasn't regarded as a good enough reason to justify approval anymore, as publicists became pickier and worried about their clients becoming 'overexposed'. Just to make things even more complicated, there'd usually be at least a couple of months in the year when no matter how many times you trawled the release schedules, there wasn't a single celeb relevant to your particular audience doing anything that you could use as a hook to get cover approval. During those dark days, you'd be scraping to find one decent cover, let alone the three different options Elizabeth was insisting on every . . . single . . . month.

'Now, before we go any further, I've already decided who I think should be on the next cover,' Elizabeth continued, oblivious to Nina's distress — and to the fact that Nina might want to have a say in who appeared on the cover of her first issue as editor. 'Get your picture researcher to look for the most recent studio shots of her, so I can choose my favourites. And you probably should email her publicist yourself to request interview time — from what I've heard, it's always better if the editor does it themselves, rather than leaving it to one of their minions.'

'Right,' Nina croaked, still in shock. 'So who is it?'

'Nicolette Rivera. I've been told she's an "it" girl who everyone seems to love,' Elizabeth declared, obviously having no idea who she was.

Nina closed her eyes as her stomach sank. Of course her new boss — her ex-nemesis whom she was determined to impress — had to choose the one celebrity she would never, ever be able to get publicist approval for. 'Stop the ride,' she begged the universe silently. 'I want to get off now.'

twenty-two

As the sound of the ringing phone interrupted Nina's copy-editing marathon, she glanced at the time. Christ, it was nine thirty already – how had that happened? Last time she'd checked, it was just nudging five pm. She hadn't noticed when the bright Sydney daylight had morphed into inky darkness, the sky filling up with the bats who embarked on their nightly ritual of chasing each other across the sky to feast on the fig trees in Centennial Park. She'd been vaguely aware of her staff saying goodbye as, one by one, they'd left the office until she was the only one remaining – as usual.

'Hi,' she said abruptly, having recognised Jeremy's mobile number.

'Hey, pork chop – I was just checking if you were still there or on your way home?'

'I'm still here. I told you I'd text when I was leaving. I haven't texted, so that means I haven't left,' she replied tetchily. She knew he was just checking in, but Nina couldn't help getting annoyed. She was busy enough as it was without him interrupting just to see if she'd left yet.

'Okay, I just thought you might have forgotten. Well, let me know if you want me to come and pick you up when you're ready to leave.'

'I can get a taxi,' she replied, her mind already wandering back to the feature article she was in the middle of rewriting.

Jeremy sighed. 'I know you can, but I just thought it would be nicer if I came to get you. It's pretty much the only time I get to see you, seeing you're always at work. How much longer do you think you'll be? It's nine thirty already,' he said, a drop of reproach seeping through his words.

'I know what time it is,' Nina said, trying not to let her irritation get the better of her, without much success. 'Do you think I'm still here just for the fun of it? Uh, no. I'm here because I've had a hectic day and I still have stuff I need to do before I leave. And talking to you is just going to make me later, so if you don't mind, I'm going to hang up now so I can get on with it.'

Not bothering to wait for Jeremy's reply, she slammed the phone down and dragged her burning eyes back to the computer screen. She felt like the world's biggest bitch, but she knew he didn't understand, no matter how many times she'd tried to explain how much work she had on her plate and the pressure she was under. They barely saw each other during the week, and at weekends she was either catching up on sleep or zonked out in front of the TV, completely brain-dead after another soul-destroying week of being beaten down by Evil Elizabeth. Even then, she was surgically attached to her BlackBerry, obsessed with checking every email that arrived, not wanting to give Elizabeth any excuse to accuse her of slacking off.

Nina wriggled out of her silver sequinned blazer – as usual, the building's aircon had been shut off at eight thirty and it was beginning to get stuffy. After editing the raw copy filed by her feature writers, she still had a pile of layouts that needed checking before they were sent to Elizabeth for her tick of approval. Not that the tick was ever granted on the first go – after Nina had given her feedback to the graphic designers, tweaking a headline here and a breakout box there, Elizabeth would then sit on the layout for hours, leaving the *Candy* team in limbo, before finally emailing back a list of changes she wanted, which usually completely contradicted whatever Nina had just approved.

At first, Nina had tried to be diplomatic about it, suggesting a happy medium that incorporated both their requests, but when Elizabeth overrode her without even trying to reach a compromise, she had tried another tack, kicking up and arguing vehemently for what she thought looked best – but that too had got her nowhere. Elizabeth had made it quite clear that she didn't value Nina's opinion at all, so now she just bit her lip and kept quiet, acquiescing to whatever random changes Elizabeth wanted, even when the art director looked at Nina

Be Careful What You Wish For

in despair. She knew she should keep fighting for what she wanted, but Elizabeth would never let her win, so what was the point? And it didn't just happen with the design layouts, it was everything to do with the magazine – the choice of stories that made it into the issues, the pictures that accompanied them, the headlines, the subheads, the captions, the running order . . . Elizabeth was a micromanaging nightmare and, in her eyes, Nina couldn't do anything right.

Realising she was parched, Nina headed to the kitchen. She'd been so busy that day, she'd made a conscious decision to stop drinking water after lunch so she didn't waste any time going to the bathroom. 'And everyone thinks being a magazine editor is the height of glamour,' she thought wryly as she opened the fridge to grab one of the bottles of coconut water that had been sent into the office by a savvy PR company who regularly had crates of it delivered to *Candy* and other magazines, knowing that eventually one of them would tweet about it and their client would score some social media love.

Sucking down the mineral-enriched goodness, she was about to kick the fridge door shut, when she spied a strangely shaped bottle hiding behind the rows of coconut water. Reaching to the back, she pulled out a large glass vessel, shaped liked a human skull. 'Crystal Head Vodka,' she read on the back, intrigued by the slightly grotesque bottle. 'Looks expensive – I wonder what it tastes like?' she thought. It had already been opened, so she pulled the stopper out and sniffed. There was a tumbler sitting on the kitchen bench; she splashed some in, then hesitated, remembering her promise to

Tess that she'd cut down on her drinking after the previous weekend's incident.

The Saturday night before, she had dragged herself off the couch to meet up with some of the old Nineteen crew for dinner and drinks, starting at China Doll on Woolloomooloo Wharf. Not that Nina had eaten much; her appetite was another casualty of her job, along with the ability to go to the bathroom whenever she wanted to. While her former colleagues had fawned over her, desperate to find out all about her 'amazing' job, how it felt to be sitting in the editor's chair and all the perks that went with it, Nina had polished off drink after drink. She couldn't bear the slightly jealous looks, the way they seemed to treat her differently now that she was an editor, how they sucked up to her in the hope she'd remember them next time a job vacancy came up. 'If only they knew what it was really like,' she'd thought, ordering another bottle of pinot grigio. But she didn't want to burst their bubble – it was easier to play along, pretending that she absolutely loved being the editor of Candy, that it was everything she'd ever dreamt of and so much more.

After dinner, it had been her idea to go to Hugo's Lounge in Kings Cross – even though the club was past its prime, Nina had a VIP card which gave her access to unlimited two-dollar drinks. She'd stayed there until it had closed, buying drinks for anyone and everyone. Most of the Nineteen crew had bailed around one am, but Nina had partied on, making new friends every time she went to the bar. When they'd shut up shop, the security guard had had to carry her down the stairs. He'd tried to put her in a taxi, but she'd insisted she didn't need one, that home was just down the road and a taxi driver wouldn't take her that short distance anyway. He'd shrugged and headed back to the club, leaving her tottering down the street. She had been doing pretty well until she'd drunkenly decided to take a shortcut through the back streets of the Cross. Stumbling down laneways, passing junkies sitting in the gutter with needles in their arms and prostitutes coming back from dealing with their latest clients, she'd stacked it a couple of times, ruining her gold Prada stilettos, but refusing all offers of help. After getting thoroughly confused about the direction she should be heading in, she'd finally given up and called Tess, who thankfully was already up, getting ready for her early shift. After slurring her way through what she'd thought was a perfectly coherent explanation, Tess had made her walk to the nearest cross street, tell her the name then promise not move until she got there. Nina didn't remember much else, but apparently Tess had found her passed out on a bus stop bench, using her Miu Miu tote as a pillow and clutching one of her scuffed Pradas to her chest like a teddy bear.

'Not my finest moment,' Nina admitted to herself in the office kitchen, then shrugged. Surely she was allowed to blow off steam now and then? Most people got obliterated on the weekend; it wasn't like she'd committed a crime. 'Stuff it,' she thought, and knocked back the vodka. The cold, clean liquid slithered down her throat, leaving a faint liquorice aftertaste. 'Not bad – who needs coconut water when you can drink swanky vodka from a glass skull?' she asked herself as she slurped down some more. Carrying a glass of the straight liquor in one hand and the bottle in the other as she made her way back to her office, Nina told herself she deserved it. It had probably been sent in by one of the many booze companies who were very generous with their products, so it wasn't like she was stealing from someone's personal stash. Technically it belonged to the magazine, and she was the boss lady of the magazine, so really she had as much, if not more, right to it than anyone else. Besides, she was the one who was working back past nine thirty for the fourth night in a row, so why shouldn't she have a little drink to make her Thursday night a bit more bearable?

Feeling slightly fuzzy around the edges after polishing off another measure of what was quickly becoming her new favourite vodka, Nina printed off the edited versions of the stories she'd been slaving over and dropped them into the tray for the sub-editors to work on the next day. Turning her attention to the stack of layouts, she belatedly noticed the small yellow envelope in the bottom corner of her computer screen, signalling she had new email. 'Probably just the scans of the weekly English trash mags from our UK office,' she thought, flicking over to her inbox, which she'd been ignoring for the past two hours while she concentrated on editing copy.

There were thirty new emails – not from the UK office, but from Evil Elizabeth. Nina's hand groped for the glass skull, splashing more liquid into the glass then raising it to her mouth. The vodka was now getting warm, but Nina was past caring. She needed some liquid strength to help her get through the barrage of emails from Her Royal Evilness. It was bad enough that she had to deal with her incessant messages and phone calls during the day, constantly checking up on her and meddling with everything she could get her hands on, but the damn woman wouldn't leave her alone, even at ten pm when Nina was still trying to catch up on everything she hadn't done yet because of all the interruptions.

Scrolling through the list of emails, Nina's fury started simmering. They were all things that could wait until the morning, yet Elizabeth couldn't help but clog up in her inbox unnecessarily, demanding to know what was happening with various bits and pieces that Nina was already on top of.

Yes, she'd sorted out the recruitment forms for Felicity's replacement – the editorial assistant had resigned after Elizabeth had yelled at her because the tea that she had made when Elizabeth had been in the *Candy* office for yet another meeting hadn't been hot enough. When Nina had stuck up for her staff member and tried to diffuse the situation by jokingly pointing out that, technically, Felicity was her assistant, not Elizabeth's, so she shouldn't have to make her tea in the first place, Elizabeth had gone ballistic, accusing her of being disrespectful and threatening to give her a verbal warning. Fun times.

Yes, she'd spoken to the fashion team about keeping the prices of the clothes they shot under five hundred dollars. Despite her time on *Marie Claude* back in the day, Elizabeth didn't seem to have a fashion bone in her body, and couldn't seem to grasp that some people were happy to drop more than their fortnightly pay on a new piece to add to their Sass & Bide collection.

Yes, she'd approached the agent of a celebrity couple, pitching the idea of an 'at home' shoot with them and their two beloved pugs. Yes, she'd made it clear that, unlike some magazines, *Candy* didn't pay for celebrity access and yes, they were fine with that.

'Yes, yes, YES – I'VE ALREADY DONE IT ALL, YOU SHREW! I KNOW WHAT I'M DOING, YOU DON'T NEED TO KEEP CHECKING UP ON ME LIKE I'M A CHILD!' she felt like screaming. Instead, Nina decided it was time to blow the joint before she got so angry she put her fist through her computer screen. Taking one last swig of vodka, this time straight from the bottle, she grabbed her stuff and headed for the lift, before the guilt about leaving the unchecked layouts and unanswered emails could get the better of her.

She could see the living room lights were on as she climbed unsteadily out of the taxi when it pulled up in front of her building. That meant Tess was still up, so she fumbled in her bag for some mints before heading up the stairs. 'Don't want her to think I have a drinking problem or anything; she needs to worry about herself, not me,' Nina thought, squinting as she tried to get her key in the lock. After five tries, she finally managed to swing the door open, almost knocking Tess over in the process.

'Sho shorry, Tesh!' Nina squawked as she fell through the door and onto the couch. 'Oops, am I slurring?' she wondered. 'Surely I didn't drink that much vodka?'

'Go out after work, did you?' Tess asked, as she helped Nina to the couch.

'No, I've binatchaoffish all night,' she mumbled.

'Bloody hell, Nina, have you been drinking again?' Tess asked, her worry and frustration obvious. 'You can't keep working like this. You've done at least sixty hours in the past four days, and it's been exactly the same for the past few months. You're stressed out of your brain, you look like a wreck – when is it going to stop? You really need to look after yourself.'

'Oh gawd, not you too.' Nina rolled her eyes. 'I've already had a lecture from Jeremy tonight, I don't need another one, thanks very much,' she managed to enunciate without slurring as much. 'If you'll excuse me, I'm going to the bathroom to get ready for bed.'

She hauled herself off the couch with as much dignity as she could, and weaved her way across the living room, ignoring Tess's concerned look. No one understood. Didn't they realise that she had to keep on trucking? Couldn't they see that she still had to prove herself, that if she quit now it would look like she wasn't up to being an editor? She could just imagine the industry gossip now: 'Shame about that Nina Morey – she had a lot of talent, but I guess she couldn't cope with the pressure. Was promoted too soon, probably. ABM did take a risk on her, you know. Sometimes it just doesn't pay off. Oh well, if you can't handle the heat, get out of the kitchen — isn't that what they say?'

Nina stared at herself in the bathroom mirror. No, she wouldn't let it happen. She wasn't a quitter. She had to keep at it, no matter how much Evil Elizabeth made her life hell — she didn't want to give her the satisfaction of winning. But . . . if she was completely honest with herself, she was so sick of feeling like she was never good enough, like she didn't have an iota of talent, like she was an imbecile who couldn't be trusted. Then there was the queasiness that sloshed around in her stomach every Monday morning when her alarm went off. And the panic that shot through her when she thought she'd accidentally left her BlackBerry at home and wouldn't be able to check her emails on her way to work. And the lies she had to tell everyone about how much she loved her job. Her bravado suddenly was nowhere to be found. 'I don't know if I can do this anymore,' she whispered, hating how pathetic she sounded. She felt like she was unravelling at the seams.

Gripping the basin with white knuckles, she hung her head in shame. The mountain of stress and pressure that was her constant companion reincarnated itself as a massive lump in her throat. Without warning, tears started running down her face and a strangled sob escaped. Not wanting Tess to hear her distress, she grabbed the nearest towel and stuffed it in her mouth to muffle the sounds of her howling. Her head bowed, she sobbed and heaved, watching the river of tears run down the sides of the basin until they disappeared down the plug hole. When there was nothing left, she sank down onto the cold bathroom tiles and closed her eyes, utterly exhausted, her BlackBerry clutched tightly in her hand.

twenty-three

Nina surfaced groggily from another crap night's sleep with the all-too-familiar lump of dread sitting in the bottom of her stomach. Her tongue was furrier than a Labradoodle and her head felt like it'd been run over by a road train of semitrailers. Holding her breath, she slowly turned towards Jeremy's side of the bed, hoping he'd already left for the day. Result! She couldn't face his all-too-regular look of concern mixed with resignation and a dollop of disdain. He'd been dead to the world when she'd ricocheted through the door at . . . wait, what time *had* she got home last night? Nina tried her best to remember as she automatically groped for her BlackBerry, then hauled herself out of bed and staggered to the bathroom. A snapshot of hitting up one of the bars near the office flashed into her brain while she sat on the loo, scrolling through the avalanche of emails that had landed in her inbox after she'd finally left the office at eleven pm. More snapshots followed, featuring Nina ordering a succession of double vodka sodas until she eventually did away with the soda and ended up drinking straight vodka while talking to anyone who'd listen to her slurred rants about how much she hated her boss.

Shit, her boss! Cutting through the pea soup in her brain, Nina remembered the eight thirty meeting she had with Elizabeth. Christ, it was already eight! There was no way she could be late, not after last time when Elizabeth had torn strips off her in front of everyone because she'd been fifteen minutes late to a production meeting. Nina had tried to explain she'd got caught up consoling her fashion editor whose father had passed away suddenly, but Elizabeth didn't want to hear it.

'Evil bitch,' Nina muttered as fiercely as her hangover would let her, while she yanked a Ginger & Smart dress from its hanger, crammed her feet into a pair of five-inch Marc Jacobs heels, slicked her hair back into a ponytail and made for the door of the apartment. 'At least I'll get the worst part of my day over and done with first,' she consoled herself as she tried to ignore her protesting stomach. Then she remembered that her art director was expecting a selection of snappy coverlines to be waiting for him when he arrived at work, so he could start designing the cover. Nina had left them to the last minute yet again, too stubborn to send them to Elizabeth for her approval because she knew exactly what would happen. She'd be summoned to the editorial director's office, where they'd spend three hours dissecting each coverline, even though Nina and her team had already slaved over them until they were the perfect combination of fun, promising and informative, tempting the reader to fork out $7.50 for the magazine.

But, of course, Elizabeth was on a completely different coverline wavelength. No matter how many times Nina tried to explain why they'd crafted them in a particular way, or pointed out the pop culture reference they referred to, her boss always tore them apart to make them as dull or as cheesy as possible. Every time, Nina swore she wouldn't let it happen again but then, four weeks later, she'd be so worn down by Elizabeth's nit-picking and passive-aggressive comments that she found herself giving up and letting her have her way. She hated herself for it, but in the end it was easier to admit defeat. Especially after that time she had decided to stand her ground and Elizabeth had retaliated by booking a meeting with HR to discuss her 'attitude'.

It had been six months since her meltdown in the bathroom, and things had gone from bad to worse. Nina's confidence had been sucked well and truly dry. Elizabeth had made it clear she didn't value her opinion at all, even though Michael had hired Nina because of her reputation as a fresh new talent. 'Pity Elizabeth didn't seem to get the memo,' Nina thought bitterly. So much for her vision of turning the struggling magazine around when she'd first accepted the job. She'd had such faith in herself back then – now she just did what she was told by the dictator, and hated herself for it.

Nina bit her lip as the ache in her stomach turned into sharp stabbing pains. Halfway down the stairs, she had to stop and lean against the wall as sweat oozed through the make-up she'd hurriedly slapped on. She unconsciously checked to see if the red light on her BlackBerry was flashing, signalling the arrival of yet another email, before sucking in a deep breath and shuffling down the street towards the bus stop. 'I'm fine,' she insisted to herself. 'So I probably drank too much last night; I'll just make myself throw up when I get to the office to get rid of the booze, then I'll be right. It's all good. Mind over matter, right?'

Just as Nina was turning the corner, she heard her name being called. 'Nina, wait up!' She gritted her teeth, before swivelling around and forcing a smile onto her face so that Jeremy couldn't see the lines of stress furrowed between her bloodshot eyes.

'Hi, J, what are you doing here? Thought you'd be at work already,' she said nervously, wishing she'd brushed her teeth before running out the door. Standing on tiptoes to give Jeremy the obligatory kiss on the cheek, she prepared herself for yet another lecture.

'I left my iPad at your place, and it has the redevelopment design on it that I'm presenting to clients today,' he explained. There was a brief silence before he asked tentatively, 'So, what time did you get in last night?'

'Um, I'm not sure, I didn't really notice the time – maybe half eleven?' Nina lied. Try more like half past one, by the time the bar staff had refused to keep serving her.

'I see.' They both knew she was lying, but neither of them was willing to come clean. 'You look like shit,' Jeremy said bluntly.

Nina blinked. They often fought about how late she worked, how much she was drinking and how stressed she was, but Nina thought they'd argued themselves dry. Jeremy had long since stopped offering to pick her up from the office when she eventually finished editing copy and proofing layouts at eleven pm after dealing with Her Evilness all day. She knew he was just trying to make her life easier, but she didn't want his help, thanks very much. He'd also stopped encouraging her to blow off steam at the pub, even though alcohol helped wipe the omnipresent spectre of Elizabeth from her mind on weekends. After a few vodkas, a bottle of red and maybe a cocktail or two, Nina felt more like her old self – the fun, happy Nina who used to love her job when she was at *Nineteen* and *Lulu*. Not the emotionally exhausted Nina who hated anyone asking about work because she felt obliged to tell them how glam it was, how many celebrities she'd met – because after all, she was the editor of a glossy magazine and thousands of women would kill for her job.

But these days, getting blind wasn't just for weekends. Since she'd started drinking in the office after *Candy*'s staff had left for the day, she found herself craving alcohol almost every night after she forced herself to leave the endless emails from Elizabeth in her inbox and the piles of work on her desk. Nina didn't see anything wrong with propping up the bar – any bar – by herself; there was always someone to talk to. She worked hard, so she deserved to play hard. Right?

'Well, don't you know how to make a girl feel good?' Nina tried to laugh off Jeremy's comment, while pulling her Tom Ford sunnies out of her bag.

'I'm serious.' Jeremy's voice hardened. 'I know you work these crazy hours because of Elizabeth, but you don't have to go direct to the nearest pub when you finally leave the office. I'm happy to pick you up but you never let me. At least that way I'd get to see you for a bit, rather than waking up every morning to find you passed out in bed, reeking of booze.'

Nina ignored her frustration and embarrassment. She knew that he and Tess were worried about her, which made her feel like a child, but quite frankly she got enough of being treated like a child at work. The combination of stress, exhaustion, her hangover, the thought of the heinous day ahead and her protesting stomach made Nina snap. She'd show him where he could stick his attempt at tough love.

'I don't have time for this,' she said furiously. 'It's my life, you can't tell me what to do. You're not the one who works fourteen-hour days and weekends too, only to be told you can't do anything right by your out-of-touch micromanaging boss from hell. You don't understand the pressure I'm under to turn this magazine around. I can't just clock off at six like you do. And it's not like I have time for a lunch break, so I'm sorry if I want to go out for a bit after work to socialise. Obviously I'm not allowed to have fun, even though I work my butt off. So thanks for telling me I look like shit – I've got a hideous schedule at work ahead of me, including a meeting with Elizabeth in fifteen minutes, so you've really set me up for the day, Jeremy. Thanks a lot.'

As Nina stalked off, she saw Jeremy's shoulders slump and his head drop. For a second, she was tempted to turn around and apologise for her dummy spit, to wrap her arms around his broad chest and bury her head in his neck, to take the day off and spend it in bed like they used to when they first hooked up. Then a fresh burst of indignation exploded inside her. 'Fuck him,' she thought. 'He's just jealous of my career and how dedicated I am. It's my life; if he feels second-best, that's his problem, not mine.'

Huddled with the rest of the wage slaves crammed onto the packed peak-hour bus, Nina wished she could call Tess or Johan and have a good bitch about how selfish and unreasonable Jeremy was being. But she didn't want to make Tess worry about her more than she already did. Although the antidepressants and therapy had helped, her cousin still had a long way to go in recovering from her mental illness. She could call Johan but it would be a bit random – how long had it been since they'd actually spoken to each other? Sure, there'd been a couple of texts over the past year, always asking each other when they were going to catch up, but neither of them ever committed to anything. Work took up so much of her time and he was always busy with Ed. Being Ed's boyfriend had turned into a full-time occupation, plus Johan didn't like to stray too far from his gay comfort zone. Nina had long ago tired of all the scene queen stories and Johan got weird if he didn't get to hang out in one of his usual haunts – the last time they'd met at a new cafe in Redfern, at her suggestion, he'd spent the whole time bitching about the 'breeders' with their prams and moaned about the lack of eye candy. The fun, sweet guy she'd worked with back at the hotel in London who had encouraged her to pursue her dream of working in magazines had turned into a self-obsessed, bitchy queen. And if she was brutally honest, she wasn't much better. 'God, what's happened to us?' Nina wondered.

Getting off the bus, she strode down William Street, gulping in the traffic fumes as her stomach heaved with the anticipation of dealing with Elizabeth. 'Maybe she'll cancel?' Nina thought hopefully. 'Maybe she's been up all night with food poisoning and she'll have to work from home? Maybe Michael will want to see her urgently so she'll postpone our meeting till tomorrow?' While offering these options up to the universe, Nina found herself pushing open the door of the seedy twenty-four-hour pub two blocks away from the office. A smattering of old men sat at the bar, staring into their schooners of Reschs, while a few guys still out on the lash from the previous night poured Jack Daniel's and Cokes down their throats.

'Yes, darl?' A sixty-something woman with dyed black hair and pink lipstick that was bleeding into the lines around her mouth looked at Nina sullenly from behind the bar.

'A triple vodka on the rocks, please.' The words were out before Nina realised she'd even opened her mouth. She pushed a twenty-dollar note towards the barmaid, clutched the glass of clear goodness like it was the elixir of eternal happiness, then downed it in one gulp. Her stomach recoiled as the fresh vodka made its acquaintance with the stale vodka from the previous night. 'That'll get me through this morning,' Nina told herself, wiping her mouth and making her way unsteadily to the office. She kept her sunglasses on in the elevator while it zoomed up to level twenty-seven. Trying to ignore the acute pain in her stomach and the fresh sheen of sweat that was making itself at home on her forehead, she pushed her way through the crowd of people in front of her as the doors opened. 'I'll just check my make-up in the bathroom — don't want to give Elizabeth any excuse to have a go at me,' she thought blearily. Opening the door to the bathroom, she was relieved to find it empty. She just managed to crash into a stall and lock the door before her stomach staged its coup d'état. Hanging over the toilet, Nina vomited up booze and bile until there was nothing left. She rinsed her mouth at the basin, swallowed three breath mints, squeezed out some eye drops while expertly managing to avoid smudging her mascara, then smoothed her hair and washed her hands. 'Right,' she told her reflection in the mirror. 'It's show time.'

twenty-four

To: Morey, Nina
From: Crawford, Elizabeth
The cover looks great.

Nina stared at the four words on her computer screen, her mouth hanging open in shock. Surely there must be a mistake? Surely Evil Elizabeth hadn't just given her a compliment? Her eyes involuntarily shifted to the window – surely the sky had to be falling in? Any minute now, she'd spot Chicken Little sprinting down the street.

She wondered when Elizabeth had got her hands on a copy of the printed cover. Obviously she had seen it before it had been sent to the printers, but when you used as many fluoro colours as *Candy* did – all the better to stand out on the newsagent's shelf and the supermarket rack – you could never quite tell how it would turn out until you had the actual cover in all its Pantone glory in your hot little hands, fresh from the printers. Nina quickly dialled her production assistant.

'Hi, Ange. Could you please call Chris and ask for a printed copy of the cover? Elizabeth has one already, so they must have been delivered to the courier dock. Thanks.'

Glancing at the bar fridge she'd had installed in her office on the pretence that the larger fridge in the communal kitchen was a toxic health hazard, Nina was sorely tempted to pour herself a celebratory drink. After all, getting her first-ever compliment from her boss after months of pain and suffering was no small feat. And there was a brand-new bottle of Absolut chilling in the freezer compartment.

'No, Nina,' she told herself sternly. 'It's only eleven twenty-five. Remember the promise you made to yourself the other day? No drinking in the office till after midday.' But surely this was a special occasion, whispered the voice that was so often in her ear these days. And if she added a splash of soda, everyone would just assume it was sparkling water. It was almost too easy.

Powerless to stop herself, she was opening the fridge when Angela walked into her office with a yellow A4 envelope in her hand. Nina jumped, slamming the fridge door closed with way more force than necessary.

'One brand-spanking-new *Candy* cover, as requested,' Angela announced, seemingly oblivious to Nina's guilty expression, as she placed the envelope on top of the overflowing pile of magazines, invitations, financial spreadsheets and design layouts in her boss's in-tray. Nina closed the office door as Angela exited. She wanted to savour this moment without being interrupted. She'd worked so hard to secure this particular cover and for Elizabeth to finally acknowledge her efforts made it all worthwhile.

Being an Australian magazine on the opposite side of the world to Hollywood meant most of their cover shots were purchased from the local picture agencies that syndicated the work of photographers who shot celebrities for the big American and English magazines — ELLE, *Vogue*, *Glamour*, *Harper's Bazaar*, *Nylon* . . . But occasionally they'd get lucky, with an A-list celebrity's publicist agreeing to a shoot that would be exclusive to *Candy*. Unfortunately they didn't have the budget to fly a creative team overseas, so instead they'd use a company which specialised in overseeing every aspect of the photo shoot in their absence. The company would book the photographer, the stylist, the hair and make-up team, plus have a production assistant on the ground to make sure they were sticking to the creative brief supplied by *Candy*.

This was how Nina had ended up with a cracking shot of Hollywood's Next Big Thing, Maia Rocket, on her latest cover. But it hadn't come easily — despite Maia cultivating a reputation as the girl-next-door-with-a-wicked-sense-of-humour, she had been a total nightmare at the shoot. In a filthy mood — thanks to an epic public fight with her boyfriend the night before that had made headlines on all the celebrity blogs that morning — Maia had bitched and moaned her way through the day. Even though the stylist had stuck to the list of her favourite clothing labels supplied by her publicist, Maia had sniffed dismissively at the majority of outfits which had been pre-approved by Nina, insisting that she wanted to wear the clothes she'd turned up to the shoot in.

If she'd been dressed in a bang-on-trend outfit of, say, J. Brand denim cut-offs worked back with a white tank and the cult Isabel Marant floral jacket that every celebrity was begging to sell her granny for, then it wouldn't have been a problem. But no – Maia had been decked out in head-to-toe black. And as every editor knows, an all-black outfit on a magazine cover never works, unless the magazine is a high-fashion title and the outfit in question is a slinky Tom Ford number, preferably slashed down to the waist and up to the thigh to show some skin. Which explains why the panicked production assistant had bombarded Nina with phone calls, desperate to know how to handle the situation.

The photo shoot had been in London, where Maia was promoting her latest movie, so with the time difference, the calls had started in the evening. Usually Nina would still have been in the office, but it had happened to be Jeremy's birthday, so she'd booked dinner at Rockpool. She had been determined to be the perfect attentive girlfriend. She'd even managed to keep her drinking under control during dinner, helped by Jeremy watching every sip of wine she took with eagle eyes. But then her BlackBerry had started buzzing angrily in the buttery leather Chloé envelope clutch she'd bought in the last David Jones stocktake sale. At first, she'd forced herself to ignore it, despite no longer being able to concentrate on what Jeremy was saying. When it didn't stop, he had sighed, looked pointedly at the bag that was gyrating around the table between them and asked resignedly, 'Aren't you going to get that?'

Nina had needed no further prompting. Dashing outside, she had spent a good half hour talking the production assistant through her conniptions. After advising her to take Maia's publicist aside to talk privately about her client's attitude, Nina had arrived back at the table to find Jeremy staring into space, looking beyond bored.

'Sorry, J, bit of a work crisis. We're shooting a cover in London and the celeb is being difficult. But it should all be sorted now. How about a cocktail?'

No sooner had they ordered a round of Negronis than her Blackberry had started up again. Shooting Jeremy an apologetic look, she'd grabbed it and run. She had spent so much time on setting up this shoot, she couldn't risk it falling apart now, she reasoned with herself as she instructed the flustered assistant to put Maia's publicist on the phone so she could speak to her directly. Thanks to Nina's not-so-subtle threat to cancel the cover if her client kept refusing to cooperate, Maia's publicist had promised to whip her into shape and keep her on the straight and narrow for the rest of the shoot.

Back at Jeremy's place after dinner, Nina had been in the middle of giving him a stellar birthday blowjob in an effort to make up for all the interruptions when she heard her BlackBerry's siren song travelling up the hallway from the bag she'd deliberately left in the lounge room. The only person who would be calling at that hour would be someone from the cover shoot on the other side of the world. Trying to concentrate on the matter at hand, she had admitted defeat after five rings. Wiping her mouth on the sheet, she'd pretended to Jeremy that she didn't want its incessant ringing to wake up the rest of the house, but had secretly been glad of the darkness which had made it impossible to see the look on his face as she'd practically sprinted out the door.

Almost forty-five minutes later, she'd snuck back into bed, the adrenalin pumping through her veins as she dissected the update from the assistant in London. After her publicist had read her the riot act, Maia had apparently sucked it up, turned on the charm, and had blitzed her way through three of the approved cover outfits plus a couple of extras for the cover story that would appear inside the magazine. 'Nothing like an ultimatum,' Nina thought grimly, staring at Jeremy's unforgiving back. She knew he wasn't asleep and she didn't blame him for being pissed off, but what did he expect her to do? It was a cover shoot with an A-list celeb on the other side of the world, and if she hadn't been on call to solve any problems, there would have been hell to pay with Elizabeth.

Now it was time to see the fruits of her labour. Opening the yellow envelope, Nina realised she was holding her breath as she slowly pulled out the cover. 'Stop stressing,' she reassured herself. 'Elizabeth has already said she likes it, so at least that's the biggest hurdle over and done with. And you were happy with the final image, design and colour palette – the only thing that could go wrong is if the printers have stuffed up the fluoros.'

Nina flipped the cover over. She blinked. Then blinked again. 'What . . . the . . . fuck?' she whispered disbelievingly. Closing her eyes for a few seconds, she convinced herself she was dreaming. Then she looked at the cover again. Nope. Not dreaming. The cover in front of her looked nothing like the one she had sent to print. Fuming, she dialled Elizabeth's extension.

'Hello, Nina,' her boss chirped, infuriating her even more. 'Did you get my email? The cover looks great, don't you think?'

'What did you do to it?' Nina managed to grind out.

'Sorry? What did I do to it? Oh, you mean the couple of revisions I did after the dyelines came in? Did I forget to tell you about those? Silly me. Yes, I decided to make some small changes; I didn't think the cover was as strong as it could be.'

'Some small changes? Are you kidding me?' Nina yelled down the phone, not caring how loud she was. 'You completely changed the colour scheme, you've rewritten half the coverlines and Maia's mini-skirt has magically become a maxi-skirt, thanks to the wonders of Photoshop. And you just forgot to tell me?'

'There's no need to get upset, Nina,' Elizabeth replied snippily. 'Remember that I'm the editorial director of *Candy* and if I don't think the cover is working as well as it should, I have every right to make any changes I see fit.'

'You had your chance to make changes when I showed you the cover BEFORE it was sent to print!' Nina shot back furiously. 'In fact, I seem to remember you asked for several things to be tweaked, as per usual, because no matter what I do you're never bloody happy. You never respect my opinion, but I put up with it because I have to. But the fact that you went behind my back and made numerous changes to a cover that I sweated blood to organise is beyond insulting. I deserve better than that. And by changing Maia's skirt, you've also jeopardised our editorial campaign in the issue that goes on sale next week – you know, the one where we've taken a stand against using Photoshop? Thank God the Maia cover is for the following issue, but it will still look like we've reneged on our own Photoshop ban if anyone realises what you've done. You need to get off your power trip or ditch whatever grudge you're still holding from our *Marie Claude* days, Lizzie, because I HAVE. HAD. ENOUGH.'

Nina knew she'd crossed a line, but she didn't care. She slammed the phone down, ignoring Elizabeth's outraged squawking on the other end. Immediately, the phone began to ring, Elizabeth's extension flashing up on the screen. Grabbing her bag, Nina headed for the elevators. By now she was about to self-combust if she didn't get a drink in her hand – all she wanted to do was to throw some hard liquor down her throat to snuff out the red-hot flames of outrage that were licking at her insides.

'Nina, wait!'

Quickly wiping her face clean of anger before turning around, Nina came face to face with Mel, *Candy*'s entertainment editor, who was waving the latest copy of *OK!* at her.

'What is it? I've got somewhere to be,' she said, diluting the terseness of her words with an apologetic smile.

'Sorry, it's just that you know the celebrity photo shoot we're scheduled to do tomorrow? The "at home" story with Aerin and Noah with their two pugs?'

'Yes, what about it?'

'It says in here that they've broken up. There are rumours that he cheated on her, although of course their reps are insisting that the break-up is amicable.'

Nina struggled to keep a lid on her frustration – today was bad enough without this unwelcome development.

'Please tell me you're kidding. Their reps didn't even bother to let us know?'

'Nope. And I just confirmed the bookings for the photographer plus the hair and make-up team this morning, so their agencies will charge us for the cancellation.'

'Great. Just what we need – a two-thousand-dollar bill for a fucking shoot that didn't even happen! Sorry, Mel, I'm not angry at you – I'm just having a bad day,' Nina explained swiftly when she saw the shocked look on her employee's face. 'I'll call the publicists when I get back and give them a serve – hopefully I can back them into a corner and they'll at least agree to pay for some of the cancellation fees.'

'Sounds like a plan,' Mel replied, scooting back into the office before Nina could blow up again.

On her way to the nearest pub, Nina felt her phone vibrate. She ignored it – why bother answering when it would just be Evil Elizabeth demanding she come back to the office straight away so she could give her a written warning or, better still, sack her on the spot? She refused to give that bitch the satisfaction. When she saw Elizabeth next, it would be on her terms, after she'd had a chance to speak to Michael about the editorial director's non-stop meddling and nightmare management style. She wasn't going to go down without a fight.

As she ordered a triple vodka tonic, she pulled her phone out of her bag along with her wallet. When the missed call flashed up on her screen, she was shocked to see that it hadn't been Elizabeth at all. It was Johan. 'God, it's been at least three months since I've heard from him,' she thought, thrown off by the random contact. While the phone was still in her hand, it beeped twice, signalling that he'd left a voicemail. Taking her drink to the darkest corner of the pub, she dialled in to get the message while sucking down the alcoholic nectar. Expecting to hear a longwinded message in his usual chirpy tone, she raised an eyebrow when she heard Johan's hesitant, choppy sentences in a weird voice she'd never heard before – he sounded absolutely shattered.

'Hi, fluffball,' he started, using his old nickname for her from their London days. 'It's me. Um, I know it's been a while since we last caught up but can you call me as soon as you can? Please? I really need to talk to you. Like, super-urgently. Okay. Call me. Bye.'

Deleting the message, Nina made a mental note to call him on the weekend – knowing Johan, he probably just wanted to have a whinge about how he had busted Ed checking out other guys and, quite frankly, she had bigger problems to deal with at the moment.

twenty-five

Walking into Bills on Crown Street, Nina ignored the tables of tourists ordering the cafe's famous ricotta hotcakes and the usual crew of fashion publicists schmoozing stylists over fat-free fruit plates. Sitting down on the chocolate leather banquette, she ordered coffee and waited for Johan to make his grand entrance. She'd eventually got around to calling him back three days after listening to his voicemail, but he'd refused to tell her what was wrong over the phone, begging to see her in person. The only time she could squeeze him in was just before she was due at the Channel 37 studios to do her monthly TV interview to promote the new issue of *Candy*. Not ideal timing, but he had insisted it couldn't wait.

Checking her schedule of back-to-back meetings on her BlackBerry, Nina didn't notice his arrival until a shadow fell across her table. Looking up, her smart-arse comment about his lack of punctuality shrivelled on her tongue as she took in Johan's appearance. Gone was the immaculately groomed god who'd had confidence dripping from every pore when she'd first met him back at the Bickford in London. In his place was a hunched figure whose clothes hung off him. If not for the green eyes that she knew so well, Nina could easily have dismissed him as a junkie who had wandered in off the street. Struggling to disguise her dismay, Nina pasted on a big smile as she leant over the table to hug him.

'It's been a while, huh?' Johan croaked, as his eyes filled with tears.

She nodded, not trusting herself to speak. She'd been expecting the old Johan — buffed to perfection and dressed in head-to-toe designer gear — to swan in, plonk himself down and immediately start gibbering on about whatever superficial drama he was having in his relationship with Ed. How wrong she'd been. 'Looks like you're not the only person with problems at the moment, Toto,' she thought as Johan wiped his eyes with a napkin, then clenched it tightly in his hands.

'How are you?' she asked gently, not knowing what else to say.

'How do you think I am? Don't worry, I know I look like shit.' He smiled weakly. 'Bit different to last time we saw each other all those months ago. But things change, don't they? Things aren't always what they seem,' he said, not bothering to hide the bitterness in his tone.

Be Careful What You Wish For

Nina decided to bite the bullet. 'Babe, what's wrong? Please tell me. I know we haven't been as close recently and a lot of that is my fault. But I'm here now, and you're one of my best friends no matter what, so come on – out with it,' she said firmly, aware that the clock was ticking and she was due at the TV studios in less than an hour, then hating herself for thinking about work at a time when anyone could see that he was obviously in desperate need of help.

'It's over with Ed. I'm moving back to London. I leave tonight,' Johan said in a rush.

'You're what? Tonight? Why so soon?' Nina stared at him, trying to get her head around the news. 'Oh, and I'm sorry to hear about Ed,' she said belatedly, trying to sound like she meant it.

'Don't be,' he said shortly. 'That bastard has ruined my life.'

'What do you mean? What happened?'

Johan paused long enough for the waitress to set down Nina's skim flat white, before embarking on his explanation.

'I'll warn you now – it's not a pretty story. I've done some things I'm not particularly proud of, but I guess I just got carried away. I lost sight of what's really important and it's come back to bite me on the butt, as you Aussies would say.' He took a deep breath, looked around to make sure that the people at the tables next to them were deep in their own conversations, then continued in a low voice. 'A couple of weeks ago, Ed and I went out with a bunch of friends. We've been partying pretty hard over the last few months, as you can probably tell from looking at me, but this night, things went a bit pear-shaped. We'd had a few lines of coke and some MDMA at home before hitting Oxford Street, and everyone was up for a big night. At Arq, one of the guys offered me some GHB and I thought, why not? I'd had it in London heaps of times before, so I didn't think anything of it. But it must have been a lot stronger than what I'm used to, because the next thing I knew, I was waking up in hospital.'

'Oh my God, Johan . . . are you alright?' Nina gasped. She'd always known that Johan never said no when it came to dabbling in illicit substances, but he'd never suffered from anything more than a hideous comedown as a result. Noticing his jittery hands as he took a hit of caffeine, she guessed he'd graduated from dabbling to using regularly since landing on the doorstep of Sydney's drug-infused gay scene.

'Let me finish,' he said grimly. 'So I regained consciousness in St Vincent's Hospital and the nurses had to fill me in on what happened, as Ed was nowhere to be seen. They told me I had overdosed on GHB, which is apparently easy to do, because the strength of the liquid varies so much and the drug depresses your respiratory system, so if you take too much, you stop breathing. Luckily, I had people with me who realised what was happening and the hospital was only down the road from the club. Of course, given the location, they see this kind of thing all the time. But while I was in hospital, they took a blood test. I didn't get the results until after I'd been discharged. When I called up to get them, they insisted I had to go back to the hospital so the doctor could talk me through them. That's when I knew.' Johan's voice cracked as he battled to maintain his composure.

'Knew what?' Nina whispered, as cold fingers of dread wrapped themselves around her heart.

'That I was HIV positive.'

His words slapped her across the face. Nina's mouth opened, but no sound emerged. She stared at him, hoping that it was some hideous joke, that any second he'd reach across the table, poke her in the ribs and crow, 'Ha ha, gotcha! Just jokes, darl!' But he didn't. Because it wasn't. She reached across the table and grabbed his hands, which were now shaking violently. She realised he was waiting for her reaction and pulled herself together – this wasn't about her, it was about Johan.

'I just . . . Johan . . . I don't know what to say . . . I'm so sorry . . .' she eventually choked out. 'What did the doctors say? Have you started treatment already? Do you have any idea how you contracted it?'

'Oh, I have an idea, alright.' The bitterness returned to his voice. 'You know how careful I've always been – "if it's not on, it's not on", isn't that what people say here? But there was one time, after another massive night out, when I stupidly thought it would be okay. It wasn't like he was some random I'd picked up at the Midnight Shift. Admittedly, we were both off our heads, so my judgement wasn't exactly razor sharp, but I had no reason not to trust him . . .' He petered off, lost in the memory of the night his life was given an expiry date.

'Trust who?' Nina asked, trying to make sense of what Johan was saying. She desperately wished she had an extra-strong drink in her hand – vodka, gin, rum . . . hell, even whiskey – anything that would numb the pain of this awful conversation.

'Ed.' He spat the word out like it was toxic. Which, in a way, it was. 'It turns out that my boyfriend has been HIV-positive for the past decade but never bothered to let me know, until it was too late. In fact, he's kept it quiet from pretty much everyone. He's so in denial about it that sometimes he even forgets himself, which is why, when we were high as kites, he let us have unprotected sex that night. Well, that's the explanation I got when I confronted him, anyway. At first he tried to deny he had anything to do with it – he accused me of cheating on him with other guys and insisted that's how I contracted it, but I knew I hadn't done anything more than grope a few strangers on the dance floor since we got together. And last time I checked, you can't get HIV by groping someone through their clothes.'

'So he admitted it was him?' A ball of fury was burning in Nina's stomach. She'd never liked Ed, but she'd never thought he was capable of something like this.

'Eventually – after I ransacked his apartment looking for the antiretroviral drugs to prove it. When I moved into his apartment, he insisted I use the guest bathroom – he said the idea of sharing a bathroom revolted him, and I didn't question it. Ed was very particular about certain things so it didn't seem that weird. You know how precious some gays can be. But now I realise it was because he didn't want me poking around in the cabinets in case I stumbled across his stash of meds. But once I'd found them he had no comeback. He broke down, begging me to forgive him. I threatened him with legal action, packed my stuff and left. If I never see that bastard again, it will be too soon,' he said blackly.

'Where did you go after that?' Nina felt like she was on autopilot, asking question after question as she did her best to absorb Johan's news. She gave up trying to ignore her craving for alcohol, waving down a waitress and ordering a double-shot Bloody Mary.

'I dragged my suitcase to the nearest bus stop and sat there like a zombie for a few hours while I tried to process everything that had just happened. When it started getting dark, I realised I needed somewhere to stay. Most of my friends in Sydney are also Ed's friends, and obviously they were the last people I wanted to see. So I got in a taxi and asked the driver to take me to one of the backpacker hostels in the Cross.'

'What? A hostel? Why on earth didn't you call me? You know you could have stayed with me and Tess,' Nina reprimanded him as she sucked down the spicy booze-laden goodness that had just been delivered to their table.

Johan raised an eyebrow. 'I did call you. While I was sitting at the bus stop, I left you a voicemail, asking you to call me urgently. But you didn't call me back, so I figured you were too busy with that bloody job of yours, or you were pissed off with me for letting our friendship slide while I gallivanted around Sydney's gaybourhood with Ed. I needed somewhere to go while I got everything sorted before I fly back to the UK tomorrow, and a hostel was the easiest option seeing you weren't picking up the phone. And I didn't want to spend too much – I need to save my pennies for specialist appointments when I get back to London. Being HIV positive ain't cheap, you know,' he said, with a weak smile. 'Where are the loos here? That coffee's gone straight through me.'

Pointing him in the direction of the bathroom, Nina stared out the window as her brain sifted through the worst conversation of her life. Her best friend was HIV positive. She hadn't been there when he'd needed her. As if that wasn't bad enough, she had totally ignored him even when he'd specifically stressed how much he needed to speak to her. In fact, it had taken her a full three days to bother returning his call. Now he was leaving the country in less than twenty-four hours, his life changed forever by one terrible decision.

And where had she been?

Too busy fighting with her power-tripping boss about a stupid magazine cover.

Too busy feeling sorry for herself and blaming everyone else for her problems.

Too busy believing that her work took precedence over everything else, and that no one could possibly understand the pressure she was under.

Too busy thinking about when she could get her hands on her next drink.

Be Careful What You Wish For

Too busy trying to hide her drinking problem from Jeremy and Tess, the two people she loved the most, while throwing their attempts to help back in their faces.

Too busy being self-obsessed, when at the other end of town, her best friend had called for help and she hadn't been there for him.

Nina hated herself. Hated what she'd become, hated what she was doing to her life and the people in it. If she'd needed a reality check, she couldn't have asked for a better one. It was too late for Johan to change what had happened to him, but she could still change what was happening to her. 'Just as soon as I finish this Bloody Mary,' she promised herself, removing the straw and draining the last half in one large gulp.

twenty-six

Sitting in the make-up chair at the Channel 37 studios, Nina squinted, concentrating hard on merging the double reflection in the mirror into one. As the make-up artists gossiped about the previous night's TV ratings and the hairstyles of the breakfast show hosts on the rival networks, she started to regret buying the bottle of gin after she'd said goodbye to Johan, having promised to take him to the airport that night for his flight back to London. The gin had seemed like a good idea at the time; a salute to the early days of their friendship, when they'd bonded over copious amounts of the liquor after a particularly stressful shift on the hotel's front desk, pouring it down their throats like it was water.

Marching down Oxford Street while trying to hail a taxi in peak hour, she'd found herself slowing down outside the hole in the wall that sold booze around the clock. Despite having sworn less than fifteen minutes earlier that she owed it to Johan to get her life sorted out, her credit card had been swiped and the bottle of Hendricks had been stashed in her bag before her brain had caught up with her body. 'It's not every day your best friend tells you he's HIV positive just before you're due to do a live TV interview,' she'd thought, finding yet another excuse to justify her drinking habit. 'Jesus H. Christ, if I can't have a drink now, when can I?'

The bottle had been half-empty by the time the taxi had pulled up outside the TV studios, and Nina was glad there hadn't been anyone in the car park to see her stumble out of the back door, the tell-tale brown paper bag poking its head out of the top of her favourite old Miu Miu tote. Waiting for the TV show's associate producer to collect her from reception, she'd used the time to nip to the bathroom and take another couple of swigs, washed down with cold water gulped from the tap, before being taken to the make-up room.

'Okay, love, you're all done. You're not due on set for another twenty minutes, so go upstairs to the green room and one of the producers will collect you when they're ready for you,' the make-up artist told Nina, interrupting her attempts to rectify her double vision.

Clambering out of the chair, she headed to the green room and was relieved to find it empty. Grabbing a plastic cup from the water cooler, she quickly splashed some of the Hendricks in and topped it up with water to dilute the distinctive smell.

'Idiot,' she chastised herself. 'There was a reason you switched to vodka, remember?'

By the time the associate producer appeared at the door, Nina was no longer seeing double, but triple. While wallowing in the mess that she'd made of everything, the alcohol had stoked a burning rage against Ed, the man she held responsible for destroying her best friend's life. In her irrational state, Ed had become a scapegoat, someone she could blame not only for Johan's problems, but her own as well. In her drunken state, she figured that she would never have become so obsessed with work if Johan had been around to give her the reality check she needed. But he'd been too busy splashing around in Ed's shallow world to notice. If Johan had never met Ed, their friendship wouldn't have been put on ice and she wouldn't be in this situation; he would have pulled her up on how she'd been acting like a selfish bitch and would have warned her that she was in danger of losing everyone she cared for, all because of a job she didn't even enjoy. Ed had stolen Johan from her. Everything was Ed's fault. And he needed to pay, not only for what he'd done to her, but for what he'd done to Johan. Oh boy, did he need to pay. Immersed in a thick fog of drunken indignation, she decided she had to get revenge, no matter what.

Nina did her best not to stagger as she followed the producer down the hallway and into the studio of *G'day Australia*, the network's top-rating breakfast TV show. Taking her place on the red couch, she smiled at the cookie-cutter blonde co-host who would be interviewing her about the big editorial campaign in the new issue of *Candy*, which had gone on sale that morning. Checking her pre-written notes, the co-host waited until the floor manager counted down as the cameras started to roll.

'Welcome back to the program! The new issue of *Candy* has hit the stands and this month they've launched a big investigation into the effects of Photoshop on women's body image. After seeing the results, the editorial team have decided to ban Photoshop from the magazine and have produced Australia's first Photoshop-free issue. I have *Candy's* editor, Nina Morey, with me now – Nina, congratulations on a wonderful initiative! Can you tell us what the reaction has been like so far?'

Nina stared at her own face that had appeared on the monitors at the far end of the studio then remembered that everyone was waiting for her to speak. It was now or never. Clearing her throat and making a concerted effort to enunciate her way through the haze of gin, she began her spiel.

'Thank you, Lucy. The response to our first Photoshop-free issue has been absolutely amazing,' Nina lied smoothly, having completely forgotten to check *Candy's* Twitter account that morning given everything else that had happened. 'But there's something more important I want to talk about this morning.' She turned to face the camera straight on, ignoring the look of alarm that tried to flicker over Lucy's Botoxed features as she realised Nina was going off on an unscripted tangent. 'And that is betrayal. The betrayal of someone very close to me who did nothing to deserve it . . . a betrayal that will affect the rest of his life, all because the person responsible was too selfish to admit the truth. Edward Butler, if you're watching this, I always knew you were a son of a bitch, but what you've done to Johan is un-fucking-believable,' she hissed. The morning's alcohol consumption came home to roost and her words jumbled together in her hurry to get them out before the sound guys cut off her microphone. 'I hope you're ashamed of yourself, you bastard! You deserve to burn in hell!' she screamed, as tears poured down her cheeks.

She was barely aware of the pandemonium in the studio as the executive producer yelled at the head cameraman to cut the live feed and go to an ad break, stat. She saw what looked like shock and pity on Lucy's frozen face, before she found herself yanking off her microphone, grabbing her bag and walking straight out of the studio, through reception and into the car park, where a taxi was dropping off a man who Nina belatedly recognised as the head of the TV network. 'Wait till he hits the shit storm inside,' she thought grimly as she climbed into the back seat. She started to giggle hysterically through her tears, high on adrenalin as the craziness of what she'd just done filtered through to her brain. 'Am I insane?' she wondered. 'Probably. But at least I went out with a bang.' She felt strangely exhilarated.

Giving the driver an address, she pulled out her phone and dialled Elizabeth's office number. Cursing as it rang out and voicemail picked up, she took a deep breath as Elizabeth's terse tone told her to leave a message.

'Elizabeth, it's Nina. I quit. This voicemail is in lieu of me handing in my notice as the editor of Candy. I will put it in writing when I get home. I'm guessing you won't want me to work out the three-month resignation period that's in my contract so I'll ask my assistant to pack up my desk and have my personal belongings sent to me. Tell Michael I'll be in touch with him later to explain. Good luck with finding a new editor.'

The next call she made was to Jeremy, who picked up on the first ring.

'Nina, where the hell are you? One of the guys in the office just said something about you having a meltdown on live TV? I was just about to call you to check if you're okay.' She could hear the concern in every word and burnt with shame at how badly she'd reacted whenever he'd tried to make her see that she was going off the rails. All he – and Tess, for that matter – had wanted was for her to be happy, and every time they'd tried to help or offer support, she'd not only thrown it back in their faces but had made out that it was their fault for not understanding what she was going through.

'Jez,' she bleated, wishing desperately he was in the taxi with her so she could give him a big hug. 'I'm okay. I'm more than okay. Yes, I just had a spack attack on national TV, but it's all good. I doubt I'll get invited back again any time soon, but that's fine, because I just quit my job.'

As Nina said the words, the reality of what she'd just done began to sink in. She'd dropped the F-bomb in a drunken rant on live TV in defence of her best friend, who'd probably be horrified if he knew. She'd quit her coveted editor's job, a role that thousands of women would mow down their best friends for, and had most likely destroyed any chance of getting another position in the publishing industry along with it. But funnily enough, she'd never felt better.

'Did you just say you'd quit your job?' Jeremy's voice was stunned.

'Sure did,' Nina replied. 'I just called Evil Elizabeth and left her a voicemail saying I was handing in my resignation. I've had enough. And I know you and Tess have, too. I'm so sorry about the way I've treated you; I've been a total nightmare and I don't know how I'm going to make it up to you. Johan told me some devastating news this morning, which I'll tell you about later, that made me realise that all the stress and pressure isn't worth it,' she explained. Suddenly it all seemed so crystal clear. 'It's not what you do that matters, it's who you are. And I don't like who I am when I'm the editor of Candy, putting my job before my friendships and my relationship. I love you and I don't want my job to come between us.' She felt tears well in her eyes as she realised just how close she'd come to ruining her relationship. Okay, it wasn't one hundred per cent perfect, but whose was?

'Don't cry, honey, it's okay,' Jeremy soothed. 'I won't lie, things have been a nightmare recently, but I guess I never gave up hope that we'd pull through. I think you need to take some time out to get back on track and work out what you've learnt from this. You've been pretty stressed lately, so I'm not surprised it all got too much for you. Sometimes people work so hard to get to where they think they want to be that once they get there it's hard to admit that it's not the right place for them after all.'

After hanging up, Nina sighed heavily, realising that, once again, Jeremy was right. She'd been too stubborn, too arrogant, too proud to admit that being the editor of *Candy* wasn't right for her. Maybe she'd been promoted too soon, maybe her personality clash with Elizabeth was to blame or maybe she would never be the right person to be an editor, no matter how old she was or who she worked under. She'd never know – all she knew was that she felt sweet relief at finally working out what really mattered, before it was too late.

There was just one thing left to do. Getting out of the taxi that had pulled up in front of a nondescript building in Kings Cross, she ignored the lure of the bars, bottle shops and pubs that lined the street. Throwing the gin bottle into the nearest bin, she walked into the building's foyer and headed for the reception desk.

'Hi, can I help you?'

'Uh, yes . . .' Nina hesitated. She pictured Johan's face in her mind, then remembered Jeremy's faith in her and Tess's strength in admitting she had a problem and getting help, then forced herself to continue. 'What time does the Alcoholics Anonymous meeting start?'

acknowledgements

A book doesn't write itself (unfortunately!) – there are a few people I want to thank who were involved along the way, so please bear with me.

Firstly, Claire Kingston, my publisher at Allen & Unwin, who emailed out of the blue to ask if I'd 'ever thought about writing a book' – BEST. EMAIL. EVER. With so many writers struggling to get their voice heard among the 50 *Shades* madness, I know how lucky I am to have this book on the shelves and it's all thanks to you.

Thanks to my editors at A&U, Christa Munns and particularly Ali Lavau, who ironed out all the kinks and polished my manuscript until it was shinier than the Taylor-Burton diamond.

In the magazine world, there are too many people to name who have given me a stack of inspiration and advice, but special thanks go to Gerry Reynolds and Peter Holder – gentlemen, I owe you a drink – and to all my magazine friendships that have continued well after we've moved on from the desks we first bonded over. I also owe Acacia Stichter, my friend, former colleague and art director extraordinaire, a massive favour after she dropped everything to design my book cover at the last minute.

Tina, Mickey, Dan and Benny – I wouldn't be who I am without you; thanks for putting up with me and being my crazy family.

Bree – thanks for being my best friend, my partner in crime, the other pea in my pod. And for being brutally honest whenever I asked you to read the first draft.

Finally, to Gareth, thanks for being my everything.